Twisted Shadows

Twisted Shadows

James Schmerer

Writers Club Press
San Jose New York Lincoln Shanghai

Twisted Shadows

Writers Club Press
an imprint of iUniverse.com, Inc.

For information address:
iUniverse.com, Inc.
5220 S 16th, Ste. 200
Lincoln, NE 68512
www.iuniverse.com

ISBN: 0-595-09566-6

Printed in the United States of America

For my daughter, Pamela Anne

Acknowledgements

For their support and assistance, my thanks and gratitude to John Boni, Donna Boni, Jack Sowards, Ralph Rosner and my parents, Louis and Margaret Schmerer.

Prologue

Shawn Parker sat up in bed and watched his lover cross the room to the chair where she had piled her clothes earlier that evening. He had promised himself that this time he would not try to stop her from leaving. Now as she picked up her jeans and started to wriggle into them Shawn knew he was going to break that promise.

"I really wish you wouldn't go," he said.

"Look at the clock. I've got to."

"Come on. Don't leave yet."

She sat down on the edge of the bed and slipped into her shoes. "Quit whining. I told you last night I couldn't stay for breakfast. Don't worry. I'll call you." She stood, tucked her blouse into the jeans and blew him a kiss before she walked out of the bedroom.

"Next time we have dinner first," he yelled, but either she did not hear him or chose not to answer because the next thing he heard was the front door close.

Shawn hated that their relationship consisted of nothing more than two or three hours in bed together. He sat there and tried to figure out a way to move their relationship onto another level. A strange sound broke into his thoughts and he looked towards the bedroom door.

A man stood in the doorway, a sawed-off shotgun cradled in his hands. Shawn made a frantic grab for the .38 on the table next to the bed. His quick reaction surprised the man in the doorway but not enough to make a difference. He pulled the trigger and both barrels of the shotgun fired simultaneously; the sound deafening in the confines of the small bedroom.

Shawn Parker felt the twin shotgun loads tear into his body, blowing him back against the headboard. He hung there for a moment, then slowly slid down onto the bed, leaving harsh streaks of blood patterning the wall.

Chapter One

Ginny Thomas, a rag-tag girl of fifteen, was wearing cut-off jeans and a tank top, both of which were worn thin from constant use. Her hair, like the wood piling she was leaning against, had been bleached from continued exposure to the brutal glare of the harsh Florida sun.

She had ditched school again and was now sitting on the walkway of the small marina wondering if she was going to go back tomorrow. She couldn't decide which she hated more; school itself or the kids in it, who walked around her as if she had leprosy or some other disease they didn't want to be exposed to.

So she had come to the only place in her world where she felt comfortable, where her only friend was likely to be. Only he wasn't there. The slip where he moored his boat was empty. With nowhere else to go, she had flopped down on the walkway to wait for his return.

Ginny looked up as the sound of an outboard motor echoed across the calm water of the inlet. Rising to her feet, she blocked out the glare from the sun with her hand and searched for the source of the sound.

Across the inlet, she saw a 24-foot boat barreling towards the outermost slip with no apparent let-up in speed. Fearing the worst, Ginny raced down the length of the dock and kicked two beat-up fenders over the side just as the driver of the boat spun the wheel hard over, which only managed to assure that the boat would neatly miss both fenders before slamming bow first into the dock, its still running props holding it fast.

Ginny jumped onto the boat, took three quick steps to the cockpit and pulled the emergency fuse cord out of the dash, whereupon the engine died. Turning, she looked angrily at the man standing at the wheel who had a can of beer in his hand and an embarrassed grin on his face.

Lou Parker, a week-old growth of beard on his fifty year-old well tanned face, moved back from the wheel and sat down on the stern bench. He nodded at the emergency fuse cord in Ginny's hand and grinned. "I was just about to do that myself."

"Sure you were."

"Absolutely. I just lost my balance there for a moment."

"Like when the boat hit the dock." She pointed at the can of beer. "And that didn't help much either. Gimme!"

Lou quickly pulled the car away, holding it over his head, out of her reach. He shook his head. "You're too young."

"And you're old enough to know better," she shot back as she leaned over, shoved one of the seat cushions aside, opened the lid to the storage locker and pulled out a rope, which she expertly threw over a cleat on the dock. Hauling in on the line she maneuvered the boat against the dock before securing the other end to a cleat on the stern.

Lou put his feet up on the remaining cushion and watched her repeat the process at the bow. Coming back to the stern, Ginny looked around the boat, and scowled at the mess at Lou's feet. A week's worth of empty beer cans were scattered among the remnants of uneaten food and unattended fishing gear. In short, the boat could have passed for a small garbage scow.

"How can you live like this?"

Lou shrugged and polished off the last of his beer. He handed the empty can to Ginny and got to his feet, but too many empties had taken their toll and he swayed, fighting to keep his balance. Ginny watched as he slowly lost the battle and slumped to the deck, where he curled up, closed his eyes and promptly fell asleep.

Ginny stared down at Lou with a mixture of distaste and compassion. She liked this man who sometimes allowed her to sleep on his boat when she had nowhere else to go. She just wished he didn't drink as much as he did. But there seemed to be nothing else that interested him. He said he liked to fish, but she'd never seen him come back with a catch and most of the time he left the dock without any bait. He seemed to be a man who was just living out the rest of his life without caring how he did it. And she'd never heard him laugh and this troubled her. As did the gun she had found one day in one of the cabin's drawers. She'd decided that something bad must have happened to him but she could never get him to tell her what it was. In fact, there wasn't a lot about his life before he came down here and bought the boat that he'd talk about.

Ginny sighed, took another look at the shape the boat was in and resigned herself to the inevitable. Jumping onto the dock, she walked down to the end and picked up the small broom laying next to a hose. She tossed the broom into a nearby garbage can, grabbed the hose and dragged them both back to the boat. She took another look at Lou laying there and grinned. It would serve him right. She twisted the nozzle on the hose and directed the stream of water right at his head.

Lou moved as the cold water hit him. Twisting away so the force of the water coming from the hose hit him in the back instead of his face, he went back to sleep.

Seeing the water was not having the effect on Lou she'd hoped for, Ginny turned the hose on the trash laying in the rear well of the boat. She used its power to push the trash to one corner where it would be easier for her to pick up. She knew she had to work fast if she was going to get it cleaned before the sun went down and she couldn't see what she was doing anymore.

The local grocery store was sandwiched between a 2-hour dry cleaners and a "No Appointment Needed" barber shop. All three had seen better days and blended in well with the run-down look of the neighborhood.

Lou pulled a six-pack from the refrigerator at the rear of the store and carried it to the front counter. Sleep had become impossible while Ginny was cleaning the boat, so he'd dragged himself up and gotten away from her.

For a reason he really didn't understand, she had taken it upon herself to see to it that his boat was always clean and maintained. She had tried to do the same with him and so far, he'd been able to fight her off. He knew he tolerated her inter-ference in his life because since she had attached herself to him he'd never had to worry about gassing up or emptying the bilge or any of those other cute things that they said had to be done when you owned a boat. Ginny saw to it all.

Lou dumped the six-pack onto the counter and looked up at Mrs. Owens, the overweight owner of the store, who'd been watching his every move from the moment he'd come in. Lou smiled graciously at her while grabbing a package of sugar doughnuts from the rack nearby and tossing it on the counter next to the beer.

Mrs. Owens made no move to ring up the purchases. Lou ran his hand over the stubble on his face and nodded. He knew what she was waiting for and rummaged through his pockets for the money to pay her. Finding none, he sheepishly looked up at her. "Couldn't you just add it to my tab? I'll come back later tonight and settle up."

Mrs. Owens had been through this with Lou too many times before. And too many times before, he'd forgotten to pay up and she'd have to continue reminding him before he finally did. Mrs. Owens had come to the conclusion that Lou never intended to cheat her out of the money, it was just that he didn't seem to care that much about money. But she had a store to run and couldn't allow customers like Lou to take things without paying for them. So she reached out for the beer and doughnuts and put them on the shelf behind her. "And these'll be waiting for you when you do," she told him.

"If I die from starvation, Mrs. Owens, it'll be on your head."

"Lack of beer and doughnuts never killed anyone, Mr. Parker."

"There's always a first time," he said as he turned away, pushed the door open and shuffled into the street.

Lou entered the courtyard of the stucco two-story building trying to remember where he'd hidden the key to his apartment when he'd left the week before. He knew that he hadn't taken it with him only because he wasn't that stupid. He'd already lost so many keys over the side of the boat that his landlord had finally threatened to charge him double the next time he lost one. So he'd taken to hiding the key when he left to spend time on his boat and was now facing the problem of remembering where he had hidden it.

He stopped in front of the door to his apartment and looked around. He knew the key had to be somewhere nearby. Reaching up, he ran the tips of his fingers across the top of the door jam and came away with nothing more than dust and grime.

He turned and spotting the potted plant that stood just down from his door, he decided that it would make a good place to hide a key. He dug his fingers into the dirt and got nothing more than dirty fingernails for his trouble. His eyes then caught the emergency fire extinguisher recessed in the wall. Walking over to it, he reached into the well at the top of the extinguisher and smiled, feeling the key laying there. He pulled it out, walked back to his apartment, unlocked the door and pushed it open.

He walked in and pulled up short. The furniture that had come with the apartment-couch, coffee table, easy-chair, lamps-were all still there. Everything else was gone. None of his pictures were on the wall. None of his magazines were scattered about where he'd thrown them. There were no dirty plates stacked in the sink. In fact, it looked as if nobody lived there at all.

He heard a noise behind him and turned in time to see the apartment manager, Kaplan, a large man who was pushing seventy and whose body still carried the hardness of a lifetime of working out, come in and his bewilderment immediately changed to an uneasy understanding. Lou gestured around the room with a sweep of his arm. "Your work?"

"Yes it is. You're moving out."

"I am?"

Kaplan nodded. "I don't want you here anymore."

"Come on. I always paid my rent."

"Yeah and sometimes you even paid it in the same month it was due."

"But I paid it."

"You just don't get it, do you? Look, it's simple. You can't live here anymore. You give the place a bad name. You come in here drunk every night. Waking everybody. I can't handle all the complaints. I'm too old for this. I want peace and quiet and the only way I'm going to get it is with you gone."

"You're a prick, you know that?"

"That could be. But right now I'm just tired of making excuses for you."

"And where do you expect me to go?"

"Anywhere as long as it's nowhere near this place."

Resigned, Lou slumped down on the couch. "Where's my stuff?"

"Boxed and sitting in the alley out back, waiting for you to haul it away."

Kaplan looked down at him. Despite all the trouble Lou caused, he still liked the man. "Look, I know what you're going through. I retired myself ten years back. But sitting around drinking and pretending to go fishing isn't what retirement's all about."

"You know nothing about me."

"I know enough to tell you that you've got to find something to do. Something that interests you."

"There're things I'm interested in."

"Besides drinking."

"Anybody ever tell you to mind you're own business?"

"Lots of people. Mostly those who didn't want to hear the truth. Leave the key on the table," Kaplan told him and walked out.

Lou sat there for a moment staring at the empty doorway before forcing himself to get up and over to the door where he turned back for one last look at what had once been his warm nest.

The aging Ford station wagon drove past the palm trees that had been planted when the first homes on the tract had been built in the late forties. The houses had originally all been constructed from a single set of plans but through the years different owners had attempted to make them their own and now they were as individual as their owners had been.

The station wagon pulled into the driveway of the yellow stuccoed home and stopped abreast of the green lawn. The driver, Diane Masters, an attractive woman in her early forties, dragged a grocery bag across the front seat and cradling it in one arm, grabbed her purse with the other and got out of the car.

She shut the door with her hip, walked around the front of the car and stopped abruptly when she caught sight of Lou sitting on the steps to her porch. She then saw the boxes stacked on her lawn. She shook her head and continued towards her front door. "No way, Lou. No way in hell."

"I thought we had something going," he said, getting to his feet and blocking her path.

Resigned, she stopped and faced him. "So did I. But I was wrong. You forget why I stopped seeing you?"

Lou frowned. He tried to remember but for the life of him couldn't and she saw that.

"I'll remind you. Maybe it'll sink in this time. I kicked you out because I couldn't stand you sitting around doing nothing. All day. Every day. From the time you got up until the time you passed out dead drunk at night. You did nothing. Not a thing. And that's not natural, Lou."

"I was thinking."

"I know. About the past."

"Sometimes."

"All the time. Well, I live in the present. The past's over and no matter how hard you keep thinking about it, it's not coming back. And neither are you."

She brushed past him to the door. This time he didn't try to stop her. When she got the door open she turned back. "And get that stuff off my lawn!"

She went inside, slamming the door behind her. Lou turned and looked unhappily at the boxes piled on the lawn.

Lou stretched out in his favorite position on the boat; legs sprawled on the deck, back resting comfortably against the rear deck with a can of beer in his hand.

The entire boat was filled with the boxes containing his belongings, as was the wooden walkway next to it. He'd left himself a two-foot passageway between the boxes and the water. Just enough room for him to get by if he ever wanted to go somewhere. Finishing off the beer, he tossed it to join the others that were piled up at his feet just as Ginny came down the dock ramp. She looked at the empty beer cans and frowned. "Come on, Lou, I just finished cleaning it."

"It's my boat. I can do what I want," he said, and reached for another beer from the cooler at his feet.

"Then you ought to think about keeping it clean yourself instead of my having to do it."

"Nobody asked you to do it."

Ginny sighed. He was right. He'd never asked her to clean the boat. Of course, he never objected either. She decided that she had nobody to blame but herself if he didn't appreciate what she'd done. "Mr. Langer says to tell you that you can't leave the boxes on the dock. You've got to stow them on board."

Lou looked around at the boxes of various sizes that filled every inch of space on his boat. "Where'd he suggest I put them?"

"He didn't say. Only that you've got to get them off the dock."

"Tell him I'm working on it," he said, and took a long pull from the can.

Ginny nodded. She'd expected an answer like that. She decided that the next time he left for a beer run, she'd straighten things out and get all the boxes on board. Having made that decision, she reached into her back pocket and pulled out a thick stack of letters and advertisements. "And he told me to tell you that he's no post office and for you to stop giving out his address for your mail."

She held out the mail to Lou who looked at it as if it was contaminated.

"I told him to just throw it out. That you wouldn't read it anyway, but he insisted I give it to you."

Lou looked up at her. "Don't you have anything to do? Like go to school or something?"

Ignoring his question, she checked through the mail. "There's a couple of your pension checks…" She stopped and looked over at him. "You know, if you cashed these things once in a while you wouldn't always be short of money." She waited for a response and getting none continued to look through the mail. "There's the usual junk stuff…and here's one that looks official…from the police, the return says."

Lou frowned. He reached for the letter and tearing the envelope open, he pulled out a single sheet of paper. A chill coursed through his body as he realized he was reading a death notice. His only son was dead, murdered in his home. By assailant or assailants unknown. Although he hadn't gotten along with his son and hadn't spoken to him in months, the notice of his death seemed to drain whatever life was left in him.

Ginny had heard of people turning white but she'd never seen it before. Now she had. The man before her had turned a ghastly white and seemed to crumple before her eyes.

"What?" she asked.

He didn't answer and she saw tears forming in his eyes. She thought he was too old to cry. Only kids did that yet here Lou was, years her senior, almost too old to be her father, with tears running down his cheeks.

Reaching out, Ginny gingerly took the letter from Lou's hand. When she finished reading it she looked over at Lou with heart felt compassion. The thought that he might've had a son, or any children for that matter, had never entered her mind and now, according to the letter, that son was dead, murdered in his bed. She had never faced a situation like this and didn't know what to do so she just stood there and waited.

Finally, he turned and looked at the young girl standing in front of him. He drained the last of the beer from the can, tossed it to join the rest of the empties at his feet and got up. He took the letter from her and stuffed it in his pocket.

"I'm sorry," she finally said.

Lou didn't respond. Instead, he pushed one of the boxes aside until he found his jacket and slipped into it. He then began rummaging through the rest of the mail until he found his pension checks and stuffed them into the same pocket. Slipping into the cabin, he opened the drawer under the port side bunk, grabbed his old service revolver and shoved it into his waistband before returning to the deck. He looked at

Ginny standing there and gestured around the boat. "Take care of her for me, will ya'?"

The request took her by surprise. This was the first time he'd ever asked her for anything and she liked the feeling it gave her of being a real part of his life, something she'd wanted for a long time. "Sure thing, Lou."

She watched him step onto the dock. "Where're you going?"

When he didn't answer, she tried again. "When you coming back?"

Lou looked around, at Ginny, at the boat, at the boxes scattered about, and shrugged before he turned and walked away.

Chapter Two

Lou stood looking down at the grave in front of him and allowed his mind to wander back over the years when Shawn was growing up, when there never seemed to be any time to do the things he'd always planned to do with his son. He looked at the ground, pictured his son laying there under the newly sodded earth and felt unwanted emotions start to swell within him. It had been his choice to leave town and retire to Florida, leaving friends and family behind. There had been nothing holding him in New York except for Shawn and spending the rest of his life arguing with him was something he hadn't wanted to do. So he'd left and hadn't seen his son since. And now he never would.

Lou reached into his pocket and pulled out a crumpled tie. He made some effort at straightening it, then gave up and draped it over the headstone. He took a final look at the grave, then walked slowly back to his rented car, got in and drove off, winding his way past other graves to the entrance of the cemetery.

As he reached the gate, a dark brown Chevy that was parked on the roadway above his son's grave, started up and followed him out.

Lou double-parked in front of the 109th precinct, got out of his car and looked over at the familiar building.

He'd worked Manhattan for the first six years on the job and the transfer to the hundred and ninth in Queens, with its preponderance of single and two-story homes instead of the apartment houses he was used to in the city, was not something he had wanted. But they'd been short of detectives here at the time and he wasn't given a choice. The orders had been cut and published and so, reluctantly, he moved across the river and reported to the one-o-nine. He had never left it. Through the years, Queens became his own personal territory and working Manhattan again was forgotten.

Lou trudged up the familiar steps and into the precinct. His clothes were the same he had on when he'd left the marina. He'd caught the first New York plane out of Miami and paced the aisle all the way into La Guardia. He rented a car at the airport and headed east on the Grand Central. He'd gotten off on Northern Boulevard and continued east until he found the first motel that had a vacancy. He'd rented a room, but as tired as he was, couldn't sleep. So he'd watched the sun come up over a cup of coffee and then driven over to the cemetery and from there to here.

Lou opened the door to the squad room and ambled in. In his rumpled clothes, he looked more like a suspect than a visitor, but since he'd gotten past the desk sergeant, none of the detectives paid him a second glance.

Lou felt a strong twinge of homecoming. The squad room looked exactly like it always had: jackets tossed over the back of chairs, half-filled coffee containers scattered about, men on phones, the smell of disinfectant mixed with the lingering odor of vomit.

Lou walked through the squad bay and up to the single office at the far side of the room. The door was closed. Lou thought of knocking but decided he didn't have to anymore so he opened the door and went in.

Captain Ned Morrison was a few years older than Lou and looked like a man who'd downed too many drinks in his time along with too many meals. It took him a moment to recognize Lou.

Morrison had never liked Lou and he suspected that the feeling was mutual. He was right. Their mutual dislike had begun the first day Lou joined the squad. Lou's rule bending reputation had preceded him and Morrison intended to lay down the law now that he was under his command. He'd called Lou into his office and informed him how things were going to be. He demanded that Lou follow the Department's written procedures to the letter. That the procedures were what Morrison lived by and he expected every detective under his command to do the same. Lou had listened politely and then got up, announced he was going to get drunk and walked away leaving Morrison standing there feeling the stares and snickers of the rest of the squad.

Morrison spent much of his time from that point on trying to take Lou down. He never succeeded. Lou and his partner, Frank Tollin, had continued doing things their own way. And they were successful, closing case after case. No matter what he'd assigned them, and he'd given them the toughest cases that came in, they closed them.

And they didn't seem to even want any reward. Commendations meant nothing to either of them. They were just doing their jobs. Morrison's emotions moved quickly from dislike to a genuine hatred for them both but it centered on Lou whose attitude made him feel worthless. He would have transferred them both out if they weren't so damn good.

As their commander, he'd shared in each arrest they'd made and it looked good on his record. He'd even gone out of his way on occasion to congratulate them when they'd solved a particularly complex case. Eventually, they'd formed an unspoken truce that lasted until Lou retired.

Now Lou stood opposite him again only this time as a civilian. Morrison looked him over and raised his eyebrows as Lou slid into the chair in front of Morrison's desk uninvited.

"You could have called and told me," Lou said without preamble. "I missed the funeral."

"We tried calling, but your phone's been disconnected."

Lou waved it off. "I forgot to pay."

Morrison stared at the man slumped in the chair in front of him. He looked like a washed-out shell of the man he remembered and this pleased Morrison. He leaned back, waited for Lou to make the next move.

"You want to tell me how it went down?" Lou finally asked.

"Why?"

"'Cause it's my son."

"And that's it? A father's curiosity and nothing more?"

Lou straightened up, a flash of anger crossing his face. And then it left. Too much trouble. He shrugged his shoulders, slumped back down. "I'll find out anyhow."

"That's what I figured," Morrison said. It was what he'd suspected from the moment Lou had entered his office without knocking. "Stay out of it, Lou. It's got nothing to do with you. We've got a murder case here and we don't need any civilian sticking his nose in where it doesn't belong."

Lou forced a grin and leaned forward. "Now that you got that off your chest you want to tell me how he was killed?"

Morrison took a deep breath. Lou hadn't changed one iota and wasn't about to. "You always have to have it your own way, don't you? Fine. He was gunned down. In bed. Took two barrels from a shotgun. Blew him all to hell. There were bits and pieces of him took us two days to scrape off the wall and we never did get it all. Is that what you wanted to know?"

Lou sat motionless for a moment, then dragged himself to his feet and moved towards the door. "It's a start."

Morrison got up and came around his desk following him. "Stay out of it, Lou. I mean it. We don't need outside help."

Lou turned back to face him. "Is that what I am now? Fuckin' outside help? Jesus. There was a time when you'd of begged for my help."

"That time's past. You should try and remember that."

Lou turned walked out without a word leaving Morrison wondering just how much trouble Lou was going to cause him this time around.

Lou sat behind the wheel of his car sipping a can of beer while he watched the small frame house across the street. He'd been sitting there for the last couple of hours trying to figure out a way to avoid going over there. Now, reluctantly, he decided there was no way getting around it. He polished off the last of the beer, tossed the can onto the floor of the car and got out, crossed the street and walked up to the front door. Before he could ring the bell, the door opened and a burly heavily muscled man stood there, glaring at him. Lou felt the hostility and tossed it off. He'd expected nothing less.

"I figured you for at least two more beers before you'd work up enough courage to come over here."

Lou shrugged his shoulders.

"You're not welcome here, Parker," Bill Warren went on angrily.

Lou grinned up at him. "Gee. And I thought you might've lightened up in time. But I guess once a prick, always a prick." Warren stiffened. Lou grinned liking the fact that he'd gotten a reaction from the man. "I want to see my wife."

"Ex-wife, asshole. And she doesn't want to see you. Now get the hell off my property before I toss you off. No. I got a better idea. Stay. Give me the pleasure of beating the shit out of you from here to the curb."

Lou looked past Warren into the house. Nothing moved. He looked back at Warren blocking the door and decided this was getting him nowhere. He turned and walked towards his car.

Most of the open spaces in the supermarket parking lot had empty carts sitting in them. Lou was too lazy to get out and move one, so he drove down one row and up the next until he eventually found a woman pulling out. He waited and pulled into her space as she drove off.

Lou settled back and watched the two entrances to the supermarket. He slumped behind the wheel, half his body on the back of the seat, the other braced against the door. It was a position Lou had learned years earlier on his first stake-out with the old veteran who had taken him under his wing. The man had told him that sitting in a car for hours on end watching a house or a door or a parked car was more tiring than a cross-country run. He had instructed Lou on how to get himself into a position that wasn't comfortable enough to allow him to fall asleep, but was comfortable enough to remain in for long periods without suffering. It had taken Lou a while to find what position was best for him, but once he had, he found he could sit for hours and his body would still be ready for anything.

As much as he hated to admit it, he felt good sitting there survailing the store, even if he weren't waiting for a bad guy this time out. He hadn't realized how much he'd missed it. He took a sip from the container of coffee he'd bought from the drive-thru up the street and then rested it on the dash.

Lou saw his quarry coming from the market, pushing a cart. She hadn't changed much. That was the strange thing about Darleen. She seemed to hang on to her youthful appearance while everyone around her got older.

He got out of the car, poured the remains of the coffee onto the ground, tossed the container back into the car and moved quickly between the cars on an interception course for Darleen. As he came out from behind a car, she saw him and grimaced. She pushed the cart faster, trying to get to her car before he got to her. Lou sped up and grabbed the cart, stopping her. Darleen slapped his hand away and continued on. Lou fell into step next to her and walked along without saying anything. He knew she couldn't stand silence and waited for her to break it. Finally, she looked over at him. "You look awful."

Lou shrugged, not understanding the concern everyone seemed to have over what he looked like.

"What do you want?" she asked.

Lou glanced at her. He'd known that seeing her was something he'd had to do, but now that she was here, next to him, waiting for him to explain why he had sought her out, Lou wasn't sure why he had. That wasn't exactly true. Lou knew why he'd wanted to, he just didn't know how to say it. Finally, he figured that maybe if he just started talking, she'd understand and pick up the slack.

"I guess I wanted to talk to you about Shawn."

"Oh, that's really good," she said in an icy voice. "Even for you."

"Come on, Darleen."

"Come on, Darleen," she said, mimicking him. "You ask about Shawn. Why? When he was alive you never called him. Never wrote him. Never asked about him. So how come now? You feeling guilty?"

Lou looked away from her. The fact was he did feel guilty. Darleen caught his expression and interpreted it for what it was. "Good. You deserve to."

Lou had forgotten what Darleen had been like, but hearing her dig at him instantly brought the memories back. He moved in front of the cart and when she tried to maneuver around him he grabbed hold of it, tightly this time. Years of suppressed anger towards Darleen boiled to the surface.

"And I suppose you think you were mother of the year. I was there, remember?"

"I try to forget that part of my life."

"Yeah, right. You forget everything that might be taken as being your shortcomings. You have an image to uphold. The perfect wife and mother."

"I may not have been perfect but I was there."

"Physically, sure. But you were never really there for Shawn and you certainly were never there for me."

"That's not true. Ask anyone."

"Oh, sure, you told everyone how good you were, but the fact is you weren't. I was there, remember? I lived it."

"Wrong! You lived with the Department, not us. You didn't care about us. The Job was all you cared about. I cared about our son."

"Then you sure had a funny way of showing it. You forget telling Shawn time and time again about how tired you were of hearing about his problems? Is that what you'd call caring? Being a real mother? I sure as hell don't."

"Get out of my way, Lou. That court order directing you to stay away from me is still in force."

Darleen stepped around him, opened the trunk of her car and started to unload the groceries from the cart and put them into the trunk. Lou stood there watching her. She felt his eyes boring into her back and turned around to face him. "I did what I had to do," she told him.

"Yeah, right. Ignore your own kid. You just had to do that."

"At least we had a relationship. Which is more than you had with him. And there was an honesty between Shawn and me."

"God, where've I heard that one before? You don't know how to be honest. Lying's a way of life with you."

"I don't lie."

"Right. Like when you self-righteously told me that you'd never lie to me. That even though we couldn't live together there was still an honesty between us."

"I wasn't lying. It was true."

"It was bullshit! You and that asshole you're now married to were carrying on all the time you were denying to me that there was another man. I'm a detective, for Christ's sake! Did you really think that I wouldn't check the phone bills? I knew all the time." Lou looked at her with a sense of triumph. He'd been wanting to tell her that for years.

Darleen picked up the last bag of groceries, put it into the trunk and turned to him. "I know you did."

Lou stared at her, unnerved. "You what? You knew? And you didn't even give a damn?"

"Nope."

Lou's shoulders sagged as he realized for the first time just how cold this woman he'd married was. How nothing meant anything to her, nothing but herself and what she wanted and what she needed. Not him. Not Shawn. No one. Except Darleen. Everything else was just for show.

Gratified with the reaction she saw on Lou's face, Darleen slammed the trunk shut and marched triumphantly around him.

Lou pulled himself together. He couldn't let her get away with this. Not anymore. And he knew how to get back at her. He smiled, determined to enjoy the moment.

"Hey, Darleen."

She ignored him. Wouldn't even look at him. No matter.

"You ever tell your new husband you cheated on him, too? With me?"

Darleen whirled on him. "You bastard!"

Lou grinned. He'd gotten to her. Finally. After all those years. "Through and through," he agreed, turned and walked away.

Furious, Darleen yelled after him. "And you were probably on the take just like your son!"

Lou stopped, turned back but Darleen was already in her car. She started the engine, gunned it and roared past, barely missing him.

This time Morrison saw him coming across the squad room and was ready when Lou pushed open the door. He stood up as Lou stepped to the front of Morrison's desk and planted himself there. "What's this shit I hear about Shawn being dirty?"

Morrison took a deep breath of resignation and sat back down. He wondered how Lou had gotten the information so fast and realized that he could have saved himself some grief if he'd told him the first time Lou had come into his office. But he was under orders to keep everything in the family and Lou was no longer family.

Morrison moved around his desk past Lou, closed the door to his office and walked back behind his desk. "Where'd you hear that?" he asked trying to buy some time.

"Jesus," Lou whispered and slid into the chair in front of the desk. "I didn't believe it until right now. Damn it! I still don't."

"Don't," Morrison said.

"Stop pulling my chain. You got evidence that Shawn was on the take, then I want to see it."

"We've got nothing."

Lou stared at him. "How come I don't believe you?"

"You're suspicious by nature, Lou."

"Come on, you can do better than that."

"Let it go. There's no good that can come of this."

Lou got to his feet leaned forward over the desk, right into Morrison's face. "My kid was not a dirty cop. No fuckin' way!"

"Let it go, Lou," Morrison repeated. "For all our sakes."

Lou shook his head. "I can't."

"Then you should know that I'll do everything in my power to break you if you stick your nose into this investigation. Your pension. That rep you're so proud of. Everything. And I won't lose a night's sleep over doing it either."

"Neither will I," Lou told him before walking out.

Chapter Three

The radio patrol car pulled into the parking lot of the coffee and doughnut shop on Parsons Boulevard and parked. Harry Carson, a uniformed officer of twenty-five, grabbed his hat from the empty seat next to him, aligned it perfectly on his head-two fingers between the bill and forehead-and opened the driver's door just as Lou came out from the alley next to the shop.

"Hiya, Harry," he called out amiably.

Carson looked over, saw Lou and his expression changed to unconcealed fear. He turned away and started for the doughnut shop but Lou grabbed his arm and pulled him back over to the patrol car. Lou gestured towards the passenger door.

"Open it," Lou told him.

Carson looked around hoping another patrol car would come in for coffee and get Lou off his back. Then he realized that was the last thing he wanted. There'd be too many questions about what he was doing here with Lou and he wasn't sure he'd be believed. He unlocked the door and Lou slid into the passenger seat while Carson hurried around to the driver's side and got in. He flipped both visors down hoping against hope that nobody would see them together. He turned to Lou.

"What the fuck do you want?" he asked with a bravado he didn't feel.

Lou frowned, confused. "What's with you?"

Carson looked away. The tough guy act never got you anywhere with Lou. He saw right through it. "Look, try and understand, Lou. I can't be seen with you. I don't need the grief."

"All I want is information."

"Try the yellow pages," Carson said, and immediately regretted it.

Lou's face had hardened and he twisted around in the seat so he faced Carson. "Don't push me, kid. You think the department wouldn't like to know where you were that night when you didn't answer that call? That you were piss-ass drunk, puking your guts all over that alley. I covered for you."

"My wife had just walked out on me," Carson whined.

"Think that'll make a difference with the board? I'm callin' my marker."

Carson looked at Lou and realized he wasn't kidding. He remembered that what Lou said he'd do, he always did. Still, he tried to save some face.

"I know I owe you."

"Glad you still have a memory, Harry."

"And this'll square us?"

Lou shook his head sadly. "Sure. The marker's burned as of this moment. You can sleep nights now knowing that I won't ever ask you for another thing."

"Lou, try and look at it from my side."

"I do, Harry, and I don't like what I see. Now what went down after Shawn got hit?"

Carson looked away. "Well…at first, we went at it like when any cop gets killed. We were out on the streets pushing and shoving like there was nothing else that mattered in the world.

Then word came down from up top that Shawn's bank account had been found and it contained more money than he could've earned in ten lifetimes. We were called off. Orders. Specific and clear. Stay out of it. Internal Affairs was working it. So we stopped."

"And that's it?"

"There were rumors, of course. Lots of them 'bout the amount in the account but nothing specific. Except nobody in IA would admit that they were working the case. Everybody seemed to be playing it close to the vest."

Lou frowned. There was something wrong but he couldn't put his finger on exactly what it was. He looked over at the patrol cop seated next to him. Carson shifted uncomfortably under his gaze. "That's all I know, Lou. Honest."

Lou nodded and turned away which gave Carson added bravado.

"So why don't you just get the fuck out of my car," he said, "before I have to do something about it."

Lou sighed and looked over at Carson. "Don't ever entertain the thought you could do anything about anything, kid. Life's too short to make mistakes like that."

Lou opened his door and got out of the car. He walked away as Carson flipped the visors back up, started the car and roared off.

Sitting in his car, Lou glanced at the house across the street. It was Shawn's home and he realized that he'd never been inside. Shawn had bought the place in Whitestone just after Lou had left to spend his retirement in Florida. He remembered how Shawn had called him when he'd bought it. Shawn had gotten the house when he made detective. It had been in foreclosure for some time and the bank had let it go to rot.

Shawn had told him he had picked it up for a song but hadn't wanted him to see it until it was fixed up.

Shawn had called a couple of months later and invited him over. He remembered how proud Shawn sounded when he explained some of the things he had done with the house. They'd set a time for him to come over, but something broke on a case and he'd never made it. There had never seemed to be enough time. There always seemed to be too many cases. Too many cans of beer. Maybe both. Now he was going to see it and it was too late to tell his son what he thought of it or how proud he was of what Shawn had accomplished.

Lou got out of the car and walked across the street. He bypassed the front entrance and went down the driveway to the side door. A Police Department Crime Seal warned everyone away.

Lou tore it off, jimmied the lock, shoved the door open and went inside. He poked his head into the first doorway he came to. It was the kitchen. Dirty dishes still in the sink. It looked like it'd been searched. Then he took in the latest appliances built into the varnished wood of the counters. No veneer for Shawn. His son had taken the time to do the job right, Lou thought proudly.

He continued on into the living room. This room had been tossed also. A black residue, left over from the department's print man, stood out on the tables, walls, television and stereo equipment. Lou looked at the various items that made up a part of his son's life and wondered just how much all these "things" really meant to Shawn. He knew that he cared little for "things" and thought that Shawn shared that view. Now he wasn't so sure.

Lou turned away and continued slowly on until he came to the bedroom. He stepped into the room, felt around for the light switch and flipped it on. He stood there motionless, his eyes inevitably drawn to and held by the dried blood stains above the headboard.

Lou took a deep breath and exhaled, forcing his body to relax before he walked over to the bed and closely examined the blood stains; their pattern. He looked across the bed at the door and decided that was where the shots had most likely come from. He felt no emotion. He was examining a murder scene with the same objective eye he'd used for over thirty years. His professionalism had taken over, as it had every time he'd come onto a scene like this. And there'd been too many in his lifetime.

Lou knew what was happening, how he was coldly scrutinizing the scene and allowed himself the pleasure of knowing that he still had the old habits and knowledge.

He looked down at the nightstand and opened the single drawer. Like all nightstands it was filled with an accumulation of bits and pieces. Lou rummaged around in it and then frowned. What the hell did he expect to find? The room had been tossed by the Department. They would've found anything of use.

Lou shoved the drawer closed with his knee, but it jammed. He reached down, grasped the metal handle of the drawer and shoved. The drawer gave a couple of inches and finally slid fully in. But it wasn't sliding like it should have.

Lou pulled it out again, bent down to look inside, and saw what was causing the problem. He reached inside and came away with a photograph that had fallen behind the drawer and onto its runner. He tossed the drawer to the floor and looked at the photograph. It was of him and Shawn taken years before. Shawn was in uniform, having just made sergeant, while Lou was in plainclothes. Lou recognized the shirt he'd been wearing. He still had it somewhere.

He slumped down on the bed and stared at the picture. He was pleased that Shawn had kept it all these years. And was saddened by it at the same time. He pulled his eyes from the picture and looked around the room. There were other photographs on the wall, but none of him. And none in the living room either. The only one had been thrown into a drawer with other odds and ends. Almost as if Shawn didn't want to remember that he'd had a father. But he'd kept one and Lou felt good about that.

Lou slipped the photograph into his pocket and pulled it right out again. He'd felt something. He examined the picture and saw that there was another one stuck to it. He gingerly pried it apart. It was a picture of a very attractive girl. Shawn's age. She'd been playing volleyball and the photographer had caught her as she was diving for a ball. Lou took a moment to admire her figure in the two-piece bathing suit, then shoved both photographs into his pocket.He got to his feet and froze at the unmistakable sound of the hammer of a gun being cocked.

He slowly turned around and found himself looking down the barrel of a .38, inches from his eyes. He refocused to the person holding it. He frowned, then contemptuously nudged the gun away from his face with the back of his hand.

Lou stepped back and looked at the woman standing in front of him. From top to bottom. He noted that she was about Shawn's age, pretty in a tough sort of way, nice figure, dark hair tightly pulled back, about three inches shorter than his six-foot height, and held her weapon as if she knew how to use it. He wondered if that was as far as it went, though. Holding a gun properly and being prepared to fire it into another person were two entirely different things. Lou's eyes came to rest on the Detective's badge pinned to the belt of the woman's slacks. Seeing it, Lou shook his head in disgust. Then, ignoring the gun in her hand, he turned and walked into the hallway.

Chris Preston didn't move. She was still trying to cope with the contempt he'd shown for her gun. She thought either he was totally without fear, had a courage she'd never seen before, or he'd known that she wasn't about to shoot him. Not for just breaking into the house. And he had walked away from her as if she didn't even exist.

Chris strode down the hallway after him and found him in the kitchen, searching the drawers in the counter. Chris raised her gun and leveled it at his head. "Close it," she ordered in her best command voice.

Lou looked over at her, closed the drawer, then turned away again, reached down and opened the next one. He rummaged inside. He closed that one and reached for the next.

"You open one more and I'll run you in for obstruction of justice, violating a crime scene, forcible entry and anything else that comes to mind along the way. That is, if I don't shoot you first."

Lou looked over at her curiously.

"Believe it," she said, as if reading his mind.

Lou leaned back against the counter.

"Okay. Now what?"

Chris looked at him. He still hadn't given the slightest indication that the gun leveled at him scared him at all. "This is a crime scene. Until forensic is finished with it, nothing get's touched."

"That's bull and you know it. Or at least you should if that badge means anything at all." Lou gestured towards the bedroom. "That was a clean hit in there. You ain't gonna find a damn thing that's gonna help ya'."

Chris knew he was right, but she was damned if she was going to agree. It was his attitude that frosted her more than anything else. "Then what the hell are you looking for?"

Lou shook his head and took a deep breath before replying. This woman was wasting his time.

"What was it he saw in you anyway?" Lou asked her sharply.

Chris couldn't contain her surprise. "How'd you know?"

Lou reached into his pocket, pulled out the photograph and held it up. "It fell behind the drawer in the bedroom and they missed it. So what was the attraction? It sure wasn't your manners."

"Fuck off," she shot back.

Lou nodded as if her response confirmed his suspicions. "Right," he said, and pushed himself away from the counter. He moved to the door, stopped, turned and tossed her the Crime Scene tape. "Lock up when you leave, will ya'?"

She caught the tape in the air and by the time she looked back he was gone.

Chapter Four

Lou carefully edged between the tables of the darkened bar. On the small stage, two bare-breasted girls were doing their best to dance and stay out of each other's way at the same time.

Lou pulled out a chair at a front row table and sat down. He looked over at the man already seated there. Amos Thornton hadn't changed a bit since the last time he'd seen him. The man still looked a good ten years older than the sixty he was. But he had looked that way twenty years ago, too.

"Don't you ever get tired of seeing naked bodies?" Lou asked after he realized that Amos wasn't going to acknowledge him.

Amos refused to tear his eyes from the girls on the stage to look at the man who'd asked him the question. But somewhere in the back of his mind the sound of the voice clicked and he grinned.

"But these are alive. I have to do something to remind me." He turned to face Lou. "I thought you'd retired down to Florida or somewhere?"

"I did."

"Then what the hell are you doing back here?" Amos asked and immediately regretted it as the reason came back to him.

"I'm sorry about your son."

"Yeah, thanks."

"Well, at least he went out with a smile on his face. If you've got to go that's the way to do it."

Surprised at his statement, Lou reached out and grabbed the man's arm.

"Talk to me, Amos."

"You didn't know?"

"Would I be asking if I did."

Amos glanced back up at the stage and then, resigned that he'd have to explain his remark before he'd be allowed to go back to what he'd come here for, turned in his seat to face Lou.

"Way I heard it, it couldn't have been too long after he came that he got blasted…within five or ten minutes I heard 'em saying…the kids that did the autopsy."

"You didn't do it?"

"Nope. I was on call, too. But they never called me. I didn't find out about it until the next day. When I asked they told me not to worry about it. That they'd gotten someone else in to do it. And they had."

"How come they cut you out?"

Amos shrugged. "Who knows? Ask the top floor, I guess. That's where I heard the order came from."

"A cover-up right from the get-go."

"That'd be one way of looking at it, I suppose," Amos agreed.

"Can you think of another?"

"Sure. I'm getting ready to retire, Lou. I've done my time. Now don't get me wrong. I've enjoyed every minute of it. But right now, I'm kind of a lame duck and they could be wanting the new kids doing things now."

"That's bullshit!"

"True enough, but that's the reason they gave."

Lou sat back. Amos was a shrewd old cookie. He was trying to tell him something, but he wasn't going to volunteer it. Lou didn't blame him. Amos was protecting almost forty years on the job. Forty years. One hell of a pension.

"So what happened?"

"You know how it works. The new kids did the autopsy and the next day they got called upstairs and when they came back it was like they'd had their mouths sutured shut."

Lou was missing something. What the hell was it? Amos was watching him. Waiting for him to get it. But what? Then it came to him.

"And the original paperwork?" Lou asked.

Amos grinned and looked at Lou as if he were going to give him a gold star.

"Beats me. Upstairs somewhere, would be my guess."

"And the one that's available is a sanitized version."

Amos pulled out a cigar and lit up. "You know what? The thing is that the kids don't even give a shit. All they care about is their machines. Running tests like there's no tomorrow. It surprises me that they even condescend to touch the body. You've got to get in there, Lou, to learn anything. Touch the body. Get a sense of what happened. Machines can't tell you that. Only the body can."

He sat back, took a large puff on the cigar and looked at Lou. "They don't care. Not like we did." Amos' face was turned to Lou, but he wasn't seeing him anymore. He was back in the past.

Lou climbed to his feet and tossed a bill on the table. The movement caught Amos' eye and he looked up at Lou as if seeing him for the first time.

"You look terrible," he said.

"Must be the weather."

Lou turned and walked away. He made his way back between the tables towards the front door. Amos watched him go, then turned away, looked up at the girls on the stage and settled back to enjoy the show.

Morrison was watching Brady blow the game, coming up with a split in the ninth frame, when the young kid walked up to him.

"You Morrison?" the kid asked.

"Who wants to know?" Morrison answered not wanting to be bothered. His team was ahead by only seven points and right now that didn't look like it was going to hold up.

"Charley said to tell you there's a call for you. He said to tell you that they said it was important." The kid didn't wait for a response and walked away.

Morrison turned back to the alley in time to see Brady's ball hang on the edge before it fell into the gutter, inches away from making the ten pin. It was a good try, but good tries meant nothing when the entire game hung in the balance. If they lost by that one pin Morrison swore that he'd have Brady on morning watch for the next year.

Disgusted, he turned away and made his way into the bar. He slid onto a stool and shouted towards the bartender who was at the far end of the bar. "You got a call for me?"

Lou moved into the seat next to him. "Who was the girl?"

Surprised, Morrison looked from Lou to the bartender.

Lou caught the look. "Don't blame him. I slipped the kid a ten spot. We were talking about the girl."

"You were. I wasn't."

Morrison got off the stool and turned to go back into the bowling alley, but Lou, in a move whose speed surprised Morrison, came off the chair and blocked his path.

"Try and understand this, asshole. I'm gonna find out who put Shawn in an early grave and anyone who gets in my way is gonna regret it and right now you're in my way."

Morrison stared into Lou's eyes. They were hard and unforgiving. "There's no way around this, is there?"

"None that I know of."

"Jesus, Lou. You sink your teeth into a case and don't let up. Couldn't you let it go, just this once?"

"Once it's solved, I'll let it go. Until then, no way."

Morrison sighed. As much as he hated it, he was going to have to deal with Lou. And now. He got back onto the bar stool. Lou moved next to the bar and leaned against it.

"Okay. There was a girl. We don't know who she is, what she looks like or what was going on between them."

"You expect me to believe that? That you don't know who he was with at the time he was killed?"

"We just don't know, Lou. Honest."

Lou rolled this over in his mind. Morrison placed a hand on Lou's arm. "Look, I know how you must feel. If Susan and I had had some kids I'd probably feel the same way. Worse, maybe. But I'm giving it to you straight. We just don't know." He saw that Lou wasn't buying it and decided to try another tact. "Tell you what. You keep me informed about what you find out and I'll do the same."

Lou stared into Morrison's face. "Why?"

"Because we're getting nowhere and you just might."

Lou laughed. "You mean, if I solve it you'll get all the credit."

Morrison grinned in spite of himself. "Why not?"

"Nothing ever changes with you, does it?"

"Do we have a deal?"

"We'll see how it goes."

Lou headed into Flushing and finally found a parking space off Roosevelt Avenue not too far from the apartment house. He looked up at it as he crossed the street. It hadn't changed much in all the years he'd been going there. He remembered that the inside had been renovated about fifteen years ago, but otherwise, the building looked exactly as it had when it was built some sixty years before. Except for the dirt and grime, of course.

As Lou went into the lobby the dark brown Chevy pulled over down the block and parked.

Lou took the elevator to the third floor. He crossed to the apartment door at the end of the corridor and pressed the bell.

"It's open," a voice bellowed from inside.

Lou grinned and opened the door. He walked in and looked around. The apartment hadn't changed. Old newspapers were scattered about. Dirty clothes piled next to the door waiting to be washed. A couple of plants that had seen better days. A large barrel next to the doorway into the kitchen that Lou knew was filled with empty beer cans. Even Frank Tollin was where he always was, sitting in his leather recliner near the window. Five years Lou's senior, Tollin's weathered face bespoke of having seen far too much for far too many years.

"I always liked this place, the way you live," Lou said.

Tollin grinned. "Got a phone, a TV, my food delivered, the newspaper's at the door each morning. I go down to Paddy's one night a week. What more do I need?"

"A life. When's the last time you saw the sun?"

"And sitting on a boat day after day waiting for a damn fish to bite is living? Look at you. You'd fit right in with the punks in the drunk tank."

"I love you, too." Lou said, and looked towards the kitchen. "The fridge still work?"

"Enough to keep the beer cold."

Lou went into the kitchen and retrieved a can of beer from the refrigerator. "I thought Paddy died a couple of years back."

"He did. But he sold the place about six months before he went. To that night watch sergeant you hated."

Lou came back into the living room and slumped onto the couch across from Tollin. "And the place hasn't changed with him tending bar?"

"Not so's you'd notice. Even cops from other boroughs come over to drink and shoot the shit after they go end-of-watch. So what are you doing here?"

"That's real friendly."

"Gee, Lou, I'm sorry. How the hell are you? What've you been doing with yourself? How's life down in Florida? Now what the hell're you doing' here?"

"Give me a break, Frank, will ya'?" Lou grumbled. "We spent over fifteen years together. Can't I just come over and…"

Tollin interrupted him. "Shoot the shit?"

"Why not?" Lou asked defensively.

"That look in your eye, for one thing."

Lou shrugged. Tollin knew him too well.

"Go for it," he said.

Tollin took a long pull from his beer, settled himself deeper into his chair before he replied. It'd been a long time since he and Lou had sat like this and Tollin admitted to himself that he'd missed it.

"That look in your eyes tells me that you're working a case again and the fact that you're here right now tells me that you hit a brick wall and that tells me that you want my help and that tells me you're not here just to shoot the shit about old times?" He took another sip of beer and grinned.

"How'd I do?" he asked, knowing full well that he was right on.

Lou nodded. "Pretty close."

"Pretty close?"

"Damn close."

"It never bothered you before to tell me I was right."

"It always bothered me. I just never made an issue of it."

Tollin nodded somberly, then grinned. Lou grinned back.

"Okay. I take it you've found out about the bank account," Tollin said, and cocked his head forcing Lou to nod in agreement.

Tollin put his can of beer on the table next to him and leaned forward. "They thought they could keep it quiet. Keep it in the family. As long as the papers didn't find out about it, they thought they were safe. And so far they've kept it out of the papers. So far the wagons they've circled around them has been doing one hell of a job."

"I found out," Lou said.

"'Cause you're a good detective. They're not used to dealing with our kind of cop. Control is the watchword now. Investigate sure. But only do it within the rules laid down in the manual. Or from upstairs. That way they're assured that nothing will ever get done that they don't want done."

"I'm glad I'm retired," Lou said.

"No, you're not. You're just glad that you don't have to fight them anymore. You miss the Job just as much as I do."

"Nope," Lou said. "The Department's changed too much for me."

"You're right on that score but not the way you think. The Department still lives in a dream world. Where it's right and everyone else is the enemy. It's always been that way and always will. But it used to be we only had a few politicians thrown in with the rest, but they're all politicians now. Worried about their image. The new guys wouldn't know how to work a murder case if their life depended on it. It's only the hangers-on, the guys who haven't retired yet, that are holding the department together."

"You really believe that?" Lou asked.

"If I didn't I wouldn't've said it."

Lou Parker stared at his old partner for a long time, trying to gauge if he really believed what he'd just said. The fact was that Lou respected Tollin. He'd turned out to be the perfect partner for him. When Lou started to run roughshod over all the rules, Tollin had kept him in check, even when he didn't understand what was pushing him. Lou explained it to him once. That he believed there was an absolute right and wrong and when the rule book prevented right from prevailing you ignored it. Tollin hadn't agreed but he'd gone along with him anyway. Maybe that was what made them so great a team.

"Okay. Tell me about the bank account," Lou said. "The Department knows. You know. Now I wanna know."

"I'm not sure you do," Tollin said flatly.

Lou locked his eyes on Tollin's and waited patiently. He couldn't force it out of him and they both knew it. It was up to his old partner to make the choice.

Tollin shrugged. "If that's the way you want to play it, it's fine with me. They came across the account a couple of days after the shooting went down. A Swiss account with over a million in it."

Lou was on his feet without even realizing he'd moved. "You're nuts! Where the hell would Shawn get that kind of money?"

Tollin ignored Lou's outburst and treated it for what it really was; fear that his son might really have been on the take.

"Interesting question," Tollin said. "It's the real reason the Department is so intent on covering the whole thing up."

"To save their fuckin' image," Lou said angrily.

"Go back to your boat, Lou. Go fishing. There's nothing here for you anymore."

"Yes, there is. I can nail the sonsabitches that killed my son. And who are now trying to frame him with that account. Just to cover their asses."

Lou calmed himself and sat down on the coffee table close to Tollin. "Look, how about we do it together? The old partnership. What'd'ya say?"

"I'm not a cop anymore, Lou."

"Sure, you are. It's who you are."

"No. I'm out of it."

"Then how come you still go down to Paddy's? You could drink right here. You just go there to be around guys who're still on the job."

Tollin shrugged. "Maybe."

"Come on, Frank. Let's put the team together again and solve this thing."

Tollin took another sip of his beer. He wiped his mouth with the back of his hand and looked at Lou. "It's appealing. It really is."

"Then let's do it."

"And the fact is, I've missed your ugly face."

"Darleen always thought I was more married to you than her."

"How is she?"

"The same."

Tollin nodded. Lou'd been hurt beyond belief when he'd found out about his wife's infidelity. Tollin now saw that the hurt had never quite healed. Lou hadn't dismissed her quite as easily as he'd said at the time.

Lou saw his partner's indecision. "We can make it happen, Frank. The two of us. How 'bout it?"

Tollin shook his head. "It won't work, Lou."

"Sure it will. Nobody knows the streets better than the two of us."

"Knew. Past tense."

"You've given up," Lou said, unable to keep the sadness out of his voice.

"I've gotten old," Tollin countered. "We both have, Lou. The world went and changed on us."

"And we haven't." Lou got to his feet. "Maybe you're right. Fact is I don't want to change. No reason to." He turned away from Tollin and fired the empty beer can into the barrel against the wall.

"You wanna talk, Lou, I'm here. But that's all I'll do. Talk. Hell, I'm retired."

Lou moved toward the door. "It's not the world that's changed, Frank, it's you."

Tollin shrugged again. It all amounted to the same thing. He watched Lou open the door. "You know you look like shit."

"That does seem to be the all 'round consensus."

"Then do something about it!"

Lou flipped him off.

Only the most determined drinkers and those who had nowhere else to go, still remained in the darkened bar. Lou wasn't sure which category he fell into and then decided that it didn't really matter. He was there because he'd felt trapped in the motel room. He was drinking because he had nothing else to do. And the bottom line was, he really didn't give a shit why he was doing what he was doing anyway.

He knew he was feeling sorry for himself and he hated himself for feeling that way. Then again, it was a feeling he was used to. He'd had it ever since he'd retired from the force. Lou remembered when he'd turned in his badge he'd felt as if his life had just ended. And in a major way it had. He knew he had to make a new life for himself. But he hadn't. Instead, he sat on his boat drinking and wallowing in self-pity. A trait that he hated in others and which he hated even more in himself.

Time after time, during the years after he'd pulled the pin, he resolved to get his act together. But he never had. There seemed to be no meaning left in living. He was a cop. It was not only what he did as a profession, it was his entire life. It was who he was. And so, without the badge, he was nothing. Intellectually, he knew that was crap, but emotionally he had accepted it and allowed it to control his life.

"It's you, ain't it?"

The voice came to him through the beer-induced haze and Lou slowly glanced from his half-filled glass over to the woman standing in front of him. She was a little younger than Lou, but not by much. He didn't think he knew her, but there was something that rang a bell in the recesses of his mind.

"Sure, it's you. Lou Parker. Right?"

He frowned. There was something about the way she stood there; hand on one hip, back arched forcing her breasts forward, an open smile. "Dee Dee?"

She smiled, pleased that he'd remembered.

"Well, I'll be damned," he said, smiling back at her.

"You and me both, Lou. You look…well, about how I feel. Lemme buy you a beer. It'd be like a reunion kinda."

Dee Dee signaled the bartender to bring a round for both of them and slid into the booth. "I'd heard you'd retired and went off to fish somewhere. How come you're back?"

Lou watched the bartender put the glasses on the table and waited for him to retreat behind the bar before he responded. "It's a long story, Dee."

"Bet you couldn't find any place to have fun. Life's like that. You go somewhere to have the time of your life and find out that you have to go back to where you came from in the first place to really enjoy yourself."

Lou laughed, unable to contain himself. "You haven't changed a bit."

Dee Dee shook her head. "Yeah, I have. This place's mine for one thing."

"Congratulations," Lou said sincerely.

"Thanks. I saved enough through the years to buy it when old man Hanlon, the guy that owned it, up and moved out west. He wanted to be with his children he said. I always wondered if they wanted to be with him. He was a nasty bugger."

"Somehow I never pictured you as a saloon keeper."

"It was a dream I had from the beginning. Now I don't have to work the streets no more. I still keep my hand in though. Got a few girls. Classy ones, too."

She leaned over to him and lowered her voice. "You interested I could fix you up. On the house. For old times."

"Thanks, but it's not a good time for me."

"Hell, Lou, it's always a good time to get laid. You change your mind, just say the word."

Lou raised his glass and took a sip and a sadness suddenly enveloped him. Dee Dee saw his expression and it triggered her memory.

"Hey, didn't I read somewhere that your son got shot? Yeah, I did read that." She placed her hand over his. "I'm sorry."

"And he had a Swiss bank account with millions in it," Lou said, just to hear the words again.

"You're kidding?"

He shook his head. He wouldn't kid about something like that. He drained his glass and looked over to the bartender. Dee Dee pushed her glass over in front of him. "Here. I really ain't all that thirsty."

Lou looked into her face and saw compassion. And an old friend.

"Come on, Dee. Let's get drunk together. We'll drink to my son's wealth."

Chapter Five

Lou woke up to the smell of frying bacon and a vicious headache. He looked around the room trying to figure out where he was and as some of the previous night's events came back to him, he very gingerly, in deference to his aching head, got out of bed.

He stumbled out of the bedroom with both hands pressed against his temples and followed the smell of frying bacon to the kitchen. He leaned against the door jam and watched Dee Dee scramble a half a dozen eggs before pouring them into a frying pan. "Was there anything in that place we didn't drink?" he whispered hoarsely.

Dee Dee grinned and gestured to the chair next to the kitchen table. "Bacon and eggs okay with you?"

He started to nod, but the throbbing in his head stopped him. He waited for the pain to subside and when it was finally bearable, looked over at her. "I guess it'd better be if that's what you're making." His eyes moved to the bedroom, then back to Dee Dee, frowning as he remembered more of what happened the night before.

"Dee…about last night…" He moved to Dee Dee's side, leaned over and softly kissed her on the cheek. "Thanks."

Embarrassed by his sincerity and not knowing exactly how to handle it, Dee Dee turned away. "Come on, Lou. We were just old friends being friendly."

Lou grinned. "I guess that's one way of looking at it."

Dee Dee played with the eggs for a moment before replying. "I enjoyed it, too."

Lou met her eyes and realized that there was much more to this woman than he'd ever thought. The Dee Dee he'd known while he was on the Job was a street hooker, smart as a whip, but without an ounce of compassion in her. This was not the same woman. Then again, he thought, I never did take the time to get to know her. Maybe she had always been this way and he'd never noticed. He realized that he'd made a mistake with her and regretted it.

Lou sat down at the kitchen table and watched Dee Dee shovel a generous portion of scrambled eggs onto a plate, add some strips of bacon, a couple pieces of toast and place it in front of him.

"It taste as good as it looks?"

"You tell me, Lou." Dee Dee went back to fix a plate for herself. "And after you've finished eating, I suggest you take a shower. There's a clean razor in the cabinet over the sink."

Lou looked up at her as if she were out of her mind. "What? Me? Shave? And confuse everyone?"

Lou came down the steps of Dee Dee's apartment onto the sidewalk and looked around to get his bearings. The rattle of the elevated train a block over, heading into Manhattan, pounded into his brain and reminded him that he'd poured too many drinks into his system the night before. He turned right and walked towards the market down the block. He went inside and over to the young girl standing behind the counter.

"This place have a back door?"

"The storeroom has a door to the alley, but customers aren't allowed back there," she told him.

Lou started towards the rear of the market. "Hey!" the girl shouted. "You can't go back there. That's not for customers."

"Don't worry about it. I'm not a customer," Lou said, and continued on his way. He found the rear door, and walked outside.

Lou loped through the alley as fast as his throbbing head would allow and went into the back entrance of a dry cleaners, half a block down from the market. He paid no attention to the protestations of this counterman either, who demanded to know what he thought he was doing barging into his store through the rear exit which was not for customers, and went out the front door.

Stepping into the street, Lou approached the dark brown Chevy parked at the curb from the rear. He walked up to the driver's window and balling his hand into a fist, banged it hard against the driver's window.

Chris jumped as if she'd been shot out of a cannon. Lou saw that she was bleary-eyed, her hair a scraggly mess, her make-up gone. She looked much as he'd expected her to look after probably spending the night in her car outside Dee Dee's apartment.

Lou impatiently banged on the window again and Chris looked up at him, frowning. She'd seen him go into the market down the block. How the hell did he get here, she wondered as she rolled down the window.

Lou grinned at her. "I can't remember. Where'd I leave my car?"

It took Chris a moment for his question to penetrate, to understand what he wanted, but when it did, she couldn't believe he'd had the gall to ask her the whereabouts of his car and was now waiting for her to tell him.

"Two blocks over. One block north," she finally said.

Lou nodded. "Thanks. By the way, sitting up in a car all night…you look like shit." Lou ambled off, his grin even wider.

Chris watched him go, then reached up to twist the rear view mirror so she could see herself in it. He was right, she admitted to herself. She did look like shit.

Morrison came into the one-o-nine with his head buried in the newspaper. He headed for his office and felt, rather than saw, something blocking his path. He looked up into Lou's angry eyes.

"Get that tail off my ass before I do it myself and believe me, you won't like the way I do it!"

Morrison was confused. "What tail? What the hell're you talking about?"

Lou frowned. Morrison wasn't that good an actor. Could he have been wrong?

Lou came out of the precinct with a container of vending machine coffee in his hand. He looked down the street, saw Chris's Chevy and decided that he wasn't about to go through life with her tailing him everywhere he went. He walked over to the Chevy and up to the driver's window. This time the window was open and he didn't get to bang on it a second time. Instead, he just bent down, looked at her and nodded his approval. Chris had showered and put on fresh make-up. She hadn't been able to do anything about the redness in her eyes from lack of sleep, but she did look better.

"We gotta talk." Without waiting for her to respond, he straightened up and headed towards the alley across the street.

He stopped five feet into the alley, turned and watched Chris cross the street, her jacket open to reveal a trim body that as far as he was concerned had no business coming in contact with a badge and a gun. Where'd she keep the gun, he wondered. Had to be somewhere on her body since she wasn't carrying a purse. Probably in a shoulder holster, he decided. Or in the small of her back. The thought that it would be fun finding it popped into his mind and he immediately dismissed the notion, finding it too much like robbing the cradle.

Chris walked into the alley and stopped in front of him. She stood there and watched Lou take a sip from the container of coffee, grimacing at its taste and then tossing the cup away.

"That's littering and carries a fine," Chris said.

"Arrest me," he said, moving around her to look up the street for an open bar. "I need something stronger than coffee."

"I'd've thought you had enough last night to last you."

"Guess you thought wrong."

"Let's stop pussyfooting around," Chris said. "What is it you want to say to me?"

Lou turned back to face her. "It's simple. You've been tailing me ever since I hit town. And I want to know why? Who do you think you are, Ellery Queen?"

"Who?" she asked, confused by the reference.

"Forget it. Why're you tailing me?"

"I thought you'd have figured that out by now. You're the great detective."

"Humor me. Why?"

"I wanted to see if you were going to try and find Shawn's killers."

"As simple as that."

"As simple as that."

"And if I am?"

"Then I want in."

Lou stepped back and shook his head. She had balls, he had to give her that, but that was all he'd give her. "You live in a dream world, kid."

She stepped over to him and looked him straight in the eye with a determination that he felt as well as saw. "You need me."

He dismissed that notion with a wave of his hand. "The last thing I need is a woman. Trust me on this one. I know."

"You know shit, Parker," she snapped back.

"I know I don't partner with a woman and that's all I need to know," he said, and stomped off.

"Too bad, she yelled at his retreating back, "because this woman knows things about your son's killing that you don't."

Lou stopped, thought about what she'd said for a moment, then turned and walked quickly back to her.

"Don't play games with me. If you know all that much how come you don't tell the Department?"

"They don't want to know."

Lou looked at her suspiciously. "You wouldn't be talking to me if you were the one with him that night. Or you might have been there and now you want to know what I'm doing so you can cover yourself. Is that it? Why you're doing this? To protect yourself?"

"What?" Chris said, not believing he'd just accused her of killing his son.

"What other reason could there possibly be? You're afraid that I might find out you were a party to Shawn's death."

Chris exploded. "You fucking bastard! You don't know dick about what went on between Shawn and me. You haven't seen your son in years much less talked to him. You don't know jack shit about him. Or me! And you've got the balls to come on like you do. Well, mister, let me tell you something. You may think he's innocent, but I know he is. I spent years on the street with him. Got to know him better than you ever did. I was his partner, for Christ sake!"

Lou was stunned. Not only was this woman his son's lover, she was also his partner. He lashed out before he even knew he was doing it.

"Then where the hell were you when he got hit? Partners back each other up. Why weren't you there?"

"You nuts? Where? In the closet? Maybe making it a three-some?"

"It was a setup. You should've been covering his ass. If you had, maybe he'd still be alive today!"

The accusation was just too much for Chris. Too unfair. She hauled off and threw a wicked right at Lou's jaw.

Lou's automatic reflexes took over and he pulled back, the blow missing his jaw by a hair. In the same motion, he grabbed her wrist and twisted it behind her. He shoved it higher, jamming her arm up her back. He wrapped his other arm around her neck and tightened.

Chris struggled, but said nothing. It had all happened too fast. She ignored the pain in her shoulder as Lou pushed up on her arm and tried to figure a way out.

Lou leaned in until his mouth was next to her ear. Some-where in the recesses of his mind, he was aware that he was pressed up against an ass that was nice and soft, but he was too angry for his consciousness to deal with it.

"You wanna help?" he growled in her ear. "I'll tell you how, kid. Turn in your badge and try another profession."

Chris's anger had continued to rise as Lou spoke. Not so much at what he was saying, although that was pissing her off, but she was furious that this old man had taken her so easily.

And there was no way she was going to let it go at that. No way in hell.

She reached back with her free hand and grabbed Lou's crotch. She found his balls and squeezed. Hard. Lou howled in pain and tried to pull away, but Chris held onto him for a split second longer before she finally released him. Lou immediately doubled over in pain, holding his crotch. His eyes involuntarily filled with tears.

She stepped away and leaned against the wall of the alley with her arms folded across her chest and watched as Lou tried to straighten up. He couldn't quite fully make it. The pain was still too much. Finally, Chris pushed herself from the wall. "Stay retired, Lou. It's probably all you're good for anyway," she said and walked across the street to her car.

Lou, still doubled over, watched her go before falling against the wall of the alley where he waited for the excruciating pain to subside to a bearable level.

Lou gently shifted, trying to find a position behind the wheel of his car that would allow the tenderness he felt between his legs some relief.

He maneuvered through traffic with one eye on his rearview mirror. Although Chris had driven off before he had recovered enough to slowly shuffle to his car, she was now behind him again. The woman was damn tenacious. He had to give her that. Maybe he'd underestimated her. And maybe, just maybe, she could be of some use to him.

Lou made his decision and hooked a hard right at the next corner, floored the accelerator, whipped a left at the next block, jumped the light at the next one, and then slowed down. He checked the rearview and grinned in appreciation.

She was still behind him. If nothing else, the woman did know how to drive. He had to give her that.

Lou turned into a fast food parking lot and drove around the building into it's rear parking lot and then into the alley behind it. He drove down the alley, hit the street, wheeled around the corner and came up behind the brown Chevy, which was parked just down from the fast food joint and where Chris was obviously waiting for him to come out the drive-thru.

Lou pulled to the curb, got out and walked towards Chris's car. She caught movement in her rear view and saw him approaching and grimaced. He was supposed to be in the drive-thru line. How the hell had he gotten here? Somehow, he had gotten the better of her again and she didn't like it this time any more than she did the last. She turned to face him as he got to her window.

"I need info on the Swiss account," Lou said without preamble. Without waiting for her to respond he turned and walked away.

Chris watched him go back to his car, get in and drive off past her. She grinned. Okay!

The record room at Queens Borough Command was a dismal place. Chris wondered why anyone would want to work there. Files stretched from floor to the ceiling. Aisle after aisle of them. A paper history of crime in the city. Some of the criminal records going back to before the turn of the century.

She knew all of them were eventually going to be entered into the Department's computers, but a shortage of funds, coupled with shortsightedness on the part of the City Council, made that prospect something for future generations to deal with.

Chris tagged along behind Anne Porter, a uniformed police officer, with whom she'd gone through the Academy. Anne had never liked the streets and when a job opened up in records, she'd jumped at the chance to work inside. In the ensuing years Anne had come to love the place. She thought of the records as she felt about her own family photo album; a wonderful reminder of things past and an indication of what was to come.

Anne stopped in front of a file cabinet and started slipping the files she was carrying into it. "It's too hot and you know it," Anne told her friend.

"All I want is the info on that Swiss bank account. It had to come in by wire. Right into our computer."

"It did. And a hard copy was made. So?"

"So I want to see it."

"Even if I wanted to take the chance and sneak you a look I couldn't. It's gone."

"What? Even they wouldn't have the guts to destroy evidence."

"I don't know what they did with it. All I know is that they came down here and took it. They properly signed it out, too."

"Any particular "they"?" Chris asked.

"Landers. You remember him. The suck-up who weaseled his way out of that misconduct charge for getting his rocks off in his squad car with a hooker he'd threatened to bust if she didn't do what he wanted."

"Oh, yeah," Chris said, the story coming back to her. "Then he went to work toadying for the top floor, didn't he?"

"Uh huh. They have something on him now and he'll do whatever they want and keep his mouth shut. Perfect for them. Sometimes he's a driver, sometimes a messenger. In this case he was a messenger and don't ask me who he got the file for because I don't know. I asked, but he wouldn't tell me. It's his signature on the sign-out form so it stops there."

"You know," Chris said, "this department is really two different places. You've got the guys on the street doing police work and the top floor playing politics and covering their asses."

"Just like any large corporation," Anne agreed.

Chris frowned. She had to get the information for no other reason than that it was her entree to Lou Parker. Then it came to her.

"Wait a minute. The brass took the hard copy, right?"

"The only one."

"But I'll bet no one remembered that it came in here by wire. Directly into the Department computer. It's still got to be on the hard disk."

Anne raised her eyebrows and nodded. "You're right. They probably never even thought of it. Then again, neither did I."

"Access it for me," Chris asked.

Anne shook her head. "You kidding? They find out and I'll be out on the streets again. No thanks."

"The street's not so bad."

"For you, maybe. But you know I'm raising a kid all by myself. And eight hours a day here gives me the time to be with her. No thanks. Here is where I want to be and here is where I'll stay."

"Then give me the password and I'll do it myself," Chris pleaded.

Anne stopped and turned to face Chris. "That'd be worse than showing you the file itself. That computer's secure. I give you the password and it's cause for instant dismissal. Yours and mine."

Chris nodded. She knew that. But she didn't care and Anne saw it in her face. "And you're still asking? I don't believe you."

"It's important, Anne. Look, I'll only need a couple of minutes. And it'll be my ass if I'm caught, not yours. I promise. It'll never come back on you."

Chris sat at the computer console, took a deep breath and slowly exhaled in an attempt to relax. She failed. She was right out in the open where too many people might come by and see her and they'd remember that fact if she ever had to face a Disciplinary Board for what she was doing. Now she was having second thoughts and had to force herself to put them aside and get the information for Lou.

She turned to the job at hand. She typed in Anne's password and waited for the computer to accept it. When it did, she typed in the commands needed to access Shawn's file and the record of his Swiss bank account.

As the computer worked, the door to the records room opened and a non-sworn officer came in carrying some files that he dropped unceremoniously into Anne's in-tray. He glanced at Chris, his eyes lowering to take in her body. He paused, liking what he saw. Chris knew what he was thinking. He wanted to kid around with her but with all the office sex-discrimination suits flying around he knew he'd be taking a chance. He smiled at her and went on his way.

Chris breathed a sigh of relief and went back to work. She looked at the computer screen and frowned. Shawn's file was there but there was no mention of the Swiss account.

She thought about this for a moment and then told the computer to search for the word "Swiss." A dozen references popped onto the screen. Chris scanned them and found that the most recent one was dated three days after Shawn's murder. She called it up and beamed happily at the monitor.

"Gotcha," she said, then reached over to flip the switch on the printer.

Lou nursed a beer while he read the computer printout Chris had brought him. She watched him from the other side of the booth in Dee Dee's bar, wondering if he understood what he was reading. Finally, he tossed the printout aside. "You make heads or tails of what all this says?"

"Not really. Other than it's the data on Shawn's bank account that came into the department."

Lou nodded. He'd hoped that she hadn't understood it either. He polished off the last of his beer, folded up the print-out, got to his feet and headed for the door. Chris scrambled after him, but he was out the front door before she was halfway down the length of the bar. The bartender saw Lou leave and Chris running after him.

"Hey, Lady. Somebody's got to pay for the beers," he demanded.

Chris stopped, impatiently dug into her purse, tossed some bills on the bar and sprinted for the door again.

She came out of the bar and looked around. Lou was nowhere in sight. She'd have to find him again. The man was infuriating. He'd gone about his business as if she hadn't even been there. Frustrated, she strode to her car, got in, and drove off.

Lou stepped out of the alley next to the bar and watched Chris's car blend into traffic. Satisfied, he turned and walked away in the opposite direction.

Chapter Six

Lou rang the bell of the small single-story, gray shingled house in Bayside for the third time and waited for someone to answer the door. When nobody did, he walked around to the side of the house and plodded up the driveway to the garage in the rear. He reached the garage door and looked in. All he could see was a jumble of electronic equipment: wires, cable, transistors, computer monitors, motherboards, VCR's, car phones and various other electronic equipment. You name it and it was there scattered about.

An aisle had been made between the jumble of goods and at the end of it a young man, lean, muscled and no more than twenty, was hunched over a wooden workbench. He had a soldering iron in his hand and was concentrating on the inside of an open VCR.

Lou entered the garage and the man, hearing him, looked up. He saw Lou and went back to work. "You want something or what?" he asked as he expertly dropped a bead of solder on a connection.

"Your father, I think," Lou answered as he came up to the work bench. "Unless you're not J.J."

J.J. slid the soldering iron into its stand on the table, picked up a magnifying glass and inspected his work. Satisfied with the soldering job he'd just done, he put down the magnifying glass and turned to face Lou.

"Take a hike," J.J. told Lou flatly.

"I didn't come here looking for a fight, kid."

"Then leave."

"Who put a bug up your ass?"

J.J. laughed, but there was no humor associated with it. Only derision at Lou's question. Lou waited him out.

"I grew up without a father because of you," J.J. finally told him.

Lou shook his head. "Oh, no. I'm not taking the rap for that one."

"It's the truth. Learn to live with it," J.J. snapped.

Lou took a step closer. "Your father's a crook, kid. It's what he does. He was boosting shit here before you were even a thought. Sometimes I'd catch him. Sometimes he got away. This time I caught him."

"You never would've if that computer hadn't crashed," J.J. said defensively.

"In your dreams." Frustrated, Lou turned away. He wasn't going to get anywhere with this kid. Then he realized that he couldn't leave. Not just yet. He came here for a reason and had to see it through. He spotted a computer on the floor and gestured towards it. "You know how brilliant your father is on one of those?"

"Better than you."

"So how'd he use his smarts? He hacked his way into a bank computer and transferred their money into his own account. Then waltzed in the next day and withdrew the money. You call that smart? I call it stealing. It's against the law. Try accepting the fact, that's what your father did. Period. End of story."

Lou watched the kid digest this. Okay, he decided. Try a little candy. "Look, I'm sorry your father had to take a fall. I really am."

J.J. picked up the soldering iron and went back to work on the VCR.

"I haven't the time for this. Where is he, kid?" Lou asked.

"Where do you think? In jail."

"He should've been out by now. What happened?"

"He had some trouble inside. Tried to protect a friend of his from a con who had eyes for him. Got a year tacked on to the original." J.J. gestured towards the door. "Now get out. I don't know why you came in here in the first place."

"I wanted your father's help."

"Sure. Like he'd help you," J.J. sneered.

Lou decided that he'd had enough. "You don't know shit, kid. You may think you do, but you don't. I'm sorry you grew up without a father. Tough. Shit happens. Try blaming him sometime instead of me. Or if you really want to clean up your act why don't you just accept what happened and get on with your life."

Lou turned and strode to the door. He glanced back. "You speak to your old man often?"

J.J. stared at Lou trying to decide of he should answer him or not. Finally, he shrugged. "I call him. Three, four times a week. We've got a schedule."

"Next time you do, tell him I was here and I need some help. See what he says. I'll be back."

Lou went out the door before J.J. had a chance to respond. He walked angrily away from the garage. The truth was that putting the kid's father behind bars was something that always bothered him. True, the father had broken the law and deserved taking the fall, but leaving a youngster behind didn't make Lou happy.

Lou reached his car and saw Chris's brown Chevy parked down the block. How the hell did she find me here, he wondered. He walked to the rear of his car and felt under the bumper. Nothing. He tried the right rear wheel well. Nothing there either. He found it in the left wheel well and pulled it out. Taking the homing device with him he trudged over to Chris's car.

"Police issue?" he asked holding it up so she could see it.

"I've got a friend works special services."

"Kinda takes the fun out of the job, doesn't it?"

"It found you, didn't it?"

"It's for pussies."

Lou tossed the device through the window past her face where it landed on the passenger seat. Lou walked back to his car, got in and drove off. Through his rear view mirror he watched Chris pull out and follow him. She was sharp. Too sharp for her own good, he thought. Shawn must have had his hands full. He wondered if she was sharp enough to have picked something up from Shawn; some little tidbit, an inkling, anything, about what his son had been working on that might've caused somebody to want to take him out.

Lou took the bag from the man behind the counter and walked out of the Italian grocery store. He threw it onto the back seat of his car, got in and drove off. Four blocks over he pulled into the parking lot of the city park, grabbed the bag and set it on the ground while he opened the trunk, reached inside and pulled out a blanket from the motel. Tossing the blanket over his shoulder, he hefted the bag into his arms, and looked back towards the entrance to the lot.

Chris had parked on the street. She was watching him from the inside of the Chevy. Lou sauntered over to her. "You coming or what?" he asked.

"You're a prick, you know that?"

Lou thought about it and then nodded in agreement before walking away. Chris watched him go, trying to decide whether or not to accept his invitation. She hadn't figured him out yet and this bothered her. It also intrigued her. He intrigued her. She got out of the car and walked over to where Lou'd set the bag down on the grass. She watched as he unfolded the blanket.

"Grab an end," Lou said, and tossed the blanket out.

Chris made no move to grab it. Instead, she just stood there glaring at him. He raised his eyebrows. "It's easier if we both do it."

"You ran out on me. I got what you wanted. I held up my part of the bargain. Then you split."

"Had something to do," he said, and gestured at the blanket. "The end…"

Frustrated, Chris grabbed the end and pulled. The blanket opened. Lou dropped his end and looked at her. "You can let go now."

Chris let go and the blanket fluttered to the ground. Lou sat down and looked into the bag. He started taking things out of it.

"I got prosciutto, mortadella, capicollo…provolone…and Swiss, if you don't care for the good things in life," he said as he took them out one by one and placed them on the blanket. "Here's some sun dried tomatoes…even got some oregano… and fresh baked rolls."

Chris stood above him and watched the show curiously. "So?" she asked when he finally finished.

"So you gotta eat. Sitting in a car all day, you get hungry. You gotta keep it well stocked or you'll starve to death."

"It may come as a shock to you but this is not my first surveillance."

"Then sit down. You can watch me eat."

"You used me."

"You wanted to help. You did. Give yourself a gold star."

"Fuck off."

"That's good. Clever. Look, you know who Shawn was seeing that night?"

Chris rolled her eyes to the heavens. "Jesus. You don't know when to stop, do you? I got just one answer for you, mister. Just one. Fuck off!"

"You should have your mouth washed out with soap."

"Screw you."

"Charming."

Lou picked up a roll, broke it apart and started to make himself a sandwich. Chris stared at him and forced herself to relax, to regain some measure of self-control.

"I suspected he was seeing someone, but I didn't know who," she finally said.

Lou tossed her a roll. "Force yourself. It's good."

Chris looked at the roll in her hand. It was still warm and did look appetizing. And she was hungry. Resigned, she dropped to her knees on the blanket and pulled the roll apart.

"And you knew about the money," he said.

"Uh huh. I suspected. He'd asked me not to ask. I didn't."

Lou frowned at her and shook his head.

"I trusted him," she said.

"Millions of dollars and you never asked where it came from? Give me a break."

"Don't pull that self-righteous shit with me. You didn't even know he had it."

"How the hell was I to know?"

"Oh, now the great Ellery Queen doesn't know how to detect. For Christ's sake, he was your own son and you didn't know dick shit about him."

Lou grinned at her. "Ellery Queen?"

Chris looked away, embarrassed. "I looked it up."

Lou was impressed, but he wasn't about to say so and give her any sort of satisfaction. He wondered why he didn't before dismissing the thought entirely. He took a bite out of his sandwich and looked at her. "So we didn't get along. He didn't like me much."

"How could he like you when you were never there. He needed you and you ran."

"You ought to try the mortadella. It's mouthwatering," he said, changing the discussion.

Chris looked at him and tossed the roll onto the blanket. She got to her feet. "Talking to you is like talking to a brick wall. I'd rather eat alone." She turned and stomped away.

"Hold on!" Lou shouted, getting to his feet.

"Fuck off," Chris said without breaking stride.

Lou forced himself not to respond in kind and instead turned away, thinking over what she'd said and finally realizing she must have been closer to Shawn than he'd thought. There was no other explanation for her to know so much about their relationship. It bothered him that Shawn had confided in her instead of coming to him and had to admit what she'd said was the truth. He hadn't been around for Shawn to confide in, wasn't the father he'd wanted to be, should have been. He'd known that fact for years and had been unable to do anything about it. It was just the way he was. Yet he'd always regretted it. And now this girl comes along and tosses it in his face. He tossed the remains of his sandwich on top of the other food and rolled the whole mess together in the blanket. He picked up the blanket and lugged it back to his car, forcing the thought of Chris completely from his mind. And failing miserably.

Lou came out of the kitchen with two cans of beer. He tossed one of the cans to Tollin and then pulled the tab on the other, pitching it in the general direction of the barrel. "And a mouth on her. Jeez. She's a bitch on wheels. And she wants to be my partner. Fat chance. If she wasn't a girl I'd beat the crap out of her. I don't know why I don't. She sure doesn't act like a woman. Anything but."

Lou slumped onto the couch and looked over at Tollin who'd been watching him in total fascination.

"You through?" Tollin asked.

Lou grinned sheepishly. "I guess."

"Alright. So you blew it. But you need her. Whatever she knows about Shawn could help."

"The price is too high."

"Okay."

"And I can do it without her."

"I know."

"You can't talk to her."

"Uh huh."

Lou brought the can of beer to his lip and took a gulp. He then looked over at Tollin. "I'll give it another shot."

"If you think so, Lou."

Lou grinned. They'd been down this road before. Too many times. He raised the can of beer.

"Up yours," he said.

Lou walked up the driveway to the garage. He opened the door and stopped. The place was still as much of a mess as before, but then, although pieces of electronic equipment had been scattered about in haphazard fashion, now they were ripped apart, smashed or crushed on the ground. The place looked raped.

J.J. stood up from behind a pile of what was now nothing more than electronic rubbish and stared at Lou. His face was a mass of welts and bruises. Beneath his torn shirt there was more of the same.

Lou's composure faltered. He watched as J.J. fought the pain as he moved slowly over to his workbench and sat down. Lou walked over and stood in front of him and waited.

"It happened last night," J.J. said through swollen lips. "There were two of them."

"You know them?"

"Nope."

"You report it?"

"Get real. Half this stuff's got no receipt," J.J. replied trying to smirk, but unable to pull it off through the swelling.

It was what Lou had expected. "That does make it tougher."

J.J. looked away from Lou, not wanting to meet his eyes. "I spoke to my old man."

Lou waited for him to continue. He could see this was hard on the kid and he didn't want to add to it.

"He said it was up to me whether to help you or not. He said he would, but that was him. This was me and my choice." J.J. looked up at Lou and met his eyes. "What is it with you two?"

"We're old friends."

"But you put him away," J.J. said slowly, trying to get a handle on the strange relationship between his father and this man his father obviously respected.

"Happens. It doesn't affect the friendship."

"I don't understand either of you."

"Maybe we don't even understand it ourselves," Lou admitted. "So. What's it going to be?"

J.J. shrugged and then shuddered involuntarily at the pain even that slight movement caused him. Lou nodded and started for the door.

"Wait," J.J. said. "What is it you want?"

Lou walked back. He pulled the computer printout from his pocket and held it out to the kid. J.J. took it and glanced at the first page, then rifled through the others.

"Swiss bank account," he said, recognizing the codes on the printout.

"I need anything you can get me about the money in it. How it got there. From whose account. Money like that has to come from somewhere. So where it came from would be the icing on the cake."

J.J. grinned at Lou's request and this time he was able to do it through his swollen lips, although it did look grotesque. "You realize you're asking me to commit a crime."

"Me? Never. I'm just wondering if it can be done."

"Yeah, right."

"Can it?"

"Of course."

"Can you do it?"

J.J. threw him a look that told Lou he really shouldn't have bothered to ask. He waited for Lou's next question. He wanted to hear him say the words.

Lou knew what he wanted and hadn't the heart to disappoint him. "Will you do it?"

J.J. had thought it would've made him feel good, hearing Lou asking for his help. But it didn't and he wasn't sure why.

He turned away and looked around the garage; at the remnants of his storehouse of equipment.

"I'm sorry about what happened," Lou said.

J.J. nodded. "The guys that did this. They came with a warning. Don't help that asshole Parker they kept saying. Over and over and over again." He looked into Lou's eyes. "I don't like being told what I can and can't do."

Lou smiled. "Seems like I remember your father saying the same thing a long time ago."

"Maybe," J.J. agreed.

Lou reached out and gently placed a hand on the kid's shoulder. "Take care of yourself," he said, and walked out of the garage. He went down the driveway to his car, opened the door, then stopped. He thought for a moment, then slammed the car door and annoyed with himself, walked down the street to Chris's car. He went to the passenger door and tried to open it. It was locked. He knocked on the window and gestured for her to unlock the door. Chris sat there and glared at him. Finally, she reached over, unlocked the door and he slipped into the seat.

"Now what?" she asked.

"Remember the bar from the other day," he answered. "If you're going to hang on like a bulldog, we might as well set some ground rules."

Lou waited for some sort of response, but Chris just sat there watching him. She was trying to figure out what was behind his offer. It wasn't in character. Hell, she decided, I really shouldn't look a gift horse in the mouth. But the fact was she didn't trust him.

Lou got tired of waiting. He opened the door to the car, got out and walked away. Chris watched him get into his own car and drive off. She stayed there for a moment trying to come to some sort of conclusion. Should she take him up his offer or shouldn't she? She shrugged. Why not?

Lou leaned against the front fender of his car and watched Chris pull up next to him. He pushed away from his car and led the way to the bar. When they got to the door, Chris reached for the handle but Lou beat her to it. He opened the door and stepped aside, gesturing for her to go in.

Once inside, Lou pointed towards a table past the bar, in the rear. When they got there, he reached around and pulled the chair out for her. Chris looked at him, bothered. She wasn't used to this kind of behavior from him and it made her uncomfortable. First, he'd offered to work together, then he'd opened the door for her, then he'd pulled her chair out. He had something up his sleeve. She was sure of it.

Lou took the chair opposite her. "Beer okay?"

Chris nodded and Lou looked over at the bartender and held up two fingers. "Two beers," he said, and watched for a moment as the bartender went to work. He turned back to look at Chris and found her staring at him. There was a heavy silence. Finally, Chris broke it.

"It's your show," she said.

"Tell me about you and Shawn."

Chris shook her head. "I tried that. You don't listen too good."

The bartender came over and put two beers on the table and left. Lou took the interruption to gather his thoughts. He leaned forward.

"Look," he began. "I admit I wasn't the best of fathers. I know that. And I regret it. The thing is, I did what I did and I have to live with it. I can't even make it up to him anymore. I'm not even sure I would've if he wasn't dead. But right now the only thing I know is, I gotta try. I have to find out who killed him. It's not going to bring him back, but I gotta do it. And I need your help."

Lou sat back, picked up his beer and took a long swallow. Chris watched him. She'd listened closely to what he'd just told her and had to admit it sure sounded like he'd meant it and that it had come from the heart, but it had also come from Lou Parker and with him you never knew what he really meant and what was pure con. And she had to know. To make sure. Too much was at stake for her to take it at face value.

"So all this is just to ease your own guilt," she finally said.

Lou frowned. She went straight for the jugular. He shrugged. "I don't know. Maybe." He took another gulp of beer and met her look straight on.

Chris felt for him. She couldn't help herself. But there was something more. Something she couldn't quite put her finger on. It was all too pat. She looked at him closely. He was returning her look as if he were sitting in a poker game, face frozen in place, on a bluff. Damn him! She sat back and looked at him with admiration.

"Boy, you're good. I almost bought that bullshit."

Lou looked at her innocently.

"Any of it true?" she asked.

Lou shrugged.

"All that just so I'd partner you?"

"Whoa…nobody said anything about a partnership. All I want from you is some info on my son. I work alone."

"Then what the fuck was Tollin?" she shot back.

Lou winced. "You really have to talk like that?"

Chris ignored the question. "He was your partner for over twenty years."

"We were a team. Besides…," Lou trailed off.

"He's a man," Chris finished for him.

Lou shrugged. Chris leaned forward. "I don't want to fuck you, if that's what's worrying you. I just want Shawn's killer." She pushed her chair back and got to her feet. "Think about it."

She strode away, down the length of the bar and out the door.

Dee Dee watched her leave, then picked up her drink and walked over to Lou's table. She sat down in the seat Chris had just vacated.

"I'm surprised at you, Lou. She's young enough to be your daughter."

"Gimme a break. She was Shawn's girlfriend."

"I see."

"You don't, but that's okay."

"She likes you, you know."

Lou shook his head. "She hates my guts. Hasn't said a civil word to me since we met."

Dee Dee sighed. "Okay. Have it your own way. Look, I don't like being the one to tell you this, but one of my girls heard something. About your son."

Chris went out of Lou's thoughts immediately. "I'm listening."

"Now don't you get all worked up about this," she said, seeing his sudden interest. "It's just rumor. Street talk."

"The best kind," Lou said. "Give."

"Well, one of her clients works down at City Hall. He's got some friends in the Department. High up. The word is that they found big-time drugs stashed at Shawn's house. Over two kilos."

Lou couldn't help laughing. "Next thing they'll discover is an ax and pin the latest serial killings on him. Jesus, what the hell is going on here?"

"Beats me, Lou. I'm just telling you what I heard."

"It's not enough that they find some Swiss bank account in his name with a couple of million in it. Now they come up with a drug connection. And Internal Affairs is nowhere to be seen. They must really want to dirty him good."

"But why?"

"Dee, if I knew the answer to that one I could go back to my boat and fish."

"You mean, go back to your boat and waste the rest of your life."

"I think I may have talked too much the other night."

"Or maybe not enough."

Lou sensed a presence and looked up. Two burly plainclothes detectives stood above him. He recognized one, Brady, from outside Morrison's office.

Brady looked down at Lou. "The Captain wants to see you," he growled.

Lou looked over at Dee Dee and grinned. Dee Dee leaned back to watch the show. Lou picked up his beer and took a sip, ignoring their command and the other detective, Conklin, stepped closer.

"Now," Conklin ordered.

Lou nodded. What choice did he have, he seemed to be saying. He reached into his pocket, pulled out some bills and tossed them on the table. He got to his feet.

"See ya, Dee."

He leaned over and kissed her on the cheek. As he straightened up, he uncoiled a hard right uppercut with all the force of his body behind it.

It caught Conklin square on the jaw. He went back over the table behind him, hit the floor and stayed there, out cold.

Brady looked at his partner for a moment, then turned to Lou, at the same time pulling a sap from his pocket.

Lou saw the sap and immediately stepped back, out of range. Brady moved in, the sap held out from his body. He swung the sap at Lou's head.

Lou ducked and kicked up with his right foot. The sap missed its target. Lou's kick didn't. It caught Brady right in the balls and he doubled over in pain. The sap dropped from his grasp as he clutched at his crotch. Brady dropped slowly to the floor and threw up.

Dee Dee looked from Brady to Conklin and then over to Lou.

"Nice and dirty, Lou. I see you haven't forgotten," she said, a huge grin on her face.

"Do me a favor, Dee. Your girls. Ask them about Shawn. The drugs. Maybe the money. But most important. Did they ever see him with a woman?"

"Other than the one that just left?"

"Other than her."

He looked over at Conklin who still hadn't moved, then stepped around Brady and walked out.

Morrison pulled into the driveway of his home, still reflecting on his disastrous day. It had started first thing this morning when an idiot Assistant D.A. refused to file on a perfectly good arrest. She'd said the warrant had expired. But the asshole hadn't come home until after midnight. Twenty minutes after the warrant expired. What the hell did she want them to do? Ask him to wait while they got another? Then, two of his men had totaled a car when they busted a red light on a surveillance. They were both okay, but the city was going to be sued for big bucks when the driver of the other car got out of the hospital. And lastly, the team he'd assigned to the shooting over in Flushing Meadows had come up with nothing, after three weeks of telling him that they were about to make an arrest.

The day had definitely not gone well. Now, as he got out of his car and saw Lou sitting on the steps to his house he knew his day was about to get worse.

Lou got to his feet and waited for Morrison to come to him.

"We have to talk," Lou informed him.

"I wanted to talk to you earlier today and look what happened," Morrison said.

"You want to talk to me you find a better way than sending two goons to do it."

"You bastard. Those "goons" as you call them are New York City Police Detectives. Now I got one with a broken jaw and another who won't be able to walk for a month."

Lou smiled. "They're not very good. You won't miss 'em."

Morrison's anger dissipated. He knew that Lou was right.

"Now, what was it you wanted you had to send them to get me?" Lou asked.

Morrison looked towards the front door of the house and then back at Lou trying to decide which was more important. "Look, Susan's waiting dinner for me. She's probably got enough for you, too. She's a great cook. We can have a nice dinner. Then talk."

"I already know about the drug connection."

Morrison scowled. How the hell did he find that out, he wondered. And how much did he actually know or was he just fishing? He had never learned how to read Lou. Morrison looked wistfully towards his house as he tried to figure out how to handle it. Thinking on his feet had never been one of his strong points. He knew he needed more time to think it through. How to deal with this.

"Susan's gonna skin me alive if my being late ruins her dinner," he finally said.

"Then go eat."

Morrison stepped closer. "Don't push it, Lou. Trust me. There are things going on…let the Department handle it. It'll be okay."

"How?"

"I've got some ideas. Together maybe we can wrap this whole thing up. And get what's best for each of us. You for Shawn and me for the Department."

Lou turned and walked away. Morrison called after him. "I'm on your side, Lou."

"Nobody's on my side but me," Lou answered and continued on his way.

Chapter Seven

Lou pulled into the parking lot of his motel, parked and walked to his room. As he reached the door he noticed it was open about an inch. He stepped to the side and reaching down, pulled a .38 Colt from his ankle rig. With the gun in his right hand, he pushed the door wide open with his left and waited. Nothing happened. He was deciding on his next move when Chris called out from inside the room.

"If you're through playing cops and robbers why don't you come in?"

Lou sighed. He lowered his gun and stepped in.

Chris was seated in the only chair in the room which was small by any standard: just enough space for a nightstand, the chair and a small dresser. Lou's clothes and other stuff were tossed about haphazardly much in the same way they had been on his boat. Chris, neat and clean, stood out against the clutter of the room.

Lou put his foot up on the bed and returned the .38 to his ankle holster which gave him a moment to recover from the surprise of her being there and which had reminded him of the numerous times over the years either he, or Tollin, had come home to find the other sitting there waiting. For a while they'd even changed locks and set traps for each other. Then, when it became apparent that both were too good at breaking and entering for the traps to mean anything, they gave up and got used to coming home, not knowing if the other would be there waiting for them.

Now Chris had done the same thing to him and he wasn't sure he liked it. Or did he? He wasn't really sure. Ignoring her, he reached under the bed and pulled out his suitcase. He opened it, pulled out a belt rig, and clipped it to his waistband before picking up a 9mm automatic. He ejected the clip and checked it to make sure it was full.

"He wasn't into drugs," Chris said.

Lou looked over at her. "You knew about that, too?"

"Only a little while ago," she said, shaking her head. "That woman, Dee Dee, told me. I went back, but you'd already gone. She's worried about you."

"We go back a long way."

"I gathered that."

"You're sure about Shawn and drugs?" Lou asked.

"Absolutely. He was death on the subject."

Lou nodded. He'd expected no less from his son, but he'd had to ask. "First the money. Now the drugs. I figure they were setting Shawn up."

"No shit."

Lou winced, still hating her language. He slammed the clip into the butt of the automatic and slipped it into the belt rig.

Chris gestured to it. "If you need that along with the one on your ankle, I'd say you could also use some back-up."

Lou glanced at her and shook his head. "You'd drag me down, kid. When I work with a partner I need to trust he'll be there."

Chris eyes blazed, mirroring the anger she felt inside. She could take the personal attacks, but when he ridiculed her professional ability he'd pushed the envelope too far. Furious, she jumped to her feet and strode angrily across the room right into his face. "What the hell makes you think you're the only one who can get this thing done? I'm a cop. A damned good one. But with your limited imagination that's something that just couldn't be. Well, you won't get shit done without me! You'd better start accepting that fact right here and now. And you'd better start thinking of me as a detective, because that's what I am, whether you like it or not."

"Wait a minute," Lou objected.

"For what?" Chris asked, jumping in before he could continue. "So you can make another feeble attempt at conning me?"

"I never conned you?"

"Horseshit!" Her eyes locked with his, daring him to deny it again.

Lou finally shrugged. "Okay. So I conned you a little," he admitted. "I needed some information."

"Then you ask. But all that's in the past. This is now and there's a new game starting. And we're going to play it by my rules."

"I don't want to hear them."

"Who gives a shit what you want? Mister, I'm going to be on you like glue. Where you go, I go. What you get, I'll get. That should be simple enough even for you to understand."

"And if I refuse?"

"You can't."

"Watch me."

"And you won't."

Something in her tone made Lou pause. As much as he hated to ask, that something forced him to. "Why not?"

"Because you're not that stupid. Deep down you know I'm right, that you need me, but you're just too fucking stubborn to admit it. Besides, you have no choice in the matter. I'm here and here I'm going to stay, so you just damn well better get used to it!"

Lou believed her. Not that he was about to get used to her being around, but that she was going to be there. And as much as he hated to admit it, he did need her. He also had to admit he liked her toughness. He also knew he'd never tell her that. "You're a pain in the ass, you know that?" he said instead.

"I always thought I had a nice ass." She grinned, meeting his look head on.

"Okay," he agreed. "You want to help? Fine."

"It's about time."

"Don't gloat. I hate gloating."

"Like I care."

"Start. If we know how each other thinks we can get things done without getting bogged down in personalities."

"Says the man who's been bogged down with the fact that I'm a woman with a badge."

"Don't you ever ease up? This isn't a battle."

"What would you call it?"

"Look, somewhere downtown there's got to be a record of the second search. The time they found the drugs. I want to see it."

"We already went that route. It didn't work."

"That was then. This is now."

She stared at him and tried to determine whether or not to believe him. He returned her look with total innocence. But she still didn't trust him. He could see it all over her face.

"Okay. I give you my word. That good enough for you?"

She took a moment to let what he'd said sink in. Then she grinned. A full winning smile. "And where're you going dressed up like an armory?"

"Out."

She scowled. "Some partnership."

"Best you're going to get."

Lou walked up the narrow steps leading into the pool hall. It took him a moment before his eyes accustomed themselves to the room, which was lighted only by the harsh glare of the lamps above the green felt tables. The players' faces were in shadow as they stood next to the tables which made it very difficult for Lou to find who he was looking for.

At a table in the far corner of the room, Danny Hanlon grinned in anticipation at the setup his opponent had left him. An almost straight-in shot on the nine ball. As he bent over the table to line up the winning shot his face entered the pool of light from above. Lou saw the now lighted face, walked down the length of the room and slid into a chair opposite Danny's table.

Danny looked up, saw Lou and frowned. "You retired. What the hell're you doing here?"

"Slumming. You interested in a cup of coffee?"

Danny pocketed the nine ball and stood up. "You buying?"

"Don't I always?"

Danny turned to his opponent and took the money the man held out. "You want to go again?" he asked him.

The man shook his head. He'd had enough and walked away. Danny broke down his stick, picked up his cue case from under the table, opened it and put the two pieces inside. He closed the case and turned to Lou.

"Well?"

"Lead on."

Danny's idea of having someone buy him coffee was to order an entire meal to go with it. Lou watched as Danny bit into the largest deli sandwich he'd ever seen. How Danny could get it into his mouth was even more amazing than how he could fit the sandwich, an order of potato pancakes and an enormous side of cole slaw into his slim frame. Although he'd seen him do it any number of times it never ceased to astound him. Danny finally looked up at Lou with a mouthful of food and raised his eyebrows.

"I need some information," Lou told him.

"So what else is new," Danny said, and took another bite of his sandwich.

"They found some drugs in my son's house."

"Bullshit! Your kid was cleaner than you."

"Nevertheless, they found what they found."

"This was after he got gunned down, right?"

"When they searched his house," Lou agreed.

"You figure a plant?"

"I know it was."

"But you can't prove it."

"Not yet. But I will."

"So what's this got to do with me?"

"The drugs had to come from somewhere. Who's top dog in town now?"

Danny wiped his mouth, sat back and looked at Lou. "Is this what brought you out of retirement? The drugs they found?"

"Partly."

"And the other part is you want to find who killed your kid, right?"

"Right."

Danny thought about this and decided that it was a worthy cause. Something he might do himself. That is, if he'd ever had a kid. "You know, Lou, I thought that when you retired, I'd be off the hook. I know you kept me out of jail, but I repaid that with good information ten times over."

"That you did, Danny. No question about it. This has nothing to do with the past. I'm just asking for a favor. You can say 'yes' or you can say 'no'. Either way I'll still pick up the tab on all that food you're putting away."

Danny nodded. "I figured that's the way it'd be. You're something else, you know that?"

"So?"

"So if I were looking to score some shit, there'd be a couple of guys I'd call, depending on how much I needed. How much did they find?"

"I don't know for sure, but the word I got is that it was around two keys."

"How badly had it been stepped on?"

"That I don't know," Lou told him.

Danny nodded. "Tell you what. You find that out and give me a ring. I can probably trace it to one or two guys up the ladder with that info."

"I can reach you at the pool hall?"

"Anytime. Leave a message if I'm not there and I'll get right back to you."

Lou nodded, got up, and tossed some bills on the table. "You'll hear from me."

"Like old times, huh, Lou?"

"Like old times, Danny."

Chris walked into the police building cafeteria and spotted her quarry eating by himself in a corner of the room. She grabbed a cup of coffee, paid for it, and walked over to Landers. She pulled out the chair opposite him and sat down.

"You mind?" she asked him.

Surprised, Landers shook his head. He didn't mind simply because nobody ever sat with him. He worked for the brass on the top floor and therefore was not to be trusted. He had long ago accepted that this was the way of things in the Department, but could never quite accept the loneliness it brought with it.

"Aren't you afraid of being seen with me?" he asked, unable to keep the bitterness from his voice.

"Fuck 'em if they can't take a joke," Chris said with a smile.

Landers grinned back. "I appreciate the sentiment, but this is the first time you've said boo to me in years. Or since I went to work up top. I suspect there's more to this than just a friendly chat," he said shrewdly.

"You're right," Chris agreed. There was no sense beating around the bush. He knew people didn't sit down with him without a damn good reason. "It's about Shawn's murder."

"You and he were pretty tight there for a while the way I hear it."

"You heard right. And the way I heard it you took the files on his case out of records."

"Where'd you hear that?"

"I checked the sign-out sheets. You've got custody."

Landers shook his head. "Not really. I just got them for the brass. They've got them now and don't even ask. There's no way in hell that I could sneak you a look."

"Come on. Shawn was my…friend…I want to know what happened."

"Forget it. It's not happening."

Chris had been carefully watching his face and came to the conclusion that this man was not about to jeopardize his position for her. Yet she needed him to help her. She decided to try another tact. "Okay. I understand your predicament and I'm sure you'd help me if you could."

"Absolutely. I just can't on this one."

"Then don't show me the files. Just tell me what's in them."

"How the hell should I know that? All I did was go down and get them and bring them upstairs."

"And you read them on the way."

"No way, lady. You know the trouble I'd be in if I'd done that."

"No more than you're already in."

"What trouble you talking about?" Landers asked too quickly.

"I know you got yourself into some trouble and the brass covered for you and are holding it over your head. My guess is they figure as long as they keep it quiet, they've got themselves someone who'll keep his mouth shut and do exactly what they want."

Landers shrugged. "And if that were true, and I'm not saying it is, you're still asking me to go against them. Come on, give me a break."

"You used to be a good cop," Chris said.

"No," he disagreed. "I never was. Not from the first day I went into the Academy. I should never have joined the Department in the first place."

"You could always quit," Chris said gently.

"And do what? I made my own bed and now I'm going to have to sleep in it."

"That's a lousy way to live your life."

"It's not so bad. The paycheck's good. I don't have to get involved in any dangerous stuff. I'm going to school. In a couple of years I'll graduate and maybe get my masters. Then I'll tell them what they can do with their job, but until then…," Landers trailed off and took a sip of coffee.

"You read that file, didn't you?" Chris said, only this time it was a statement, not a question.

"What makes you say that?"

"You're looking for a way out from under and you thought that maybe the file would do that for you. Come on, all I need are some specifics," Chris pleaded. "And nobody would ever know you'd already sneaked a peek."

The threat hit home and Landers glanced away to see who else was in the cafeteria. He looked back at Chris with a worried look on his face. He'd lived with being blackmailed for a long time now and since he didn't stand up to it before, he knew he wouldn't do it this time either.

"They found two kilos alright," Chris explained to Lou back in his motel room.

"Did he remember what the chemist's report said?"

"Not all of it, but the bottomline is that it was good stuff. It'd only been stepped on about twice."

Lou picked up the phone, dialed the pool hall and asked for Danny. He wasn't there and Lou left a message that he'd call back. He hung up and turned back to Chris.

"Who found it?"

"A detective that just made 2nd grade. He goes end-of-watch in about thirty minutes. I checked."

Lou grinned. She'd anticipated what they needed. Not bad. Not bad at all.

Chris watched the emotions play across Lou's face and couldn't help sympathizing with his dilemma. She'd done the job for him and he didn't know how to handle it and while she understood that, she wasn't going to allow him to get away with it. Not this time.

"Thank you, Chris. Good job, Chris. I appreciate what you've done, Chris," she said, lowering her voice to mimic his.

"You always talk to yourself like that?" he asked, refusing to give an inch.

"You're a real prick, you know that?"

"That's the second time you've called me that. The next time you'll wish you hadn't."

"Anytime you think you're man enough to back that threat up, you're welcome to try."

Lou looked at the woman opposite him, fists clenched, feet balanced, body taut. Just like a man would be and it unnerved him. He turned and walked to the door. "You look silly," he said as he went out.

Chris took a deep breath, forcing herself to relax. He did know how to get to her. She had to give him that. She followed him out the door and over to her car. Lou was standing at his own car watching her. She looked over at him. "You coming?"

"We'll take my car this time," Lou said.

"You can take your car if you like, but without me in it. I'm the one who knows where we're going. You come with me or not at all."

Lou thought about it and decided that he wasn't going to win this one. He slammed his door shut and walked over to her. He held out his hand. "Gimme the keys. I'll drive."

"Try and get this through that aging skull of yours. I'm perfectly capable of driving a car. And probably better than you."

Chris opened her door and slid behind the wheel. She looked back to Lou standing there staring at her. She smiled pleasantly. "You coming or what?"

Lou realized he wasn't going to win this one either. Zero for two. Somewhere along the line he was going to win one of these confrontations and couldn't help but wonder when? He walked around the car and got in.

Chris followed the detective's car away from the precinct and through traffic. "I think I know where he's going," she said.

"You want to let me in on it?"

"There's a watering hole a lot of the guys go to after watch. It serves breakfast, lunch and dinner at all times of the night and day. Along with drinks. Most of the detectives like to go there. Not many uniforms, though."

"Paddy's?"

"You know it?"

"From before you were born. Let's take the chance you're right and get there first. I'd like to talk to him before he gets inside."

Chris nodded, turned down the next block, sped up, and made another turn. She was now traveling parallel to the detective, but going much faster than he was.

"How come you don't ever check in?" Lou asked her. "Don't you have an assignment or anything?"

"I took some vacation days so I could be with you full time."

"Lucky me," Lou said, and then frowned. "And Morrison bought that? You wanting vacation time? He's stupider than I thought."

"Don't sell him short. He knew why I wanted the days off as soon as he knew you were in town. He probably figured that if we do come up with something, I'll go to him first and he'll get the credit."

"And will you?" Lou asked.

Chris shot him a look. "I'll do what I think is right, not what Morrison wants. And not what you want, either. What I want," she told him firmly.

Lou nodded, realizing again the woman he was seated next to was not going to be easy to control.

Detective 2nd Grade Scott Henderson drove into the parking lot of the all-night eatery and bar. He'd been looking forward to a good stiff drink for hours and couldn't wait to get inside. He pulled into a vacant parking space, shut off his engine and saw another car pull up behind him, blocking his car from backing out. He watched as two people got out and approached. The woman came over to his side while the man walked to the passenger side. He slipped his hand onto the grip of the gun on his hip and was starting to pull it out when the woman reached his window and flashed a Detective's shield in his face.

"Chris Preston," she said by way of introduction. "We'd like a few minutes of your time."

"About what?" Henderson asked, wondering what a Detective wanted with him and having to brace him in a parking lot.

Lou knocked on the window of the passenger door, gesturing for him to open it.

"Who's that?" Henderson asked Chris.

"A friend. You'll love him."

Henderson wasn't sure what was going on, but she was a fellow police officer and his curiosity got the better of him, so he reached over and unlocked the passenger door. Lou slid into the seat and Chris got into the back.

Lou held out his hand. "Lou Parker," he told him.

Henderson shook Lou's hand and suddenly everything became clear to him. "You're Shawn's father."

Lou nodded and then gestured toward Chris. "And Chris was his girlfriend."

"I'd heard that," Henderson said. "I just didn't put the two together until just now. I'm sorry about what happened to Shawn."

"Thanks," Chris said.

"You searched my son's place and found the stash."

"That's right."

"Where'd you find it?"

"Inside a broken TV in a closet."

"Shawn didn't have a broken television set," Chris objected. "He'd just bought an entire new entertainment center and threw the old stuff out. I helped him."

"Maybe so. But there was a broken set in the closet and it contained two kilos of cocaine."

Henderson looked at Lou, then over to Chris.

"You two think it was planted," he said.

"The thought had crossed my mind," Lou agreed.

"Mine, too," Henderson said, surprising both Lou and Chris.

"Talk to me," Lou said.

"Well, I had an off-the-record conversation with the guys who made the initial search and they told me that they'd found no television other than what was in the wall cabinets in the living room. But when I went in, there it was, so I figured they'd missed it the first time through."

"No, there was more that raised your suspicions than that," Chris suggested.

Henderson thought for a moment before replying. "You're right," he finally said. "That place had been sealed. It'd been torn apart by the best we've got. And they had come up empty. Then three days later, I get ordered to make another search. And I find the coke. It just didn't ring true to me."

"I can hardly imagine why," Lou said.

"You have any thoughts on why?" Chris asked Henderson.

"Only the obvious one. Somebody wants Shawn to look like he was dealing. I know the coke was there. I found it. Before that I'd heard rumors about a Swiss bank account. When I found the coke I realized they might be true."

"They are," Lou said.

"It all fit. The coke. Swiss bank accounts. All the same I still think that coke was planted."

"I'm sure it was," Lou told him.

"But what I don't understand," Henderson said, "is why go to the trouble of planting the coke if he's already dead? Why go to all that trouble?" Henderson looked first at Lou, then at Chris, for an answer. But none was forthcoming. They just didn't know either.

Chris pulled up to the front of Lou's motel room. "What time you want to get started in the morning?" she asked as Lou got out of the car.

Lou turned back and leaned into the car. "I'll meet you here at eight."

"There must be something more we can do tonight."

"If you think of anything, go do it. Me? I'm going to turn in. I'm beat."

He took another look at her and grinned. "You don't look so terrific yourself. A good night sleep would do you some good, too."

Lou shut the door and Chris watched him walk to his room, turn and wave, then go inside. Satisfied, she put the car in gear and drove off.

Inside his room, Lou picked up the phone and called the pool hall and was told that Danny still hadn't come back. He sat down on the bed to wait for Danny to call.

Chris went home and took a long shower, something she had been dreaming about doing for most of the day. She came out of the bathroom and looked lovingly at her bed. Lou was right, she thought. She was tired. She wondered if Lou was asleep yet and decided he was. He'd looked beat, but then she realized he looked beat every time she'd seen him. She smiled as her mind replayed their parting this evening. Lou'd been really nice, concerned about her. Something he hadn't shown before. He'd even wished her a good night's sleep. Chris frowned. Was he being sincere or was it all just a con?

Chris quickly threw on some clean clothes and drove back to the motel. She pulled into the parking lot and breathed a sigh of relief. His car was still there. She thought about going home again, to her nice warm bed, and rejected the idea. She just didn't trust the man. So she parked and settled in for a long night keeping watch deciding she wasn't going to give him the chance of going off without her.

Chapter Eight

Lou was jarred awake by the strident ringing of the phone. He was stretched out on the bed in exactly the same place where he'd fallen asleep the night before. He reached over and picked up the phone.

"Yeah?" he said, fighting grogginess.

"It's me. Danny."

"What time is it?"

"A little after seven. Sorry I didn't get back to you last night but I got involved in a poker game and it just broke up. What is it you wanted?"

It took Lou a moment to remember why he'd called Danny, then it came back to him. "The stuff they found at Shawn's. It had been watered down twice."

"High grade stuff," Danny admitted.

"We're all agreed on that, Danny. What we don't know is where it came from."

"Okay. Well, stuff like that is way out of my class."

"Gimme a name, Danny. I'll do the rest."

"There's a guy I know who might be able to help you," Danny said slowly. "But if he ever found out I told you, I'd wind up in a sewer someplace."

"The name," Lou said coldly.

"You'll cover my ass?" Danny wanted to know, unable to mask the fear in his voice.

"I never even heard of you," Lou said flatly.

"Willie Anderson. Big Willie. Guy eats more than I do. You'll love him."

"I need an address."

Lou walked out of his motel room and looked for the dark brown Chevy. He wasn't sure why he thought she'd be there he just knew he did and he was right, finding it parked across from his room. He strode over to it and knocked on the driver's side window, waking Chris out of an uncomfortable sleep.

"You didn't trust me," he told her, knowing he sounded like a petulant child and hating himself for it.

Chris straightened up in the seat. The muscles in her entire body felt twisted out of shape. "I'm sorry. I just thought that…forget it. My mistake," she said, feeling not a little foolish for spending the night in her car, instead of in her warm, comfortable bed.

Lou walked around the car and got into the passenger seat. "You thought I'd run out on you again."

Chris nodded. She felt ashamed that she hadn't trusted him. He watched her squirm. He saw no reason for him to tell her that if Danny had called last night, he'd intended to follow up right then and there, without her.

"You capable of driving this morning?" Lou asked innocently.

Chris turned the ignition and put the car in gear. "Point the way, partner."

Lou frowned. She wasn't his partner and never would be. He was tolerating her because he had to, but that was going to end soon. Sooner than Chris thought.

Lou led the way to the rear of the house where he bypassed the doorbell and started pounding on the back door with his fist.

It didn't take long for them to hear movement inside. Then the door opened and Big Willie stood staring down at them. Lou took the measure of the man and decided Danny had underestimated his size. He guessed his height at close to six-four and his weight at probably the same with just another zero added to it. And that didn't take in the .45 that Willie was holding in his fist.

"You better have a good reason for waking me up like this, asshole," Willie said coldly.

Lou turned to Chris. "Not very polite," Lou told her dryly.

Lou turned back to Willie, only this time he had his 9mm automatic in his hand. Willie saw the Beretta and glanced over at Chris. Her .38 Smith and Wesson was pointed at him.

"A big mistake," Willie told them. "Very big."

Lou shrugged. "It wouldn't be the first time. Now you got one gun pointed at us and we've got two guns pointed at you. You want to do something about it or not? Choose."

Willie didn't like the odds. "What's this all about?" Willie asked lowering his gun.

"First off, you can relax. I'm not here to rip you off. I want to talk. Nothing more."

"I don't talk so good with guns pointed at me," Willie informed them.

Lou nodded. He could understand that. He holstered his gun and out of the corner of his eye saw Chris follow his lead. Willie watched the guns disappear, surprised that they'd do it while he still had his own gun out. He found their behavior intriguing.

"Come in," Willie said, and stepped back.

Lou and Chris went inside. They entered a kitchen that could have doubled for the best in any fine restaurant in the world. From the look of the house on the outside, one would've never expected something like this. Lou slowly took it all in, then turned to face Willie.

"Nice. I'm impressed."

"I like eating and I like cooking. Kinda hobby of mine," Willie explained.

"The eating or the cooking?" Chris asked.

Willie smiled. "Both. Now whatta you two want?"

Lou slid into the chair at the table and made himself comfortable before answering. "Information. Nothing more and I won't settle for anything less, so let's get that straight right now."

"That's crap and you know it," Willie answered. "I don't want to tell you something, I don't, and there's not a damn thing you can do about it."

"Maybe you'd want to," Chris suggested before Lou could respond.

"Why?" Willie asked simply.

Lou looked over at Chris. It was her move now and he was curious to see how she was going to handle it.

"Simple. What we want to know is something that isn't going to hurt you one bit," she told him.

"Not good enough."

"Of course not, but I just wanted to make that clear at the outset. You ever been married?"

Willie laughed. "Look at me. Who'd want to marry me?"

"You weren't always that big, were you?"

"No. And I was married once. She divorced me when I passed four hundred pounds."

"Any children?"

"One. I don't see her anymore. She don't like what I do for a living. Where's all this going? You figuring on writing my biography?"

Lou was watching Chris closely. He had an idea where she was heading and was getting ready to play his role. At the same time he marveled at the way she was playing Willie.

"Tell me," Chris went on. "If anybody did something to your daughter, what would you do?"

"More'n I'd tell you, that's for sure," Willie said.

Chris gestured at Lou. "This man sitting here had a son. His son was murdered. He wants his killer. Bad. And nothing's going to stop him from getting him. Or her. You could help him find that killer."

Willie nodded. Revenge was something he understood. He turned to Lou. "How'd your son get himself killed?"

"Two blasts from a shotgun. In his own home. In bed. He never had a chance."

Willie glanced from one to the other. He believed they were telling him the truth. But there was something else. Something in their attitudes, their bearing, their tone of voice, the guns they carried, that was sending up red flags in his mind. "You guys are cops," he announced to them.

"Used to be. I'm retired now."

"And her?" Willie asked, cocking his head towards Chris.

"She doesn't count," Lou said, and ignored the look Chris gave him. "It was my son that bought it. And I want the person who killed him," Lou said, with an intensity that surprised even him.

"You're Shawn Parker's old man," Willie said, all the pieces finally falling into place in his mind.

"Uh huh," Lou agreed.

Willie made his decision. "What is it you want to know?"

"They found some dope in Shawn's house. Good stuff, too. The thing is Shawn never used. And never dealt. He was death on drugs."

"So?" Willie asked.

"So that stuff was planted there. To make Shawn look dirty. To make the cops back off going after his murderer. It was made to look like it was a falling out among drug dealers and Shawn came out on the losing end."

"And you think if you find who planted the stuff…"

"I'll find who murdered him," Lou finished the sentence for him.

"Could be," Willie agreed. "But I don't know nothing about the hit. Zip. So I can't help you. Even if I wanted to."

"Listen, the stuff they found in Shawn's place was prime. It'd been only stepped on twice. It wasn't even ready for the street yet. Get my drift?" Lou asked.

Willie nodded, then shook his head. "I don't know how you got to me, but you're way off base. That kind of stuff, that quality, is way beyond anything I'd ever see."

"Then who would see that grade of coke?" Chris asked.

Willie shrugged. "I don't know. Look, I'd like to help you, but the whole thing's way out of my league. Besides, if I did know and did tell you, odds are, I'd wind up dead."

Lou got to his feet. Faced Willie head-on. "You know who's head man. You may not know him personally, but you know. Now I need to know."

Chris moved over to stand next to Willie. She placed her hand on his arm. "We won't force you to say a thing, Willie. Just think about your daughter for a moment. And what you'd do if you were in Lou's place. Think about it," Chris implored.

Willie thought about it. What he'd do if somebody had killed his daughter. There was no question in his mind what he would do. The question was, would Lou do the same thing? No matter what the law said. The answer was written all over Lou's face.

"I can't tell you who murdered your son. Or who planted the shit in his house. But that kind of stuff…you might check out Pace Beaudine."

"My God," Lou exclaimed. "That asshole still alive?"

"More than just that. He runs all the dope in and out of this city now," Willie told them. "He's top dog in town."

"He hasn't the brains," Lou said. "I can't count the times I busted him for selling nickel and dime bags right out in the open."

"Maybe not. But he's come a long way since. He works out of a country club he financed. Does the walk with all the big shots. Owns all kinds of other legit businesses, too. From parking lots to meat plants. If anybody could get his hands on the kind of quality stuff you're talking about, it's him."

Lou thought about it and nodded. "Thanks, Willie. I appreciate it. You know the address of this country club?"

Willie grabbed a pencil and wrote on a pad, then tore off the top sheet and handed it to Lou.

"I hope you get whoever it was killed your kid."

"I will," Lou told him. "Count on it."

Chris pulled up in front of Lou's motel room and shut off the engine before she turned to him. "I still think we should go see Beaudine right now. Before he hears that we're on his case."

Lou shook his head. "From what Willie told us, getting in to see Beaudine isn't going to be easy. It's going to take some planning."

"Then lets get to it. Unless you really want to blow this lead entirely."

Lou hated being pushed and being pushed by this girl seemed even harder to take. He looked over at her and nodded. "Okay. But first I need a shower."

Chris ginned. "I didn't want to say anything, but it wouldn't hurt."

"Why don't you go get us some coffee? By the time you're back, I'll be out of the shower and we can plan our move."

He got out of the car and walked into his room while Chris locked the car and strode to the coffee shop. As soon as she entered the coffee shop Lou came out of his room, went over to his car, got in and drove off. He'd be damned if he was going to brace Beaudine on his own turf with a woman in tow.

Lou drove across the Bronx-Whitestone Bridge onto the Hutchinson River Parkway and headed north towards New Rochelle, where it took him about ten minutes and two wrong turns before he finally found the country club.

Its centerpiece was a glass and brick clubhouse that sat on a grass covered hill overlooking the golf course complete with a liveried doorman guarding the front gate. It was the kind of place where money and power were left at the door because everyone in the place had both.

A garbage truck lumbered up the driveway that led to the rear of the clubhouse where deliveries could be made without the members ever seeing them. It pulled to a stop near the kitchen door and Lou jumped off the rear bumper. He walked into the kitchen and made his way past the cooks and waiters who were too intent on catering to the whims of their demanding clientele to take the time to wonder about things that didn't directly affect them.

Lou reached the main hall, saw a sign that said "Private" and decided that was as good a place to start as any. He strode past the sign and down a corridor towards the door at its end. He'd taken three steps before his way was blocked by two suited men, who had stepped out of a small alcove to his left, their jackets bulging slightly over holstered weapons.

"Something we can do for you, sir?" the smaller of the two asked.

"I've got an appointment with Beaudine," Lou said casually.

"I don't think so. Mr. Beaudine told us he was expecting no one this morning."

"He'll see me," Lou said, and started around them.

The bigger one grabbed Lou and he found himself against the wall while the smaller one frisked him. He found the gun at Lou's waist and pulled it out.

"I wonder how that got there," Lou said innocently.

Sam Riley, an older, more muscled version of the two men, came down the hallway behind Lou and the smaller man held up the gun so he could see it.

"Nobody sees Mr. Beaudine without an appointment," Riley said. "And carrying certainly doesn't get you one."

Lou turned and stared into Riley's face. Recognition took only a moment. For both of them. "Gee, Samuel," Lou said. "I didn't know you'd become a secretary. Sharpened your typing skills, did you? That's sweet."

Riley grinned. It had been a long time coming and he was going to enjoy this. "Hold him," he ordered his two men and they immediately grabbed Lou's arms, pinning them to his sides.

"I guess wishes do come true," Riley said. He shifted his weight to his rear leg and pushed off, driving his fist hard into Lou's rib cage. Lou wanted to fall, but the two men held him rigidly in place. Riley sent a second blow hard into Lou's face. Lou's head spun. He watched, helpless, as Riley set himself for his next shot. Lou saw it coming and closed his eyes. He knew he'd feel it soon enough and decided he didn't have to watch it coming. Only nothing happened. The blow didn't land.

Lou opened his eyes in time to see Riley collapse to the floor. Out cold. Lou looked around.

Chris stood to one side. Her .38 was in her fist and pointed at the two men holding Lou. "Let him go," she ordered.

The two men looked at the gun Chris was holding on them and wisely figured they had no choice. They dropped their hold on Lou.

Lou fell back against the wall and stayed there trying to catch his breath. Chris waited for him, her eyes glued on the two men under her gun. "Stupid thing to do. Coming here alone," Chris said to him.

Lou wiped blood from his lip. "I didn't come alone. You're here." He moved away from the wall and straightened up.

Right, thought Chris. A simple thank you would be too much to expect.

Lou moved in front of his two captors who were standing in his way. "Excuse me, please," he said politely.

Only too aware of Chris's gun, they moved aside and Lou walked past them, stopped to retrieve his automatic, then continued on.

Pace Beaudine, a good twenty years younger than Lou, was working a computer keyboard with unexpected expertise at his desk in the far end of his office. The place was lush. Dark wood paneling and deep pile carpet. He looked up at the sound of a sharp crack and watched as the door to his office door splintered, then flew open and Lou walked in.

Beaudine worked hard at composing himself. "It wasn't locked," he finally said.

Lou shrugged.

"You know what that door cost? I had it made special. Hand carved. From China."

Lou glanced at the broken door. "Nice work," he said admiringly.

Beaudine frowned. "You're supposed to be retired."

"I came back."

"Shit. I really don't need this."

Chris came in and moved over to stand beside Lou. Beaudine raised his eyebrows. "I didn't know you had a daughter, Lou."

"I don't."

Chris reached into her purse and pulled out the small black case containing her badge. She flashed it at Beaudine who looked over at Lou.

"I'm retired. She's not."

Beaudine sat back, resigned to having to deal with them. "Then let's cut the bullshit and get to it."

Lou looked around the room admiringly. "You've come a long way since we last tangled."

"Times change."

"Don't they?" Lou said.

"Let's cut to the chase, huh? I'm a legitimate business man. This is my place. I own it. And it's for members only. Which you are not. Now, how about you say your say and go or should I call the police and have them throw you out?"

Lou shrugged. "Do what you want? But before the police get here I'll know what I want to know."

Beaudine remembered that Lou wasn't averse to using strong arm tactics and now that he wasn't carrying a badge anymore there was no telling what he'd do. "Ask your questions."

"My son's dead. A couple of kilos of coke were found in his house. The way I hear it, there isn't a grain that comes into this town that doesn't go through your hands. I figured you might know something about how it got into my son's house."

Beaudine glanced at Chris. He was not about to say a damn thing with her there.

"I'm not here," she said, reading his mind.

"You look here," said Beaudine.

"It's an illusion. Now answer the man's question, asshole."

Beaudine looked over at Lou. "What's with this bitch?" he asked.

Lou shook his head. "You don't know the half of it."

Beaudine thought about it for a moment and then shrugged in resignation. "Okay. She's with you. I forgive her mouth."

"Don't do me any favors," Chris said.

Beaudine got up, walked around his desk and started towards Chris. She held her ground. Lou quickly moved between them. "Forget her," he said to Beaudine. "She's not here. Deal with me."

Beaudine nodded and turned to face Lou. "I heard about the stash. The thing is, I got nothing that ain't accounted for." He waved a huge paw at the computer. "It's all in there right down to the last grain. Nothing's missing." He turned back to face Chris. "And don't get no asshole ideas, missy. Anybody touches that computer, tries to get in without the password, and the whole thing goes up in smoke. Just like on television."

"You're a careful man," she said.

"I'm still alive 'cause I think of things like that."

"You don't have the brains to think of when to go to the bathroom without someone telling you," Lou said.

Beaudine walked back behind his desk and sat down. "Think what you like. I'm telling you all my merchandise is accounted for."

"Then where'd it come from?" Lou demanded to know.

"You get me a chemical breakdown on the stuff and maybe I could tell you. But until you do, stay outta my face. You don't carry a badge no more and she ain't got the muscle to go with hers. I said what I said 'cause you lost your boy. But that's it. We ain't friends. Never have been. Never will be."

"You have no idea how disappointed I am," Lou said, turned and walked out of the office. Beaudine watched him go and looked over to Chris. "You planning on moving in?" he asked.

Chris had been fuming since Lou walked out. She couldn't believe he'd left her behind. Furious, she turned and stormed from the room.

Chris walked down the drive at the rear of the country club, got to the street and looked around. Lou was nowhere in sight. She turned around when she heard someone else coming down the drive. It was Lou and she saw he was carrying a six-pack of beer he'd obviously appropriated from the kitchen.

"You drive. I'm drinking."

Chris was still angry. "Not in my car you're not. You want to drink and drive, do it in your own car."

Frustrated, he grabbed her arm and pulled her against the wall of the alley. "Look, I said I'd work with you, but that doesn't make you my mother. What I do, I do. You don't like it…tough. Keep it to yourself or split."

He stepped away from her and pulled a can free. He popped it and took a long swill. He was taunting her and she knew it. She looked back at the country club and gestured towards it. "You believe that scumbag?"

"Hardly. He knows. The question is why he's keeping it clammed up."

"A double-cross?" she suggested.

"Like Shawn was dealing for him and holding out? It'd never happen."

"Because it was Shawn?"

"Of course."

"People do change."

Lou finished the beer and tossed it. He opened another. "Sure. But if he had, Beaudine would've screwed that fact into me. And he didn't. No. There's something else." He moved away from her. The sudden movement made him wince, a reminder of the beating he took at the hands of Riley.

"There's a doctor I know…," she offered.

"I'll live. The rib's not broken. Cracked maybe but not broken. But I think I will sit down for a minute."

He slid down the wall to the street, his back propped against the wall. Chris moved to his side. She reached for the can of beer. "You don't need this." She took the can before Lou realized what she was doing. He made a grab for it but pulled back quickly clutching his side in pain.

"Okay. You can hold it for me," he agreed.He tried to take a deep breath but the pain stopped him.

"So that's why you wanted me to drive. You can't right now. You figure to come back and get your own car when you're feeling better."

"I can drive."

"Yeah, right. You know something? You are one stubborn son-of-a-bitch."

"Hell, don't mince words. Say what you mean."

She laughed. Lou looked up at her, stared into her face. "You know something? It is kinda nice knowing what you think at the time you think it. I'm not used to that from a female type."

"We're not all the same."

"Yeah. Mostly you are. My ex… I never knew what she was thinking. She'd never come out and say it. I spent all my time trying to figure out what she wanted. By what she didn't say."

"It's called passive-aggressive behavior."

Lou looked at her and frowned.

Chris smiled at him. "I minored in psychology."

"Well, whatever it's called it's the most frustrating thing in the world to live with. Used to infuriate me something fierce. I'd ask her something and all she'd do was stare at me. And when I said I wanted her opinion, she wouldn't respond or she'd say `I'm thinking'. Never could get an honest answer out of her about nothing."

"Which is why it's so aggressive. Toughest thing in the world to cope with."

She moved to one side of him, gently shoved him forward from the waist, got her arms under his armpits and helped him to his feet. "Come on. We stay here much longer, you'll get your ass arrested for D & D. And you do look the part."

"Be nice. I hurt."

Lou sat on his motel bed with his shirt off, watching Chris tape his ribs.

"Where'd you learn?" Lou asked.

"High school. Took a class in sports medicine after school. Then the trainer got busted. He was handing out steroids to the football team like it was candy. I stepped in. Shoulders and ankles were my specialty."

She stepped back. Admired her work.

"Shawn played football," Lou said.

"Before my time."

Lou nodded and got to his feet. He slipped his shirt back on. Chris walked over to the chair and slid into it.

"We were partnered for about a year before anything happened between us," she said pensively. "Neither of us saw it coming. But one night we were in a shoot-out. Two guys thought it'd be fun to stickup a man at a Ready-Teller machine. There'd been two robberies at the place the week before."

"So you staked it out."

"If they'd come back before, we figured they might be stupid enough to try a third time. When we braced them, they opened up. We returned fire."

"They live?"

"Nope. But the intended victim did. He got through it without a scratch. Afterwards, we were so hyped up, neither of us wanted to sleep. But we did want other things. That's when the affair started. We found we needed each other. It didn't hurt us on the job and life became a lot more fun. It ended about three months ago."

"Mutual?" Lou asked.

Chris shrugged her shoulders. "I guess. But it was over long before then. Just neither of us wanted to admit it."

"Yeah. I've been there."

Chris cocked her head as she watched him tuck his shirt into his pants. "He was a lot like you, you know."

"Come on. We were never alike."

"But he wasn't as tough as you. He doubted himself. A lot." Chris thought about this for a moment. It's the first time she'd put it into words. "Maybe that was part of the reason that I stopped loving him," she wondered aloud.

Lou turned to her. "Give me a break. You think I don't have doubts?"

Chris got to her feet. "It never even crosses your mind that you can't do something."

Lou found himself feeling very uncomfortable. Probably because he knew she was right. He moved to the door and held it open for her.

"You know, I'm fully capable of opening doors for myself," she informed him.

"A gentleman does things like that for a lady."

"Since when did you become a fucking gentleman?"

Lou thought about that for a moment and then nodded before he turned and walked out. He slammed the door behind him so Chris was forced to open it for herself. After all, it was what she wanted, wasn't it?

Lou leaned against a tree down the block from his ex-wife's home. He straightened as he saw Chris come towards him. When she reached him, he fell into step beside her.

"Boy, does she hate your guts," Chris told him.

"Naa…she's just afraid of me."

"Please don't tell me you used to hit her."

Lou shook his head. "Never hit a woman in my life. Never will either. She's just afraid I'll tell her new husband things she doesn't want him to know."

Chris turned to look at him. "Would you?"

"Depends. It doesn't really matter though. He'll find out for himself in time." He turned to Chris expectantly. "So?"

"She says that Shawn never mentioned he was seeing anybody since we broke up."

"Then what the hell is it? Was he ashamed of her? Was he balling a married woman? A hooker? What?"

"Beats the shit out of me."

She glanced down the block and frowned. There was someone in her car. "Fucking kids. Hey!" she yelled and started to run towards the car. Lou loped after her, favoring his hurt ribcage.

The man in the car heard Chris yell. He looked up and saw her running towards him. He grabbed the door handle and pushed the door open.

And the car blew sky high, the blast lifting both Lou and Chris off their feet. They were blown backwards, onto a lawn as the car went a foot into the air before it smashed back down into the ground. Then the secondary explosion came as the gas tank blew. Flames shot into the sky and pieces of the car flew everywhere.

Chapter Nine

Lou was getting bored very quickly. He was sprawled in one of the chairs in front of Morrison's desk. Chris was in the other. They were both watching Morrison read the initial report of the explosion. He finally looked up at them and shook his head.

"From the bits and pieces left, the only thing we're sure of, is that you two are damn lucky to be sitting here." He fixed his gaze on Chris. "What the hell were you doing hanging around with him anyway?"

"Lay off her," Lou said, before Chris had a chance to respond. "She was just in the wrong place at the wrong time."

Morrison brushed him off with a wave of his hand without taking his eyes off Chris. "Well?" he repeated putting more of a command tone in his voice, a tone that usually scared the hell out of the people working for him.

"I was looking into Shawn's murder," Chris explained evenly.

"And who the hell gave you that assignment?"

"I did. All by myself," she replied.

"Oh. So that's the way things are around here, huh? You decide on your own assignments. Did I miss something or did someone change the ladder of command around here?"

"Let it go," Lou warned.

Morrison ignored the threat and kept his eyes locked on Chris.

"You knew what I was doing," she said.

"You asked for a few days off. I gave them to you. I felt you deserved them. That's all. And what do I get in return? You go off with this beat-up relic of a cop and start an investigation on your own without any so much as a by-your leave. Is that how you made Detective? By writing your own rules? Well, maybe that promotion you got was something that should be re-examined."

"You don't hear so good, Morrison," Lou said. "Let it go!"

Morrison knew he couldn't allow Lou to speak to him that way, to take over in front of one of his officers. He forced himself to turn and look at Lou. "Oh, now you think you can tell me what I can or can't say to one of my officers?"

"Your officers? I thought she worked for the Department or is she your personal cop now?"

Morrison shot to his feet. "You can't come into my office and talk to me that!"

"Shut the fuck up! The two of you," Chris yelled and both men turned to look at her.

She turned to Lou first. "I can take care of myself. I don't need your help." She then turned to Morrison. "You want to bring me up before a board, do it. You want to suspend me, do it. Until then I'm going to do my job the best I can in the best way I know how. And if that means I have to associate with people that you don't like than you'd better put any order to stay away from him in writing, Captain, or just learn to live with it."

Morrison sat back down and stared at Chris. He'd get this bitch for what she'd just said to him. He had a long memory and he knew that he could make life just perfectly miserable for her and he intended to do just that. At the right time. Right now he forced himself to take a more reasonable tone.

"What the hell is it with you? You meet this dinosaur and now you're acting like him. He was an embarrassment to the entire force when he was on the Job and he's making you the same thing."

Chris shook her head. "He had the best solved rate in the department or have you forgotten that?"

"I haven't forgotten a thing, Detective. But that was then. His methods don't work anymore."

"They work well enough to scare the shit out of somebody and get them to try and kill him," Chris shot back.

"And to kill you," Morrison said with more patience than he thought possible.

Lou headed for the door. He'd had enough.

"Where're you going?" Morrison called out. "I haven't finished with you yet."

Lou didn't bother to respond and continued out. Chris got to her feet and started to follow him.

"Oh, no, you don't," Morrison told her. "You sit your ass right back down, Detective Preston. I'm not through with you yet."

Chris stopped at the door. It was one thing to talk back to a superior officer, quite another to disobey a direct order, so she allowed her training to take over and sat back down.

Amos was enjoying himself. He was cutting into the charred remains of what was once a human being. He was in his element.

Lou came through the door and sauntered over to him. Amos looked up from the cadaver and smiled at Lou. "I hear this should've been you," he said, indicating the corpse with a nod of his head.

"You don't have to look so damn pleased about it," Lou said and hoisted himself onto a nearby gurney.

"Hell, you've caused more excitement around here than we've had in years. You're not going to hear me complaining. Not one bit."

Lou gestured at the thing on the table. "That going to tell you anything?"

"This mess? Not likely. Too close to the center of the explosion. But…"

Lou watched as Amos moved down to the end of the table and picked up a blackened object. He brought it back and held it in front of Lou. "This now. This is something else again. Or was." He turned it over, examining it one more time, his scientific mind totally engrossed in it. "Still is, I guess," he finally said. "Technically."

"Okay, I'll bite. What is it?" Lou asked.

"Forearm. Wrist. Hand. Blown totally off from the blast. Charred, I admit, but nevertheless…"

Amos looked at Lou expectantly. He was proud of what he'd done. He watched Lou mull over the unspoken challenge and wondered if Lou would get it.

Lou continued to stare at the charred remnants of the arm. He took longer than he should have, but finally he looked up at Amos. "You're kidding. From that?" he said, unable to keep the incredulity out of his voice.

"Why not?"

"How is more to the point?"

"A little of this. A little of that. You'd be surprised what the right combination of chemicals can do," Amos said proudly.

"So how many did you raise?"

"A complete set from this one hand. I couldn't get a palm print because the burning went too deep but I got five perfect fingers." Amos set the burned mess down. "I sent them upstairs half an hour ago. You can thank me now."

"Before I see the results? Not likely."

"I wait in full anticipation of the outcome."

Lou jumped off the gurney and moved to the door. Amos called after him. "Having fun yet?"

"Starting to."

Lou pushed through the stainless steel doors and came face to face with Chris. He moved around her and walked down the corridor. She was immediately at his side.

"I'm going to have to put an anchor around you. What'd Amos have to say?"

Lou ignored her question. "He ream you good up there?"

She tossed her head. "Not bad. Think of my career. Be sensible. A couple of threats. A complete trashing of Lou Parker. And a direct order to stay away from you."

"Then what're you doing here?"

"Fuck him."

"You should do something about that stubborn streak," Lou said.

Chris grinned. "Hell. It gives us something in common."

Lou stopped and turned to face her. "We've got nothing in common. Listen to what you've been told. You've got your whole life in front of you. Mine's over. That makes me dangerous. So stay away before you get hurt."

Lou didn't wait for a response, but turned and strode away. Chris ran after him, grabbed his arm and pulled him around to face her. "Look, I put my ass on the line for you up there and all you do is piss and moan about your life and how it's over. If it's over then go back to your boat. If you're going to stay you should at least thank me for keeping your sorry ass out of jail."

Lou stepped closer to her. "Try telling the truth sometime and maybe you would get a thank you."

"I don't understand."

"Yeah, you do."

Chris shook her head. She didn't.

"Okay. Let me lay it out for you. You say you put your ass on the line for me up there. You kept me out of jail. Okay. How'd you do all that? Just what did you have to promise Morrison to get all that accomplished? Answer me that one."

Chris looked into Lou's face in astonishment. How the hell did he figure all that out? Reluctantly, she nodded. "You're right."

"I know that."

"Well, you don't have to be so smug about it."

"Why not? You just got caught in a lie. That's your problem to deal with, not mine."

"Morrison suspended me for working with you and for insubordination and for a couple of other things that went by so fast I didn't catch them all."

"And?"

"And it'll all be forgotten if I stick with you, unofficially, of course, and report back to him with anything and everything we get."

"And you agreed."

"What choice did I have? You would've done the same thing."

"No. I'd have told him to press the charges and take my chances with a hearing board."

"You would've lost."

"Morrison's never going to press any charges. Against a member of his team? No way. It'd reflect badly on him. It's the last thing he wants. He was bluffing you. And you folded without even a struggle."

"I agreed with what he wanted, but I wasn't going to do it."

He stared into her face for a moment and then slowly nodded. "You know something. I believe you."

"Then what the fuck are you so pissed off about?"

"Because you didn't tell me from the get-go," he said, before turning and walking away.

Chris watched him go and reluctantly admitted to herself that he was right. She should have told him but she didn't want to take the chance that he'd always be wondering if she were spying on him for Morrison. She should have known he'd figure things out. Too many years on the Job had taught him all the moves and he was someone who prided himself on always being one step ahead of everybody else. And he was, she had to admit. There was no question about it. He was good.

Lou's head was buried in the refrigerator. He backed away empty-handed and slammed the refrigerator door shut. "You're outta beer," he called out and walked back into the living room where Tollin sat in his chair.

"Only because you keep drinking it."

Lou slid into the couch.

"You comfy?" Tollin asked.

"I slept a lot of nights on this thing after Darleen kicked me out."

"And I used to pray she'd change her mind just to get you out of here."

"Bullshit. You loved the company."

"I didn't love not sleeping nights."

"Yeah, you did. You loved us staying up all night talking our cases through. Figuring our next move. You never had it so good."

Tollin smiled as he remembered back. "We did clear more cases during that year than we ever did before."

"Hell, we owned the streets back then."

"Yeah. But the Department didn't give a shit. Said our methods gave them a bad name. Said we embarrassed them."

"We did what we had to do. They were never embarrassed by our results."

"No, but we never played by their rules and that they could never accept."

Lou grinned. "We did have a tendency to break them now and again."

"Never break. Bend. We hadda have some kind of edge."

"I miss those times. I really do." Lou looked down at his hands. They no longer had the smoothness of a young man. He missed those times, too.

"You getting anywhere on this crusade of yours?" Tollin inquired.

Lou tore his mind away from the past and looked up at Tollin. "Bits and pieces, but nothing's come together yet."

"I'm sorry."

"I'll get there. Don't you worry."

"I'm not," Tollin said. "You want to talk about it?"

"Nothing to talk about unless you have some idea why the Department's so set on painting Shawn a dirty cop. They have to have a reason otherwise this whole thing doesn't make sense."

"I could never find any good reasons why the brass acted the way they did."

"I'll figure it out though. One way or another," Lou promised.

Tollin nodded. If anybody could do it, Lou could. "How about this girl Detective? She any good?"

"You jealous?" Lou asked with a grin.

"I heard she was a comer."

Lou shifted on the couch uncomfortable with this line of questioning. He looked over at Tollin and saw he was waiting for an answer. He knew he had to give him one or he'd never hear the end of it. "She's not bad. Fact is, she handles herself okay."

Tollin eyed his old partner closely. That was high praise coming from him. Was she really that good or was there something more going on between them? "Anything else you want to tell me about her?"

"Like what?"

Tollin shrugged. "Whatever."

"Nothing to tell."

Tollin noted how quick the answer was in coming. There was more going on. No question about it.

"Besides, she's no longer helping me so it really doesn't matter," Lou went on, surprising Tollin.

"Oh? I would've thought you needed her."

"Yeah, right. Like a barnyard needs flies."

"What happened? She walk out on you? You should be used to that by now. I used to tell you that I was the only person in this world that could put up with you."

"I blew her off. It was getting too dangerous. I couldn't allow her to be in harm's way because of me."

"Ahhh," Tollin said, dragging the word out.

"What's that supposed to mean?"

"Nothing. But did you ever think that maybe she was there because she wanted to, and that it was her choice and not yours to make?"

Lou looked over at Tollin, surprised. "The thought never even crossed my mind."

Lou walked up the dimly lighted driveway towards the garage. He opened the door and stepped inside. The light over the workbench cast shadows throughout the room. Lou heard a noise from the darkness and pulled his gun. He moved behind a crate, into the shadows and watched J.J. come out from behind the workbench with a chrome plated .45 in his hand.

"Take it easy, kid," Lou said, and stepped away from the crate. "It's only me."

"Shit, man. You scared the hell out of me," J.J. said, and tossed the gun onto the workbench. Lou walked over to the bench as he holstered his own weapon. He picked up the .45 and turned it over in his hand.

"Nice. Commemorative model," Lou said, admiring the workmanship on the weapon.

"I wouldn't know."

J.J. went to the door and looked out. He came back shaking his head. "I get the funniest feeling I'm being watched."

"Nobody knows you're still helping me, kid. They figure they scared you off."

J.J. threw him a look. He wasn't so sure.

"Okay," Lou said. "Maybe you're right. How about you get out of here for a while? Until you feel safe."

"And what about the stuff you asked for?"

"I'll get it another way."

"How?"

"I'll think of something."

J.J. shook his head. "If you had another way you never would've come here."

"I don't want anything to happen to you."

"I'll be okay. Besides, I'll have it in a couple of hours. Then I will get out of here for a while."

"You're that close?"

"I got into their system earlier but it took so long I had to log off before they saw me."

J.J. took the .45 from Lou's hand and turned it over, examining it as if it was a foreign object. Then he tossed the gun back onto the workbench. "Dad wouldn't even let me play with toy guns as a kid. He said it'd give me bad habits. You know he never carried a gun in his life. No matter what the job was," J.J. said proudly.

"One of the things I always liked about him."

J.J. looked up at Lou. "If my father ever found out I had this…"

"Rest easy. He won't hear it from me."

"Come back after dark. I should have the stuff by then."

Lou came down the driveway and saw Chris leaning against the front grill of his car. As he approached, she moved to the door and blocked his way. "I'm sorry. You were right and I was wrong."

"I already knew that."

"This isn't working."

"What isn't?"

"Us."

"There is no 'us'."

"Look, you're the only one around who's got half a chance of nailing Shawn's killers and I want to be in on it. I have to be."

Lou shook his head. He reached around her for the door handle, but she moved her hip and blocked his way again. Lou looked at her, his expression asking how long this was going to go on. She ignored what she read in his face and kept to her own agenda. "Why'd you leave Florida anyway?"

Resigned, Lou stepped back. "To find my son's killer. Clear his name."

"Bullshit. That sounds good, but it's pure pie-in-the-sky bullshit."

"Okay. You think you're so smart. You tell me why I'm here."

She nodded. Okay, she would. "How come you retired, Lou? You're not that old."

"I'm old enough."

"Bullshit! How come?"

"I had thirty-one years on the job, isn't that enough?"

"You tell me."

"It was enough. Besides, Tollin had been forced to retire the year before and I never felt comfortable with anyone else."

"That's pretty damn lame. What's the rest?"

Lou sighed. He'd asked for this. He should've kept his damn mouth shut.

"And?" she prompted.

"And because the Department changed. And because Darleen left me. And because I had no relationship with my son. Because of a lot of things."

"So you gave up."

Damn! Where the hell does she get off saying something like that? "Think whatever you want. I did what I did and that's that."

"And now you regret it. That's why you came back. You're not here for Shawn. You're here for you. So you can be a cop again. Wear a gun on your hip again. To get into the game again. To be a player. Shawn's death just gave you the excuse to do it."

Lou's expression never changed, but inside his gut he felt an enormous desire to strike out at her. If she'd been a man he'd have decked her right then and there. But she wasn't and so he couldn't. He forced his tightly balled fists to uncoil, his body to relax. When he finally did speak it was almost a whisper. "I loved him."

"You certainly had a funny way of showing it," Chris said derisively.

Lou's anger rose again. And this time he didn't even try to control it. "Look, I loved Shawn, but the bottomline is that my son was an asshole! He just couldn't stand to be loved. You know what it's like to love someone who can't return it or even accept it? It hurts. A lot. And you should know that because you loved him, too!"

Chris felt his words hit home. He was right. It had hurt when she'd finally realized that Shawn was incapable of allowing someone to love him. It had hurt a lot. She wanted to tell Lou that but before she had a chance to, he pushed her aside, pulled the car door open, got in and slammed the door shut. She watched, unable to move, as he started the car, angrily threw it into gear and roared off.

Chris walked into the all-night hamburger joint and spotted Lou at a table nursing a cup of coffee.She walked over to the counter, ordered a coke and fries and while she waited for it to come, watched Lou through the mirror behind the counter. He seemed to be lost in some world of his own making, not here at all. Probably in the past, she thought. Her order came and she picked up the fries and the coke, walked over to Lou's table and slid into the seat across from him. He looked around, helplessly. He just couldn't seem to get away from this girl.

"You're a prick, you know that?" Chris told him as she stuffed a French fry into her mouth.

"Must you?"

"Must I what?"

Lou waved it away. If she didn't know how she talked, he decided it wasn't his job to tell her. Instead, he reached over and took one of her fries.

"Help yourself," Chris said.

Lou poured some salt on the fry and popped it into his mouth.

"That's not good for you. The salt."

Lou reached down and took another fry, poured some salt on it and took a bite. "Give it a rest, huh? I like salt."

Chris looked at him for a moment, then nodded. Her face softened. "I'm sorry for what I said back there."

Lou looked into her eyes then shook his head. "No, you're not. Why back off now?" He grabbed another of her fries with one hand and the salt shaker with the other.

"Can't anybody ever say anything nice to you?" Chris asked in frustration.

"Not if they don't mean it."

"What makes you so sure you know what the fuck I mean?"

Lou couldn't hold it in anymore. "Must you use that kind of language?"

"Must you treat me like every woman you ever met?"

"'Cause you're different, right?"

"You bet your ass I am and if you don't know that by now you're a bigger asshole than your son was."

Furious, she got up from the table, shoved the rest of her French fries in front of him. Then she picked up the salt shaker and slammed it down next to them. "Here. Kill yourself." She turned and stalked off.

Lou watched her go then turned his attention to what she'd left behind. He picked up the salt shaker, salted the fries and grabbed one. He looked at it, then dropped it and pushed the whole plate away in disgust.

Chris was sitting in her car at the far side of the parking lot as Lou came out. He could just see her head resting on the steering wheel. He walked over, opened the driver's door and looked in. Chris turned, saw it was Lou and laid her head back on the wheel.

"Get lost," she said.

"Where'd you get the car?"

"Get lost," she repeated.

"You can't have two cars on what the Department pays you."

Chris gestured at the dash. There was a rental agreement on it.

Lou held out his hand. "Gimme the keys."

Chris shook her head. "I'm perfectly capable of driving myself."

"I didn't say you weren't. Gimme the keys."

"It's my car. I drive it." Chris grabbed the door and pulled it shut.

Lou took a deep breath, trying hard to control his temper. Finally, he walked around the car to the passenger's side, opened the door and got in.

"Remember that garage you followed me to this afternoon," he asked.

"Uh huh."

"We're going there."

Lou stared out the front window studiously avoiding her look. He waited patiently for her next move, really not sure exactly what it would be. This woman was an enigma to him and that bothered him. Too much, he was forced to admit.

Chris made up her mind. She had nothing to lose by going along with Lou as much as he'd let her. She started the car, put it in gear, but kept her foot on the brake. She took a deep breath of resignation and slammed the gear shift back into Park and turned off the ignition. She stared out the front windshield into the night.

Lou waited her out, giving her the time to cope with whatever it was that was haunting her.

"It was one of the ways I used to get the guys to accept me," she finally said.

"What?" Lou asked, confused.

"The language. It was one of the ways I used to get the guys to accept me."

Lou thought about this for a moment, then nodded in understanding. It certainly was a reason. "Was it worth it?" he found himself asking, his curiosity getting the best of him.

She turned to face him. "Look, I got accepted. They…"

Lou held up his hand to stop her. Chris stopped and waited.

"That's not what I asked."

Chris knew that, but his question hit a nerve and she resented that he was able to do that. "Sure it was worth it," she finally said without much conviction.

"That's too bad."

"What's that supposed to mean?"

"It means that nobody's gonna ever accuse you of being feminine."

Chris turned away. Lou really knew how to nail her where it hurt the most. He was forcing her to face something she had chosen long ago not to. She felt the pain quickly turn to defensive anger. "Who the hell appointed you the know-all of who or what I am? You don't know shit about me!"

"I know you use the foulest language you can. And whatever the reason it's not something I think is terribly ladylike."

"Who cares what you think?"

"Nobody but me. Which is the way I like it. Drive."

Chapter Ten

Chris swung into the curb and shut off the engine. Lou turned to face her. "Follow me on this. My son gets himself killed for no reason we know of. Then drugs are found in his home. Days after his house was first searched and they'd found nothing. Now what does that tell you?"

"That the drugs were planted. But we knew that."

"But we didn't know why?"

"And now you do? Tell me."

"A cop gets himself killed and the whole Department doesn't sleep until his murderer is caught. That's just the way of things. We take care of our own. Now what's the easiest way to turn off that kind of heat?" He continued on without waiting for her answer. "You make him out to be a dirty cop. A cop who was into drugs. Dealing. Then the Department is more apt to let the whole thing slide. But look at what happens next? Your car gets blown up. A car that was supposed to have both you and me inside it. Which it would have if we'd gotten to it five minutes earlier. Someone wants us dead. And the only connection between us is we're both trying to find Shawn's killer. Someone wants Shawn's murder to remain unsolved real bad."

"So we have to find that 'someone'."

"I think you should let me take it from here on out."

Chris couldn't believe her ears. One moment he's sharing his theories as if she was his partner and the next he's tossing her aside like so much trash. "Give me one good reason and I'm gone."

"How about your life being on the line now? Look, they tried with the car bomb, but the next time it could be a long range rifle. This thing's turned more dangerous than I'd thought."

"It's just as dangerous for you."

"I've lived longer than you have. Besides, I don't have much of a life," he admitted. "Living on a boat in Florida isn't what it's really cracked up to be. What I thought it would be. I've got nothing to lose. You do."

"My life, my choice."

"And you called me stubborn?"

"Only because you are."

"It's too dangerous."

"Then I'll just have to be careful." Chris smiled. "Don't worry. I'll cover your ass if trouble does come." She got out of the car and waited for him to join her.

They walked up the driveway but as they approached the garage, Lou slowed down. He looked over at Chris and saw she was already pulling her weapon out. She had felt it, too. There was something in the air, unexplainable. Something criminal defense attorney's tore into in court. Why a cop decided something was amiss. There was no rational explanation for it. After years on the street a good cop just knew.

Lou drew his own gun and nodded to Chris. They separated and each moved silently to the side of driveway closest to them. Chris next to the house, Lou alongside the wall that divided J.J.'s house from the one next door.

They moved cautiously forward, seemingly aware of the other's movements without having to actually see them. It was as if they had worked together for years, had done the same thing numerous times before. But they hadn't. Yet somewhere in their subconscious they both realized they were acting as if they had. Later, they would think about their actions and wonder how it happened, but right now, all their concentration was fixed on what they were doing.

They reached the garage door. It was partially closed. Chris stepped quickly across the doorway, flattened herself against the wall. Lou looked at Chris. An unspoken question. She nodded and brought her weapon up next to the door frame. She was ready.

Lou, his body flat against the wall on his side of the door, pushed the door open with his foot. The door swung slowly open until it banged against the inside wall.

They waited for some response from inside. None came. Lou looked over at Chris and arched his eyebrows. Chris gestured up with her gun.

Lou nodded and pointed low with his. He held up three fingers, then made a fist. Out of the fist, Lou uncurled one finger. Then two. Then a third. They moved. Instantly. Together.

Lou threw himself through the doorway. To the left. Onto the floor. His gun arm outstretched. Chris went in on the right. Stopped behind a file cabinet. Gun arm in front of her. Covering the room.

The garage seemed deserted. No movement. No sound. Finally, Lou looked over at Chris and gestured with his head. She followed his gesture and saw the light switch on the wall behind her. She reached out, flipped it up and the single fluorescent over the workbench flickered on.

Lou swept the room with his eyes, his weapon following his look. Nothing. He got to his feet and slowly walked down the aisle. Chris followed, covering him.

Lou went past the workbench to the rear of the garage. Finding nothing of interest, he looked back at Chris. She'd stopped at the workbench and was now staring at a pile of boxes behind it, her gun lowered at her side. He walked over to her and followed her gaze.

J.J. was sprawled amidst the boxes. Arms akimbo. One leg twisted under him. Broken. His face brutally beaten.

Lou pushed past Chris, tossed the boxes out of the way and knelt down beside J.J. He pressed his finger against the carotid artery in J.J.'s neck but could not feel any blood pumping through it and rocked back on his heels.

Chris placed a hand on his shoulder. He ignored it, leaned forward and gently moved the kid's head. There was a bullet hole behind his ear. A trickle of blood had come from the wound and was already starting to congeal. Lou got to his feet and walked slowly away. Chris watched him go, took another look at J.J. before she turned and followed Lou outside. He was already halfway down the driveway and Chris had to hurry to catch up to him.

"Wait up," she yelled.

Either Lou didn't hear her or he chose to ignore her. She didn't know which. He just kept walking. When he reached the sidewalk, he turned down the block and continued on.

"Hey," Chris said. "The car's over here."

Lou trudged on. She watched him go, blending into the night.

Lou sat in a small booth across from the bar and downed a straight scotch. He washed it away with a long pull from his bottle of beer. The sickening pain he felt was because of J.J.'s death. He knew that. It wasn't as bad as when he'd found out about Shawn's, but it was close.

The last thing he'd wanted to happen was for J.J. to be killed. He liked the kid just as he'd liked his father. They were both criminals, sure, but they'd been square with him, been honest with him, and that meant something in a world where a person's word was fast becoming something meant at the moment and forgotten the next. And as much as the old professionals would never break their word to him, he would never break his word to them. Even one that was unspoken. It was how he lived his life and he prided himself on that. Which was one of the reasons that he really didn't have many friends, either on the force or off. Friends that he could trust to tell him the truth. To give their word and mean it.

And now a kid was dead because his father had trusted Lou and his son had given his word to do something. Even after he'd taken a terrible beating for it. Even when he was scared to death that someone was out there, looking to do exactly what happened. J.J.'d given his word and that was that. But Lou had really demanded it of him and that stuck in his craw. He'd put J.J. in the line of fire and that was something he'd never intended to do and as a consequence there were now two fathers without their sons.

Lou scooped up the shot glass, downed it, polished off his beer and got to his feet. He staggered out of the bar.

Tollin answered the persistent knocking on his door and found Lou leaning against the doorjamb. He stood back and watched Lou stumble through the door, find his way to the couch and fall into it.

Tollin closed the door, walked slowly over to his chair and sat down. He could smell the liquor coming off of his former partner from across the room. "You got a reason to be piss-ass drunk or is it something that retirement does to you?"

"I killed a kid tonight, Frank. I didn't actually pull the trigger but I sure as shit killed him."

"Oh, boy," Tollin said as he realized what he was in for.

"You said it. Oh, boy."

"Okay, Lou. Give it to me straight."

"I needed some help with the Swiss bank account. I asked the best computer wizard I knew to find out for me."

"I thought John J. was still in the pen."

"He was. Is. I asked his son."

Tollin nodded as he realized where this was going.

"And now his son is dead. Because he helped me, Frank. Because of me."

Tollin got off his chair and went into the kitchen. He needed some time to think, to figure out a way to deal with Lou. He opened the refrigerator and took out a can of beer. He pulled the top off and returned to his seat.

"Got one for me?" Lou asked him.

"You've had more than enough."

"You're wrong. I haven't had near enough."

Lou struggled to his feet but Tollin got up and pushed him back onto the couch. "I'm telling you you've had enough and in my house I decide what's enough."

"You always were a shit, you know that?"

Tollin returned to his chair and settled into it. "So John J.'s kid got killed because he was helping you. Well, that should tell you that you're up against more than you thought."

"But why?"

"Beats me, Lou."

Lou sat there and stared at Tollin. "Follow me on this. My son gets killed. They find he had millions in a Swiss bank account. I get someone to try and trace where the money came from and he gets killed.”

“So?”

“So the money’s the key. Don’t you see that? I know it. You know it. And the guys that planted it on him know it otherwise they wouldn’t have killed the kid.”

“Sounds about right.”

“You know damn well that it’s right.”

“So?”

“So I don’t know where to go now?”

“I do.”

Lou looked up, relieved. Tollin had always been able to come up with another angle whenever they’d hit a brick wall in an investigation.

“Go back to Florida,” Tollin told him. “Let it go. Get on with your life. Nothing you can do now is going to bring Shawn back and if you keep going on like this you’re liable to get some other innocent person killed. Or yourself.”

Lou was surprised. He hadn’t expected Tollin to tell Lou to give up. Lou shook his head. “I can’t do that. Not now,” he said, and got to his feet.

“Sure, you can. Lou, I’m your friend. I hate seeing you like this. You’ll destroy yourself over this and probably never even find Shawn’s killer.”

“You don’t get it, do you?” Lou asked in measured tones. “I’ve got nothing to go back to. There’s nothing in Florida for me. I’m a cop. That’s who I am. That’s what I’ll die being.”

Tollin snorted. “The great Lou Parker’s last case. You’ll never solve this one. It’s too big.”

Lou headed for the door. “Maybe. Then again you never know.”

“Where’re you going now?”

"The motel. I need some sleep. I can't take this drinking shit like I used to."

Chris was sitting on her apartment floor dressed in sweats and doing her morning sit-ups when the doorbell rang. She decided to ignore it but its insistent ringing forced her to get to her feet and answer it. She crossed the living room to the door and pressed the intercom button, holding it in as she spoke into the speaker grill. "Who it is?"

"It's me. Buzz the door."

"Lou?" Chris asked, unable to mask her surprise.

"Come on. Hit the buzzer."

Chris pressed the buzzer, held it for a moment, then released it. She turned to look around the room. It looked okay. Then she looked down at herself. She didn't. But there was no time to do anything about it now.

There was a knock on the door. She opened it and stepped back, wide-eyed. Lou stood there. He'd shaved and showered. His suit was pressed. Kinda. Tie straight. He looked good.

"You own a dress?" he asked as he brushed past her.

Lou'd insisted they take a cab out to the country club to pick up his car which he was now driving way over the posted speed limit. Chris glanced over at him for what she was sure was the hundredth time since they'd left her apartment but his eyes were fixed rigidly on the road as if telling her he didn't want to talk. In fact, he'd said nothing since arriving at her house that morning, since asking her the one question at her door. She'd gone in to shower and change and when she'd come out, he was still standing by the door where she'd left him. She'd asked him where they were going, but he'd refused to respond. She decided to try again. "What's with you?"

Lou frowned, annoyed at her attempt at conversation. "Let's just say I'm moody and leave it at that."

Chris turned away and looked out the window. It was his hand to play and she knew she'd just have to wait until he exposed it to her.

Lou pulled off the highway and onto a paved road leading off onto the flats. In the distance, Chris could see a high chain link fence. It was topped with coiled razor wire. There was another fence inside that one. Brick towers stood at the corners and there was a walkway bridging the towers. It was the State Prison Facility.

Chris had never been there before. She'd had to no reason to, but she knew what it was. A medium security prison, it had been built in the thirties and hadn't been renovated since. It was not a pleasant place to be in was what she'd heard.

She looked over at Lou again. His expression had changed. It now seemed to combine a sadness and an inevitability that she hated to see in anyone.

Chris followed Lou through the steel doors. She checked her weapon at the counter-Lou had left his in the car because he had no license to carry-and they both signed the requisite forms. Then they trailed behind a guard to a visitor's room. The guard unlocked the door for them, ushered them in and left, closing the door behind them.

The room had a table and four chairs and nothing else. The door had a window in it. Like the window in the wall it contained wire mesh. Lou and Chris waited in silence until the door opened and the guard ushered in a prisoner. The guard left, locking the door behind him.

John J. was dressed in prison blues. He was just a shade over sixty and there was not an ounce of fat on his body. He had been surprised when they'd told him he had visitors. When they had told him it was Lou Parker, he figured his son had decided not to help him and Lou was there to try and get John J. to persuade his son to change his mind.

John J. waited until he heard the guard pull his key from the door before looking at Lou and breaking into a wide grin. He held out his hand and crossed the room to take Lou's and shake it. "Jesus, Lou," he said. "It's good to see you."

Lou took the offered hand and forced a smile in return. John J. stepped back and looked at Lou from head to toe. He noticed Lou's attempt to look good and coupled with the expression on his face, John J. thought he may have been wrong about the reason for Lou's visit. Something was up. He glanced over at Chris.

Lou followed John J.'s look and explained. "Chris Preston. There's a badge that goes with her."

John J. reached out and shook Chris's hand. He then turned it over. He stroked it gently with his other hand, then looked down and examined it. "I'd almost forgotten what a woman's hand feels like." Then he looked into her face and grinned. "Well, almost."

Chris smiled. John J. reluctantly released her hand and turned back to Lou. "Okay. This isn't a social visit. Get to it."

"It's about J.J." Lou said in a neutral tone.

"He called the other day. Told me you wanted his help."

"He gave it," Lou said.

John J. pulled out one of the chairs. He slid into it and looked up at Lou. "I was hoping he would. He's a good kid."

John J. looked from one to the other. He saw their expressions and braced himself. "Let's have it, Lou."

Lou took a deep breath, composing himself. Then he moved closer to John J.

"J.J. was murdered early this morning," he said quietly.

John J. stared at Lou for a moment, then tore his eyes away and looked over at Chris. She nodded, confirming what Lou had just told him. He got to his feet and moved around the table to the window. He stared out.

"I'm sorry," Lou said.

"How?" John J. asked without turning.

Lou took a single breath and plunged ahead thinking it was better to get it over with as quickly as possible. "Single shot. To the back of the head. It was over in an instant."

John J. didn't turn back from the window but kept his back to them. "Think they'll let me out for the funeral?" he finally asked.

"I'll work on it," Chris promised him.

"There's something else you should know," Lou said. "I think…" He stopped, then started again. "I'm sure it happened because of me."

John J. turned and looked at Lou. There were tears in both their eyes. John J. nodded. He'd figured that out by himself. He walked over to Lou and stared into his face. He looked as if was going to tear Lou's head off. Lou didn't move. He'd already decided to take whatever John J. decided to give him. There was a horrible anger in John J.'s eyes and when he spoke it was with a deadly cold anger.

"You get the son-of-bitch that did it, Lou."

Lou nodded.

Satisfied, John J. turned away and moved to the door. He kicked at it, then looked back. "I'm counting on you," he told Lou. Then he glanced over at Chris. "You, too."

The door opened and the guard stood there. Without a glance back, John J. turned and left.

Chris wasn't enjoying the trip back anymore than she enjoyed the trip up. Lou drove with his eyes glued to the road and wasn't speaking again. She stared at his profile and tried to figure him out. What he'd done back there was nice. Decent. Thoughtful. He hadn't had to go up there personally to tell John J. that his son was dead. The prison authorities would have done that.

Then why, she asked herself. Sure, it was partially guilt. But Lou hadn't pulled the trigger that killed J.J. and she knew that he'd been a police officer for too long to start blaming himself for things he couldn't control. If that were true than Lou was carrying a lot more baggage than she'd ever thought.

Or was it more than that? Was he just doing what he thought was right? She knew that he was very big on doing things the right way and this was the right thing to do. And it showed a lot more compassion than she'd given him credit for.

So which was it? Where had all this decency come from? Could she have misread him? Was there more to this man than she had thought?

Lou came out of his reverie and felt her watching him. He looked over at her. "What?" he asked.

Chris shook her head and turned away. She was confused. She laid her head against the door window and closed her eyes. They drove on in silence.

Lou had dropped Chris off at her apartment and driven away without another word. Now he and Tollin were raiding the grocery store cooler. Their cart was half-filled with six-packs of beer. "I'm glad to see you've given up the hard stuff," Tollin said.

"Last night was just that. Last night. I was feeling sorry for myself."

"Then you know the truth of it?"

"Yep."

"That it wasn't your fault."

Lou shook his head. "Yeah, it was. He thought somebody was watching him and I blew it off."

"Instead of what? Moving in and guarding him day and night."

"I should of done something."

"You're breaking my heart," Tollin said, and turned away. Lou grabbed his arm and pulled him back around. "I'm gonna get 'em, Frank. I don't care what it takes. Their ass is mine."

Tollin shook his head, disgusted.

Chris walked into the records room at Borough Command looking for Anne. She found her in the last aisle. "There you are," Chris said as she walked over to her.

"I didn't know you were looking for me. There's a bell on my desk, you know."

"I could never use one of those things to get somebody. It seems demeaning."

Anne grinned. "It's better than waiting for me to get back up there. And it allows me to get away from the desk and get my filing done. But I appreciate the thought."

"I can't find old Amos anywhere," Chris said. "You seen him?"

"He's on vacation. And the way I heard it he had no choice in the matter."

"Damn!"

"I heard you aren't in the best of positions either."

"Morrison?"

"Who else?"

Chris waved it away. "He's just covering his ass if things don't go the way he's hoping they will."

"You ever really been able to tell which way he wants things to go?" Anne asked with a grin.

"Not really. But I don't seem to have a choice anymore."

"Look. I can give you Amos' home address and number, if that'll help."

"I appreciate it but I need more than that."

"Come on, Chris, give me a break."

Chris looked around. "I did a month down here about five years back. If I remember correctly all reports from everyone, everywhere, eventually end up here. Right?"

"Except the ones I need," Anne said with a smile.

"There one I need. On Shawn's murder."

Anne shook her head. "His case file is upstairs with the brass and there's nothing I can do about that."

"I know. But that's the entire case file. What about the individual reports? Don't they come in here?"

"Sure, they do. Eventually they do. First Homicide gets their copy, then us."

"Just in case someone's got to protect their ass."

"You got it," Anne agreed and then saw the look on Chris's face and grimaced.

"Aren't you in enough trouble as it is? What gives?"

"Morrison's not going to do anything to me. He likes me too much."

Anne arched her eyebrows.

Chris grinned. "Not like that. He's too hooked on that wife of his to even think of me that way. I'm his chance of showing the brass just how good his command is. Besides, he loves playing both ends against the middle. The only way I can get in trouble is if I fail and I'm not going to."

"Morrison might not be able to protect you even then, is the way I hear it. Who've you got on your tail?"

"Everyone" Chris said.

"Not good."

"Fuck 'em all. Nobody gives a damn about Shawn's death or the bogus drug case against him."

"You're taking a big gamble. And if Morrison should ever decide to cut his loses…" Anne let the words trail off.

"He won't," Chris said. "If it works out he'll get the credit. If it doesn't then he blames it on me. Either way he'll come out a winner."

"Don't you just love the way things always work out for some people," Anne said sarcastically.

"He's got to live with himself, not me."

"Word is that you're working with Shawn's father. That must be a trip an' a half."

"It has its moments," Chris admitted.

"He's got quite a rep as a hardcase."

"Don't believe everything you hear." Chris said, and instantly regretted it.

Anne looked at Chris shrewdly. "This isn't just about Shawn, is it?"

Chris shrugged. She really wasn't sure anymore.

Anne shook her head, annoyed at herself for what she was about to do.

Dee Dee sat on her usual stool at the bar nursing a beer. Lou came up next to her. "You got it?" he asked.

Dee Dee handed him a piece of paper. "She's expecting you."

Lou slipped the paper into his pocket and headed for the door.

"Nice, Lou. I guess I shouldn't expect a good-bye when you never even said hello," she shouted after him.

He stopped, turned back and grinned. "Sorry. I don't seem to be thinking right nowadays."

"Is it the girl?"

"What girl?"

Dee Dee laughed triumphantly. "I knew it. Good for you, Lou."

Lou forced a laugh. "It's not what you think."

"Right," Dee Dee said, her tone of voice telling him that she didn't believe him.

"Jesus. First her. Now you. What the hell is it with you women? Everybody's a damn shrink. Think they know just who the hell I am. How I feel. Which is funny 'cause I'm not even sure myself."

"I know," Dee Dee agreed. "And it's about time you found out."

Behind them, the door opened. Sunlight spilled in and framed Chris standing there. Lou walked past her out the door. Chris followed him. Outside, he turned to face her. "Where're you parked?"

"Around the corner."

"At the garage last night. You weren't half bad," he said, and walked away.

Shocked at getting a compliment from him, Chris stood motionless and watched him go as if nothing out of the ordinary had been said. He'd already turned the corner before she pulled herself together and hurried after him.

Chapter Eleven

Chris pulled into the red zone at the curb in front of the apartment building in Forest Hills, Queens and followed Lou inside. They rode the elevator up to the twelfth floor, found the apartment and Lou rang the bell.

The door was opened by a woman who was not more than twenty-five and whose figure was sensually outlined by the expensive silk robe she had on.

"Lou Parker?" she asked pleasantly.

Lou nodded and Fawn led them across an elegantly living room. Glass and wood stood out against a background of muted beige. There was just enough furniture for entertaining, but not enough to diminish the feeling of open space.

"I didn't really expect you this quickly. It's okay, but you'll have to bear with me. I've got a date and I can't be late," she said, and continued on into the bedroom.

Lou and Chris exchanged a look. Follow her into the bedroom or not? Fawn solved their dilemma for them. "You coming or what?"

They walked into the bedroom that was as tastefully decorated as the living room. Fawn sat down at the make-up table and shrugged the bathrobe off her shoulders. She was now naked from the waist up.

Chris looked over at Lou and saw that he was studiously trying to keep his eyes from straying to Fawn's well-formed breasts. Chris thought she even saw a little embarrassment in his face.

Fawn looked over at them through the mirror. "Something the matter?"

"My partner's led a sheltered life," Chris answered. She was thoroughly enjoying Lou's discomfort.

Fawn realized that Lou was embarrassed by her near nudity. "I'm sorry, but if you want to talk now, then this is the only way."

"That's okay. I'll suffer through it," Lou said dryly.

"Thanks a lot," Fawn said, feigning hurt.

"I didn't mean that the way it sounded. Honest," Lou said, and looked at Chris for some kind of help.

Fawn looked at Chris. "Is he for real?"

"He's still living in another age. Around the turn of the century is my guess. But it could be even earlier."

"Okay. If you guys are through I'd like to get to it," Lou said.

Fawn went back to putting on her make-up. "I hate these last minute things. If he wasn't flying out first thing in the morning I wouldn't've accepted." She looked at her face in the mirror and frowned at what she saw. She picked up a small brush and applied some more blue eye shadow.

Chris glanced at Lou. She couldn't decide which interested him more. Fawn's beauty, her lack of inhibition or her bare breasts. Chris decided it was probably all three and realized she'd better take the initiative or they'd never learn anything. "There's no question it was Shawn you saw?"

"It was him," Fawn said. "Trust me on this one." She laughed as she thought back. "I was fifteen when Shawn first busted me. Got ten bucks a throw back then. Now I'm ten years older and get a minimum of a thou." She looked over at them in the mirror. "I guess experience is worth something these days. Anyway, you don't forget the first time you got laid or the first cop to bust you."

"But you didn't know the woman he was with, right?" Lou finally asked, tearing his eyes away from her bare breasts.

Fawn finished the eye shadow, got up and tossed her robe on the bed. Now she was wearing only a pair of panties. "She wasn't a working girl if that's what you're thinking," she told him as she turned to the closet and opened it. She rummaged through her clothes, finally pulling out a dress and holding it against her body. She looked over at Chris. "Too flashy?"

Chris winced, but quickly regained her composure. Flashy was an understatement. "It's certainly flattering," she said, trying to be diplomatic. But she wasn't fast enough. Fawn had seen her first reaction and put the dress back. She pulled out a black sheath and held it up.

"Better?"

Chris nodded. Fawn slipped the dress over her head and then backed up to Lou.

Lou glanced at Chris who was making no attempt to hide a grin. He grinned back, then reached for the clasp on the zipper and zipped it up.

"Thanks," Fawn said crossing the room where she grabbed her purse and emptied it on the bed. She pawed through the items she'd dumped out, picked some and transferred them to a smaller one.

"Anything else you can tell us about her?" Chris asked. "Anything at all would be a help."

"She's married. Either of you got an extra…never mind…I know where I put some." She moved over to the nightstand

and opened the drawer. She rummaged around in it. "How do you know?" Lou asked.

"She was wearing a wedding ring. How do you think? Besides she had that look," Fawn said as she found three colorfully packaged condoms.

"What look is that," Chris asked.

Fawn slipped all three into her purse before looking over at Chris. "You know. Excited. Scared. She's got something new. Different. And it's a secret. Which is a turn on. She had that look."

Fawn looked at herself in the mirror, straightened her dress and then turned to them. "I don't mean to rush you but...," she said, and pointedly checked her watch.

"Thanks," Lou said.

"And the dress is perfect," Chris told her.

Fawn wondered if the compliment was condescending. She decided it wasn't and smiled appreciatively. "I'll ride down in the elevator with you."

Chris drove away from the apartment. Lou sat slouched against the door.

"You know the most interesting people," Chris said.

"It takes all kinds."

"Think you could pick her out of a line-up?" Chris asked innocently.

"Of course. What kind of a question is that?"

"Fully dressed?"

Lou frowned. He hadn't seen that one coming. Well, he'd deserved it. He'd acted like a school kid seeing his first naked woman. Worse. He'd made an ass of himself in front of Chris and she'd probably never let him forget it. Lou braced himself for her next crack.

"Well, at least we know why he never showed her to anybody," Chris said instead.

"Because she was married," Lou agreed.

"I guess that narrows it down. But not by much."

"I can't accept him seeing a married woman."

"Why not? It happens all the time."

"Doesn't make it right."

"You going to tell me in all your years you never cheated on your wife or any girl you were seeing?"

"Nope. Never did. But they did. Believe me."

"You don't think much of women, do you?"

"I did once. Thought the sun rose and set on them. Then I got older. Saw more. Experienced more. Saw them cheat. Lie. Manipulate. They're all the same."

"That's bullshit and you know it."

"No. I don't know that. In fact, I know it to be the truth."

Chris was astounded and thought he was putting her on. "I don't believe you believe that."

"Believe it! Women have their own agenda and they'll say and do anything to get what they want. You just can't trust any of them."

Chris now realized that Lou did mean every word of what he had said. He actually believed it and was more than she could take. She jammed on the brakes and the car skidded to a stop.

Lou's hand shot out against the dash in an effort to prevent himself from being thrown through the windshield. He regained his balance and looked at Chris as if she was crazy.

Chris reached across him and opened the door. "Get the fuck out," she said coldly.

"You're kidding?"

"Out!"

Lou saw the look on her face and realized that she was serious. Her eyes blazed with an anger he hadn't seen before and that anger was directed at him.

"Out, you fucking asshole!" Chris ordered through clenched teeth.

Lou got out of the car and before he had a chance to slam the door, Chris floored it and peeled away. He watched her drive off not believing she'd leave him here. But as the car sped into the distance he changed his belief. She wasn't coming back. Now what the hell did he say to cause that reaction, he wondered.

Tollin had decided to say nothing and just sat in his chair watching Lou pace back and forth in front of him. He had angrily burst into Tollin's apartment thirty minutes earlier fuming and none of the anger had started to dissipate yet.

"I mean, can you believe her? She tosses me from the car and leaves. In the middle of nowhere. It took me an hour and a half to walk here," Lou ranted on angrily.

"Cabs stop running?" Tollin asked dryly.

Lou stopped his pacing and looked over at Tollin. "Couldn't find one," he said. Then he frowned. "What difference does it make? The thing is she tossed me. Didn't give a damn about how I'd get back. What happened to me."

"Is she supposed to?"

Lou cocked his head at his former partner. "Whose side you on anyway?"

"Oh, I see. We're in a contest now."

"Shit. Where the hell're you coming from?"

"Tell me," Tollin asked as he leaned forward to grab his can of beer from the coffee table. "All bullshit aside. What do you really feel about her?"

"That's not the point!"

"Answer the question, Lou. It's not that difficult."

"I hate her fuckin' guts."

"I know. She threw you out of the car in the middle of nowhere for no apparent reason and you had to walk here and so you hate her. Aside from that, what do you think of her?"

"I just told you. I hate her."

"We know, Lou, but that wasn't the question."

"The fuck it wasn't!" Lou shouted. "I heard what you asked and I answered it."

Tollin grinned, sat back and took a drink of beer. Lou slid onto the couch. "Okay. What is it you want?"

"Since you won't deal with how you feel about her then tell me about her as a cop. She any good?"

Lou shrugged, then under Tollin's glare forced his anger aside and thought back over the last few days. "She's a good cop. Could be a first-rate detective."

"Very good, Lou. Now how about as a person. How do feel about her as a person?"

"You deaf or what? I just told you. She's a good cop."

"That's not what I asked and you know it."

Reluctantly, Lou nodded. He knew exactly what Tollin was talking about, but it was not something he wanted to think about. He also knew that Tollin wasn't about to let it go. His former partner was wearing his bulldog interrogation look and it was focused on him. He tried another tack, anything to get him off his back. "Come on, Frank. She's young enough to be my daughter. Hell, she's younger than Shawn even."

Tollin shook his head. "Try again."

"I just told you how I feel. What more do you want?"

Tollin grinned.

"That's all I'm going to say on the subject," Lou said. "Period. End of discussion."

"Well, now that I know the answer, when are you going to get it?" Tollin asked.

"You're a prick, you know that?"

Tollin shook his head and decided to switch to another tact. He was enjoying himself. "How does she feel about you?"

Lou threw his hands in the air. "How the hell should I know what she feels? What am I? A mind reader?" He tossed his empty beer can in the general direction of the barrel and sat back. "Besides, she's not stupid. She knows the age difference."

"But does she care?" Tollin persisted.

"Christ, Frank, I thought you'd understand. I mean, can you imagine me walking into a restaurant with her? What people would say?"

"Right. Like you were always the one to give a shit about what other people said."

Lou took a deep breath and looked at Tollin. "You're getting to be one large pain in the ass. You know that?"

"Seems I've heard you say that to me once or twice before."

"Yeah. And I was right then and I'm right now."

Lou stretched out on his motel bed and stared at the ceiling. He had left Tollin's and come back here intending to think the case through but found his thoughts drifting to Chris, instead. He had admitted to Tollin she was a good cop with good instincts. He had also told him that she was stubborn, tenacious, had her own set of rules, wasn't afraid to bend the Department's rules and had no love for bureaucracy. Tollin had listened and then said nothing. Not a word. He'd just sat there with a know-it-all look on his face. That's when it hit him. He'd heard Darleen say the same things about him that he was saying about Chris.

Forget her, Lou told himself. Get back to the case. He forced Chris from his thoughts by concentrating on facts of the case. Nothing seemed to make any sense. Or bring him closer to his son's murderer.

From time to time he looked over at the phone on the nightstand as if willing it to ring. But who was going to call him, he wondered. Chris? Fuck! Get her out of your mind, he told himself. She's too young for you. Way too young. Besides, she wants nothing to do with you. The idea that he should call her flitted through his mind. Explain to her what he'd meant. But he'd meant what he'd said. Or did he?

Lou sat up on the bed. This was getting him nowhere. He grabbed the phone, dialed a single digit and waited. "Yeah…is the coffee shop still open?…thanks." He hung up and looked back at the phone wondering if Chris would be home if he called her. Maybe she was exercising like the day he'd gone over to her place. He had to admit she looked good in her workout clothes. He shook his head, got off the bed, grabbed his jacket, slipped it on and walked to the door. He reached for the door knob but before he could touch it, the door burst open and he was slammed back against the wall.

Riley's two men were on him before he could recover. They pulled him away from the wall and then slammed him back into it. They grabbed both his arms and when he tried to pull away, the bigger of the two buried his knee in Lou's stomach. The wind went out of him and he doubled over gasping for breath. The man then grabbed Lou's hair and slammed his head back against the wall. Lou felt his head spin and waited for it to clear while the two men held him rigidly against the wall.

Riley sauntered through the door, closed it behind him and grinned with satisfaction. "It's payback time, Parker."

Lou watched helplessly as Riley took off his jacket and folded it neatly before laying it down on the bed. It was his own fault, Lou thought. His son had been murdered. J.J. had been beaten up and killed. The car had been bombed. And he'd been moving as if he wasn't in a danger zone. Like a fucking amateur.

Riley walked up to Lou and looked him in the eye. "You have any idea how much pleasure this is bringing me?"

Lou smiled at Riley. "Like I give a shit."

Riley's fist hit him high on the cheek with the force of a cannon ball.

Lou's head snapped back, hit the wall and snapped forward again, leaving him groggy. Lou wasn't sure if it had been the fist that had made his head spin or the blow to the wall. It really didn't matter because the result was the same.

Riley patiently waited until Lou completely regained his senses. Then he stepped in again. Lou knew he was about to get the shit kicked out of him and there was nothing he could about it.

Chris was doing sit-ups, trying to work off her anger while at the same time trying to decide what her next move was going to be. Could she continue to work with a man who so hated her sex? Did she even want to? Fuck no, she decided. Let someone else deal with his shit. She would find Shawn's killer without him.

The buzzer sounded and Chris frowned. She wasn't expecting anyone. She crossed the living room to the front door and pressed the intercom button.

"Who is it?"

"It's me," Lou said.

At the sound of Lou's voice, Chris's anger towards him returned full force. "Get lost!" she yelled into the intercom.

Chris released the button and turned away. She got one step back into the living room before the buzzer started again. This time without letup. She decided to ignore it. If Lou wanted to apologize then he could just take his apology and shove it. She'd had enough. Though she had to admit she did want to hear him say the words.

She walked back to the door, pressed the door release and waited impatiently until she heard him knock. She decided not to open it. He could apologize through it. "What do you want?" she said through the door.

"Let me in," Lou asked. His voice was muffled by the door, but Chris could hear the slur in his speech.

"You're drunk."

Chris waited for a response from the other side of the door, but there was none. Then she heard him knock again. "I have nothing to say to you, Lou."

The knocking continued. Chris sighed and resigned herself to the inevitable. He wasn't going away. She decided that she had no choice but to let him make his apology face to face and then she would toss him out. She unlocked the door and pulled it open. Lou, who had been leaning against the door, pitched forward onto the floor, face down.

Chris looked at him at her feet in disgust. "That's all I need. A drunk on my hands." She kneeled down and rolled Lou over. She saw his face and recoiled in horror. His face was a mass of cuts and freshly clotted blood. Bruises were starting to discolor his skin everywhere. Swelling puffed up his skin. He was a mess.

Lou lay sleeping in Chris's bed. She had tried to get him to go to a hospital but he'd been adamant. No doctors! No hospitals! He had made her promise not to call an ambulance and then he'd passed out again. So she had dragged him into her bedroom and cleaned him up as best she could. His eyes had been swollen shut, his lips twice their normal size and his body a mass of yellow and purple bruises.

Chris sat in a chair next to the window, her knees drawn up to her chin, staring at Lou. Having him lay there, helpless while she gently administered to his battered body had brought back childhood memories.

She'd been awakened one morning by the screech of tires outside her parents' home, followed by a jarring thud. She had jumped out of bed and run to the window just in time to see a car speeding away and a dog laying motionless in the street.

Throwing on some clothes she'd run outside to the dog. He was a mixed-breed but had enough Terrier in him to pass for one. She saw that he was alive but just barely. She'd kneeled down next to him and when the dog had looked up at her she couldn't stop the tears from rolling down her face. The dog had needed help and seemed to be asking her to give it.

Chris remembered how she had gently picked the dog up and carried him inside. Her parents hadn't been too thrilled with Chris's determination to nurse the dog back to health. They'd told her that the animal was not going to make it but Chris refused to accept their evaluation. She'd bandaged the dog as best she could and then carried him the two miles to the nearest vet.

The veterinarian had examined the dog and told her that the dog was probably going to die. He offered to put him to sleep but Chris had refused. Instead, she had accepted some pain pills from the vet and took the dog back home. She had cared for him as best she could over the next few days but in the end wasn't able to save him. She had buried him in her back yard.

The police psychiatrist, when he'd heard the story, had told her that she'd never gotten over the incident. That she was attracted to her job because of it. And to men because of it. He'd told Chris that she was a care-giver. That she wanted to help people. To make up for what she couldn't do for the dog.

Chris thought that the shrink's evaluation of her was way off base. But then she started to realize that it might be true. Lost people had become a part of her life and, like the dog of her childhood, they always disappointed her by leaving in the end. She'd nurse them back to health, comfort their insecurities, build up their self-esteem, and then they'd leave. So she'd promised herself some years ago that she wouldn't get involved with emotional cripples anymore. And she'd done it. Until she'd met Shawn.

Shawn was the first man she'd gotten deeply involved with since she'd made that vow to herself. The first man who wasn't an emotional cripple. He was confident, had a strong self-image, no self-pity and was dynamite in bed.

Then he had started working on a case that he wouldn't talk to her about. Finally, when the pain of his shutting her out of a part of his life became too much to bear, she had broken off with him. It was one of the hardest things she'd ever done. As time went on, however, she came to realize that she'd been wrong in her original assessment of him. He was not as strong as she had believed. Over an occasional lunch, she saw that his strength came not from inside, but rather from his work. He lacked compassion about others and would do anything, sacrifice anything, for his work. And he had this enormous drive to be better than his father. When they'd been going together she had thought it was an admirable goal. Later, after their breakup, she decided it was really an obsession and it was slowly destroying him. Instead of being a better detective in his own right, Shawn had been trying to behave as he thought his father would have and that meant she'd done it again. She'd taken in another emotional cripple.

Now Shawn's father was laying here in her bed. She watched him sleep and suddenly realized why Shawn had wanted to emulate him. He was ten times the man Shawn ever was or could have ever hoped to be. He had the same qualities that had attracted her to Shawn. But with Shawn they hadn't been real. He was only trying to be like his father. Now she had met the real thing. And despite some of his attitudes, which she hated, she had to admit that he excited her as no man had ever done before.

Lou moaned and Chris went over to him. She wiped his forehead with a wet cloth and sat down on the bed next to him. She picked up his hand and held it tightly. Then slowly brought it up to her lips and kissed it as tears flowed freely down her cheeks.

Sunlight poured through the window and woke Chris up from a fitful sleep. Instantly, she glanced over at Lou and saw that he was still asleep. She got up from the chair and tiptoed out of the room and into the kitchen where she mechanically went through the motions of making coffee. She was dead tired and half asleep. She stood there and stared mindlessly at the coffee maker as she waited for it to finish brewing.

She heard a sound behind her and turned to see Lou shuffle slowly into the living room. He was wearing her pajama bottoms. Ugly black and blue bruises showed between the white strips where Chris had taped his body.

"Smells good," he said.

"You shouldn't be up," she admonished him.

He made his way to the table and sat down as gingerly as possible. He slid his hand over his face and felt his beard.

"How long was I out?"

"Two days."

Lou forced a smile through his pain. "I must look like hell."

Chris grinned. "You've looked worse,"

Lou looked up at her. "Yeah? When?"

"Two days ago," she said as she picked up the pot, grabbed two mugs and went over to the table. "I'm getting used to it though."

"Thanks a lot," he said dryly.

Chris laughed. At least he hadn't lost his sense of humor. Chris liked that in a man. She looked at him and decided that she liked it even more in the man sitting opposite her. She filled both mugs, shoved one across to Lou, picked up the other and walked out of the kitchen. "I'm going to get a shower. If you're lucky I'll leave you some hot water. And a used razor."

Lou watched her go, then turned and picked up the mug. He very gently brought it to his swollen mouth and tasted the coffee. It was good. Very good. Point for her side, he thought.

Chapter Twelve

Chris walked into the crowded 7th Avenue restaurant and looked around for Anne. She saw her at a table near the rear and made her way over to her. She hugged her friend before sliding into the seat across from her.

This was Chris's first time out of her house except for quick food runs in over two weeks. Lou's face was no longer the swollen balloon it was when he had first come through her door and he no longer winced every time he moved. This she took as a sign his bruised rips were healing. About a week ago she had talked him into using her exercise machine and he now reluctantly admitted that he was probably getting into better shape than he had been in years.

Chris had first felt the jolt of fear in the pit of her stomach about three days before. It had happened when they had been discussing the case and this had quite naturally spilled over into police work in general. They had started trading anecdotes about the dumb things they'd each done over the years on the Job. As they sat in her living room laughing she had become aware of just how much she enjoyed his company, how comfortable she felt with him and how deeply she had come to care for him. That was when the fear had hit. She had decided she needed to talk to someone about it and so she'd called Anne, made a date with her for lunch, told Lou she had some shopping to do and left. Now, sitting opposite Anne in the restaurant, Chris wasn't sure she really did want to talk about it.

Anne watched the different emotions play across Chris's face and decided to prompt her. "On the phone you said you had something very important to talk to me about. I'm getting the feeling you may have changed your mind. It's okay. We can have lunch without talking about it."

"You're right," Chris said. "I did want to talk to you about something, but now, sitting here opposite you, I'm not so sure I do…or can."

"So how is Lou Parker these days?" Anne asked shrewdly.

Chris looked at Anne and wondered if she was really that that transparent or if it had just been just a wild guess on Anne's part that had found it's mark. "He's fine," she finally said.

Anne picked up her menu and looked at it. "By the way, I meant to ask you. What is it that I shouldn't believe about Shawn's father?"

"What?"

"A couple of weeks ago I said something or other about Shawn's father and you said I shouldn't believe everything I heard about him."

"Oh, yeah. I'd forgotten."

"That's what this whole thing is about, isn't it? Why we're here? You and Lou Parker?"

Chris shrugged. "I suppose."

"Then what shouldn't I believe?"

"I don't know. I mean, the two of them are so much alike…but they're different, too. Shawn wanted to be like his father, but I don't think he ever understood him. I don't think Shawn ever even understood himself. On the other hand, Lou is who he is and he's comfortable with it. And that's a quality I…"

Chris stopped and looked away. She wasn't sure she wanted to hear herself say the words.

Anne realized that Chris had stronger feelings for Shawn's father than she was willing to admit. Even to herself.

"You're falling for him," Anne said, deciding to get it out in the open.

Chris heard the words and shook her head vehemently. "Hey, ease up. I like him sure, but nothing beyond that. Absolutely nothing."

"I retract what I said."

"Thanks."

"I was wrong. You're not falling for him. You've already fallen for him."

"Bullshit!"

Anne grinned.

"Fuck off," Chris said with a smile.

"You do have a way with words, Chris. Especially when there's something you don't want to talk about."

"Then let it be."

"Okay. But this lunch was your idea. You wanted to talk to me about something. That something turns out to be Parker. Now you don't want to talk about him. Seems to me you've got a good case of avoidance."

"Maybe you're right," Chris admitted reluctantly.

"As your friend I'm telling you that you'd better get your feelings for him straight in your head before it drives you crazy."

"Don't you think I've tried? If I had it straight I wouldn't be here avoiding talking about it." Chris grinned. "That sound as crazy to you as it did to me?"

"I've heard worse. Especially when the person talking won't admit she's…"

Chris cut her off. "Don't say it. I don't want to hear it."

"Okay, but tell me. What does he feel about you?"

"I'm not really sure but I'll bet my bottom dollar that he thinks I'm too young for him. That he'd be robbing the cradle if he ever got romantically involved with me. Or even go to bed with me."

"I see you've thought of that, too."

"Oh, for Christ's sake, Anne, of course it's crossed my mind. I've spent night and day with him for the past week."

"And?"

"And what?"

"How's the thought go down with you?"

"I try and put it out of my mind and concentrate only on Shawn's murder."

Anne sat back. "Another avoidance."

"Look," Chris said. "He's going to find who killed his son and then he's going back to Florida to wither away on his boat. And I'll be here working the streets for the Department. There's no future for us. Even if I wanted it. Even if he did, too. Which he doesn't."

Anne leaned forward. "Let me tell you something, Chris. We've been friends for a long time and I think I know you pretty damn well. And I've never seen you not go after something you wanted. You've got to ask yourself what's stopping you now?"

"I already know that. Fear. Total abject fear."

"That you might get him and live happily ever after or that you won't make it together?"

"Both," Chris admitted.

"Too bad. Then you'll spend the rest of your life wondering what might have been and that's a horrible thing to live with."

"What do you suggest I do, jump him?"

"It's a thought but it wasn't what I had in mind. Let it happen, Chris. You know how you feel. What you don't know is how he feels."

"The way he treats me sometimes I can guess. And I don't like it one iota."

"Fine. Then you have nothing to worry about. On the other hand, if he does care about you he's going to have to let you know. What will happen will happen and you can't force it."

"Go with the flow, huh?"

"Something like that," Anne agreed.

Chris nodded. What the hell? She didn't have much choice anyway.

Lou was bored. He'd had enough of her exercise machine for one day and now, without Chris there to talk to, there was nothing for him to do so he began to roll the case over in his mind once again. He knew he was missing something, but he couldn't put his finger on what. He was mindlessly looking at the books she had on her wall shelves when it popped into his mind.

Moving faster than he had since the beating, he took a quick shower and headed out. He thought about leaving her a note and then decided against it. Leaving notes were for married people. Sort of like having to tell your parents where you were going when you were a kid.

Chris returned to her apartment to find Lou gone. He'd done it to her again. The man had a mind of his own and nothing was ever going to stop him from doing what he wanted when he wanted. Chris knew the feeling. She was the same way. She wondered if they really did have as much in common as it appeared? Chris buried the question and put her mind back on the case. There was something nagging at her. Something she felt they had missed. She paced the room as she began to run the events of the case through her mind.

Driving over to J.J.'s, Lou remembered that he and Tollin had often left each other notes. But that was different, he decided. They were partners. Chris was not his partner, no matter how much she thought she was.

Lou broke the clasp holding the lock that the police had put on the door, walked in and started working his way through J.J.'s garage. He picked up each piece of smashed equipment and examined it before tossing it aside. He picked up a computer monitor and winced at the effort, reminding him again of the beating he'd taken.

"Still hurts, huh?"

Lou whirled at the sound of the voice and then quickly masked his surprise at finding Chris there. She was leaning against the doorjamb watching him. "How'd you find me?"

"I figured that we'd missed something," Chris explained. "That whoever killed J.J. might have been after something else. And that maybe they hadn't found it. And when I'd came home and found you gone I figured you'd come to the same conclusion."

Lou had to admit it was not bad thinking on her part. Especially since it was the same reasoning he'd used. He turned away from her and went back to his search. There was no way he was about to acknowledge his admiration for her a second time. He looked up and saw she hadn't moved. "You going to help or what?"

Chris walked into the garage and picked up a broken VCR. "We looking for anything specific?"

"A computer printout."

Chris put the VCR down and started slowly down the aisle of stolen merchandise. She looked but didn't touch anything. Lou noticed she wasn't really doing anything.

"Don't bother. I can handle it," he said sarcastically.

Chris grinned. "I see we're feeling better."

"We? I was the one who'd had his ribs cracked. Not you."

Chris ignored him and continued to look the place over. "What's different from when you were here before?"

Lou looked around at the mess. Was she kidding or what? "It hadn't been searched then."

"Come on, I didn't mean that. What about his things? Where were they before? Your mind sees things that you pay no attention to on a conscious level. But they do register subconsciously. You just have to bring it to the surface."

Lou grimaced. "More shrink stuff."

"Humor me," Chris said.

Lou took a deep breath and forced himself to look around at the garage.

"No," Chris told him. "Look away. Stare at the wall. Picture the place then. What was where. Where he was. What he was doing."

Lou figured the quicker he did what she wanted, the quicker he could get back to doing a proper search, so he fixed his eyes on the wall and tried to get a picture in his mind of what the place looked like the last time he was there with J.J.

"This is silly," Lou said, feeling exactly that.

"Fine. Feel silly. Just do it."

Lou saw the determined look in Chris's eyes which meant an argument if he didn't do what she wanted. "There were boxes over to the side. Unopened. I remember thinking that Robbery would have had a field day in here."

"Where was J.J.?"

"By the workbench. Soldering something. There was an open VCR on the bench. The cover was off."

Chris looked around the room. "What kind of VCR?"

Lou turned and looked at her, annoyed. "How the hell should I know? A VCR is a VCR."

Chris scowled at Lou and he turned away and looked back at the wall again. He closed his eyes. "A black one, I think. Maybe. With a red logo on the cover. Maybe. I don't know."

Lou turned away from the wall. "Can I now go back to what I was doing before you started this nonsense?" he asked and without waiting for a reply started to search again.

Chris looked around. "You see it here anywhere?"

"What?"

"The black VCR with the red logo."

Lou looked over at her and saw she was paying no attention to him. She was intently searching the garage with her eyes. He did the same and finally shook his head. "I don't see it."

"Neither do I. Now where'd you suppose it went?" Chris thought aloud.

"Donno. But he was a smart kid. And he knew he was being watched."

Chris turned and walked past him out the door. He was right on her heels. She walked straight to the back of J.J.'s house and tried the door. It was locked. She looked at Lou.

"Well? Work your magic like you did at Shawn's," she challenged him.

Lou accepted her challenge, bent over and examined the door lock for about three seconds before straightening up again. He looked down at the lock admiringly. "J.J. knew what he was doing. This would take hours to pick."

"I'll send out for lunch," Chris said sarcastically.

Lou threw her a look and then stepped back away from the door. He looked around.

"Come on," Chris said, realizing what he was looking for. "The kid was a thief. He wouldn't..." She broke off as she saw Lou's eyes come to rest on the rain gutter. She watched as he stepped over the flower bed under the kitchen window, reached into the spout of the gutter and pulled out a magnetic key holder. He held it up to Chris, making no effort to hide the triumphant grin he was sporting. "Never met a thief yet who didn't think it could never happen to him."

Chris stepped away from the door as Lou inserted the key in the lock, unlocked the door and with a sweep of his arm, magnanimously allowed her to go in first.

They walked through the kitchen and on into the living room where their eyes locked onto a VCR with a red logo which was sitting on top of the television set.

"That the one?" Chris asked.

"We'll know in a minute." Lou said as he strode across the room. He turned on the power to the VCR. Nothing happened. He turned the VCR around. No power cord. He turned the VCR over and ran the tips of his fingers over the locking screws.

Lou looked over at Chris and saw she was holding a screwdriver out to him.

"Don't ask," she told him.

"Okay. But I saw you pick it up on your way out of the garage."

"Like hell you did."

Lou unscrewed the holding screws and slid the cover off. There was a sheath of computer printouts inside.

Lou jammed both of his arms against the dashboard, bracing himself for the accident he was sure Chris was going to have. She reached an alley and spun the steering wheel over while at the same time flooring the accelerator. The car fishtailed and Chris fought for control.

"Hey! Take it easy!" Lou yelled at her.

Chris ignored him and concentrated solely on her driving. She regained control and the car blasted down the narrow alley and came out into the next street. She reduced speed and kept her eye on the alley behind her through the rear view mirror. When nothing came out she relaxed and continued on at a more moderate speed.

Lou settled back in his seat, but just in case, he kept one hand on the dash. It had been a neat piece of driving. He knew if someone had been following them they sure weren't now and that took a certain amount of talent and expertise.

"There she is," Chris said with an obvious relief in her voice.

Lou looked ahead and saw a beat-up station wagon parked at the curb about twenty yards in front of them. Chris pulled up behind it and got out of the car. Lou followed her over to the station wagon. Chris took the front seat, so Lou opened the rear door and slid inside.

Anne was behind the wheel and twisted around to get a good look at Lou. He smiled at her and she smiled back, then turned to Chris. "You're sure you weren't followed?"

"Not a chance. I'd have seen anyone on our tail."

"What she's not mentioning is the speed she drove at or the vicious unannounced turns she took. I'm not even sure I'm alive," Lou moaned.

"You're safe and sound, aren't you?" Chris told him. "Quit bellyaching."

"You're sure?" Anne asked again.

"I'm sure. You can relax," Chris assured her.

"I better be. My whole life is on the line here. Morrison ever finds I did this, I'm out and my kids don't eat. Being a single parent isn't all that it's cracked up to be."

Lou realized that this woman was Chris's pipeline into the Department and was curious why, if her job was at stake, she would help him. He decided to ask her. "Then why do it?"

Anne looked back at him and frowned. She had thought he would have understood. "Because it's the right thing to do. That may sound corny, but it's who I am. What I believe." she told him in a calm, tolerant tone. "Besides, Chris needs my help and friends help friends."

Lou felt as if he'd just been talked to like a child who'd said something stupid and should've known better than to say it. He didn't like the feeling. But the fact was she was right to speak to him that way. He should've known better.

Anne reached down and pulled a large envelope from under her seat. She handed it to Chris.

"Thanks, Annie. I really appreciate it," Chris said as she leaned across the console and kissed her friend on the cheek.

"I just hope it helps."

"Me, too," Chris replied. "I'll talk to you later." She opened the door and got out.

Lou did the same but before he closed the door he turned back and leaned in. "Your kids are lucky to have you. And your ex is an idiot for not knowing what he had when he had it."

Anne was surprised. She hadn't expected something like that from him.

Lou straightened up and found Chris staring at him. "What?" he asked.

Chris didn't know what to say. What Lou had just said to Anne had come as a shock. Times they are a-changing, she thought as she followed him back to the car.

Lou turned the car's dome light on and started reading the file that Anne had given them. Chris divided her time between watching the road and glancing impatiently over at Lou. She wanted to know if he'd found anything of use but didn't want to ask, hoping that this time he would tell her without her having to prompt him for it.

Lou turned a page and read the next one. Then he went back and read it again. He suddenly ripped the page out, crumpled it up in his hand and tossed it against the windshield. Then the entire file went the same route.

"Okay. You've gotten it out of your system. Now let me in on it," Chris said, hating herself for giving in and prompting him for information.

Lou turned to face her. "Two weeks ago that charred idiot in the morgue got caught walking out of a construction site at three in the morning with some of the site's dynamite and blasting caps stuffed into his jacket. Walked right into a patrol car. Then guess what? The case is dropped because the department loses the evidence. Want to guess when he was released?"

"The day Shawn was murdered."

"Shit," Lou said, and turned away. "Take a left up here," he told her.

Chris got to the corner and made the turn.

The porch light went on and Morrison saw Lou and Chris standing under it. He opened the door and ushered them inside.

"You know what time it is?" he asked closing the door behind them. "You could have at least called first."

Lou's face was a mask of anger. "There's a lot of things I could've done. And there's a lot of things you shouldn't have."

Morrison took a step back and tried to match Lou's anger. "Oh, it's going to be that way, is it? Well, if you think you can wake me up in the middle of the night with some wild accusation you'd just better think again. You push this and I'll have your ass behind bars quicker than you ever thought possible."

"Try it," Lou said, baiting him.

Morrison tried to stare Lou down and lost. He turned to Chris. "Susan's in the kitchen making coffee. Introduce yourself. You'll like her. I want to talk to Lou. Alone."

"There's nothing you can't say in front of her."

Morrison raised his eyebrows before realizing it had been bound to happen. But he didn't have to play. "Then there's nothing I have to say to you."

It was a standoff. Chris watched the two of them glaring at one another and decided. "I'll find your wife. Leave you two alone," she said, and walked towards the rear of the house.

Morrison watched her go before he turned and gestured towards the den.

"You want a drink?" Morrison asked as he crossed the room to the small bar set in the far corner.

Lou shook his head. Morrison fixed himself one. "You gotta understand, Lou. There's more going on here than just Shawn's death."

"Enlighten me."

"I'm not sure I can."

"Try. Start with the release of that scumbag who blew himself up in Chris's car."

"How'd you find out about that?" Morrison asked unable to contain his surprise.

"What the hell is the Department covering up?"

Morrison's wife Susan called out from the kitchen. "You two want some coffee or something?"

"No. We're fine," Morrison shouted back. He turned to face Lou again.

"Please, don't push it."

"A felon is released from jail and that same day he gets blown to hell and back planting a car bomb meant for me and you don't want me to push it?"

"I know how you feel, Lou, but I just can't help you."

"Who got him released? Who supplied him with the explosives which somehow disappeared from the evidence lock-up? And why would the Department want to cover for him?"

Morrison looked away, unable to meet Lou's hard stare. "We're working on it," Morrison finally said. "As soon as I know the answers to those questions, you'll know. That's the best I can do."

"It's not good enough," Lou said. "And even if it was I'd bet you wouldn't tell me a thing until someone upstairs gave you permission."

"What the hell do you expect me to do? I get orders from my superiors and I carry them out. That's the way things are done. Now lay off, Lou. I mean it."

Lou lowered his voice to a whisper. "I'm gonna find out and the Department can go screw itself. And you'll take the fall with them." Then he turned and headed for the door.

"Lou! Wait!"

Lou stopped, turned back and waited.

"Can we make a deal?"

"Like what?"

"I don't know. Something. Anything."

Lou stared at Morrison and realized that the man was caught between a rock and a hard place. If he gave Lou complete cooperation he'd catch hell from his superiors, if he didn't Lou might bring the entire Department down. He knew Morrison wanted neither and so he could be used, manipulated, and he thought he knew just how to do it.

"Tell you what…you give me what I want to know and when I find out who killed Shawn I'll let you make the arrest," Lou offered. "Who knows? You might even get a promotion out of it if you play your cards right with the news media."

Visions of promotion coming out of this whole damn mess flowed through Morrison's mind and for the first time since Lou had come in, Morrison relaxed. "I'm telling you the truth about the asshole that tried to blow you up. We haven't come up with anything concrete yet."

"And Shawn's so-called drug connection?"

"We're caught in the middle on that one. If Shawn wasn't involved with drugs, than it was a plant and we don't know why. If he was involved with drugs, then the Department's in for one hell of a public relations mess. We just can't afford that right now."

"What's the rest of it?" Lou asked, knowing there was more. "I'll find out anyway so do yourself a favor and tell me now before it all blows up in your face."

"You never give up, do you?"

"What's the rest and this is the last time I ask."

Morrison knew he had no choice. "Shipment after shipment of high grade drugs have been moving through the city as if we didn't exist. Every time we make a move they're one step ahead of us. There has to be an inside leak."

"And the Department believes it was Shawn?" Lou asked incredulously. "That's the reason they're willing to let his murder slide? Because they think he was the leak?"

"Not me, Lou. Not me," Morrison said quickly. "I wanted it investigated. Fully. But I was overruled. From upstairs. They don't want another rogue cop's face blasted all over the papers."

Lou looked at Morrison with total disdain. "And you're just going along with the program."

"Look! The Department's my whole life. Without it where the hell would I be? Drinking my life away on some boat like you? No, thank you. The Department's where I want to be. Right or wrong." He took a long gulp from his drink. "Besides, I have no choice."

"We all have choices. That's what life's about," Lou said, and walked from the room.

Chapter Thirteen

Lou tossed the printout he was reading aside and looked over at Chris hoping that she was going to be able to understand what they meant more than he did. From the expression on her face she seemed to be just as frustrated with them as he was.

"You know what our problem is?" she asked with looking up from what she was reading.

"Yeah, we're just plain stupid," Lou said disgustedly.

She ignored his comment. "We don't know what to look for. We need someone with an eye for finance. Someone who's used to working with this stuff day in, day out."

Lou grabbed the phone. "I know just the person."

"And I'll bet he's on the other side of the law, too."

Lou held out his hand and rocked it. "Depends on where you're standing."

"And you can trust him?"

"Look. J.J. was killed getting this stuff and it's doing us no good at all. It makes his death more of a waste. I'm not going to let that happen."

"I agree. But you need someone you can trust not to…"

Lou held up his hand for Chris to stop talking. "Mr. Tennant, please," he said into the phone. Lou waited for the operator to put him through to Tennant's office.

"Mr. Tennant's office," he heard the secretary say with a smile in her voice.

"Hi. This is Lou Parker. I want to speak to your boss."

"I'm sorry, but Mr. Tennant is busy right now. I can take a message though. What did you say your name was?"

"Lou Parker and if you still want to be working there tomorrow I suggest you ask your boss if he wants to speak to me or not."

Lou heard her intake of breath, then the click as she put him on hold.

"You should've been a diplomat," Chris observed.

Lou ignored her comment, turned his back on her.

"Lou?" Tennant asked when he came on the line.

"Yeah, it's me."

"I thought you left town."

"I came back. I need your expertise."

"I can't help you right now, Lou. We're in the middle of a huge audit and I can't get away," Tennant explained.

"Tomorrow then."

"Sure. How about my house. Early. Around seven."

"You got it. See ya' then," Lou said. He hung up the phone and grinned at Chris. He may not win any awards as diplomat of the year, but he did get results.

Chris saw the smug look on his face and nodded in appreciation. "I take it you've got us an interpreter."

"Top of his class at Harvard Business. I'm meeting him tomorrow morning at seven."

"Way to go, Lou."

"Let's see if what he comes up with does us any good before you go celebrating, huh?"

"You're no fun."

"Yeah. Well, right now I don't feel much like having fun."

"Then I'm leaving."

"You giving up?"

"Not a chance. I just have this funny feeling you're about to spend the rest of the day getting yourself shit-faced drunk and I'm not going to stand around and watch you do it. I'll meet you here in the morning and we'll go over and see this Harvard guy together."

Chris grabbed her purse and walked out. Lou sat on the bed for a minute, then grabbed his keys and left.

"For a guy who came in here six hours ago with the intent of getting himself plastered, you're not doing a very good job of it," Dee Dee said as she slid into the rear booth where Lou was sitting.

"I'm trying, Dee. Believe me I am."

"Bull. You've been nursing that beer for the past two hours."

"You counting what I drink now?"

"You bet. And that's only the second one you've ordered since you walked in."

Lou pushed the glass of beer away from him and leaned back. "I guess I just don't feel like drinking."

"The case not going well?"

"It's moving along."

"And the relationship with the girl cop. Is it just moving along, too?"

"There is no relationship. I told you that before."

"Yeah. And I told you then I didn't believe you and I still don't."

"Jesus. Give me a break."

Dee Dee leaned in closer. "Lou, from what you told me you've got just two things going for you in your life right now. Solving your kid's murder and the girl. If one's not the problem then it's got to be the other."

"Chris isn't a problem. I mean, she is. She's a pain in the ass. But not in the way you mean."

"No?"

"No," Lou said with finality. "She's a good cop and that's it. Period."

"And that's the decision you've come to?"

"Yep."

"So how come you can't seem to be able to live with it? How come it's making you so glum?"

"She's working the case with me. That's it. And I'm not glum."

"And you have no other feelings for her."

Lou got to his feet. "Look, I didn't come in here to have you analyze me. I hate when people do that to me."

"So where're you going now? To another bar and sit and stare at a glass of beer."

"I'm going back to work."

"In the middle of the night?"

"It's better than sitting here listening to you rag on me," Lou said with a grin. "You got a phone in this place?"

"Use the bar phone. Tell Eddie I said it was okay."

"I thought you'd be plastered by now," Chris said when she picked him up outside Dee Dee's bar.

"See how wrong you can be," Lou said before giving her directions out of the city.

Chris got onto Grand Central Parkway into the Long Island Expressway, got off at the Great Neck exit and headed north towards Kings Point. The farther she drove the bigger and more expensive the houses got. She finally drove up to the gate of what appeared to be one of the biggest homes. Lou gestured for Chris to use the call box mounted in a brick stand next to the driver's side of the car. Chris rolled down her window and had to push the call button three times before a light went on in the mansion and a grumpy voice came out of the speaker.

"Do you know what time it is?"

Lou leaned across Chris and yelled into the speaker. "It's Lou Parker. Open up, Arnold."

"Lou?" the voice repeated with a note of disgust. "I thought we set a date for tomorrow?"

"Life's a bitch. Open up," Lou shouted.

There was a pause before the gate started to slide open. Chris released her foot from the brake and drove towards the house. "Nice place. I didn't know you had any friends in this tax bracket."

"I wouldn't call him a friend exactly."

"What would you call somebody who lets you past their guard gate in the wee hours of the morning?"

"A couple of years back he got himself into some trouble. Nothing big, but enough to scuttle his career. I looked the other way."

"You let him go?"

"It was one little mistake. Something to do with a stock transfer. He'd been conned into it by the guy I was really after. I traded his stupidity for enough info to put my guy behind bars."

"So he owes you."

"And I'm about to collect."

Lou and Chris were seated in a far too comfortable leather couch watching Arnold Tennant read the printouts while seated behind an ornate desk in his home office. He had been reading them for the past hour and both Lou and Chris were starting to get edgy. Finally, Tennant folded the printout and looked over at them. "Your son was a rich man, Lou."

"Not so's you'd notice," Lou said.

"Oh, that I don't doubt. I'll bet he never even knew it. Look…" Tennant motioned them over to the desk and turned the printouts around so they could read them.

"See here. These are all deposits." Tennant used a pen to point at a section on the printout. "Nothing was ever withdrawn. And there was never even an inquiry about the balance. That's not normal."

"You're sure about that?" Chris asked.

Tennant leaned back supremely confident. "I've got money put away for when I retire in accounts just like these. And I make damn sure they're as clean as a whistle. I know what I'm doing. My guess is somebody else opened these accounts without Shawn knowing about it."

Chris looked at Lou. "Then we're right. He was being set up. Someone wanted to ruin his reputation."

"Can you tell who made the deposits?" Lou asked Tennant.

"Nope. But look. They came from all over the country. These numbers show where the wire transfers originated. Miami. New York. Corpus Christi."

"Drug centers," Chris said.

"I wouldn't know anything about that," Tennant said. "Tell you what though. You give me a little more time and I could probably trace where else the money from those accounts go."

"You could do that?" Lou asked.

"It's possible. I figure that the money probably goes from those accounts not only into an account like your son's but also into other accounts and then into other accounts, ad infinitum, but eventually it has to land somewhere. And I'm assuming you'd like to know where or what that somewhere is."

"How long will it take?" Chris asked.

"A couple of days. A week. I'm not saying it's going to be easy but it can be done."

"Is all this legal?" Lou asked.

"Not really," Tennant admitted. "But I've always wondered if I could trace something like this and this'd give me a chance to find out."

"You wouldn't be seeing how it's done so you could do it yourself, would you? Kind of looking to the future." Lou said with a grin.

Tennant shrugged his shoulders, non-committingly. "I suppose anything's possible, Lou."

Lou nodded. He couldn't care less why Tennant was offering to help as long as he could get the answers. "Thanks, Arnold. I really appreciate your doing this."

"One hand always washes the other. But next time, could you make it after sunrise? I'd really appreciate it."

"Count on it," Lou promised. "Next time, only after the sun's up."

Chris stood in the doorway to Tollin's kitchen and watched the two ex-partners go at it in the living room.

"That's bullshit thinking and you know it," Tollin said, his voice rising. "What the hell do you think Beaudine's going to tell you? You've got nothing on him to push with, for Christ's sake!"

"What do ya' want me to do?" Lou shouted back. "Go to the Department? They're in this up to their eyeballs."

"It's not the whole Department," Chris said.

They both ignored her.

"So they're covering their asses," Tollin shot back at Lou. "So what? That's something they've been doing since time began. And if they won't help, then Beaudine's certainly not going to. He's got more to lose than they do."

"This whole case leads back to drugs and Beaudine planted them."

"Prove it," Tollin challenged.

"I can't and you know it. But he's the one all the evidence is pointing to."

"Fine. So you waltz in and he's going to admit he deals in drugs and was responsible for a cop's murder. Is that the way it plays?"

"Something like that."

"You've gone soft in the head from all those days under that Florida sun."

"Look. Beaudine planted those drugs. Or knows who did. I'll get it out of him one way or another."

"Lou, you're not carrying a badge anymore. He'll blow you away if you try to strong-arm him. And he'd get away with it, too."

"I'll take that chance."

"I just don't wanna go to your funeral."

"If you're that concerned about my welfare, why the hell won't you help?"

"Because I'm concerned, that's why!"

"I'm touched."

"You should be. Damn it, Lou, we're talking about some heavy shit here. Dangerous shit. You gave that up when you retired. Hell, I did, too. Now you want to put your life on the firing line again? You're crazy."

"I have no choice."

"Well, I do."

Lou was clearly disappointed. He turned to Chris and gestured towards the front door. "Come on, we're going," he said, but making no move to do it.

Chris stayed where she was suspecting this was only a ploy on Lou's part and deciding she wasn't going to become a player in their little game.

"And you're not even sure it is Beaudine," Tollin yelled in frustration.

"He deals in drugs," Lou told him calmly. "Big time according to what I hear. Which means he's got access to the kind of money that was in Shawn's Swiss account."

"A couple of million dollars to just toss away, huh?"

"It'd be worth it if Shawn was on to him and about to bust his entire operation."

"Pure conjecture."

"We've moved on less."

"If Beaudine is as big as you think, and I don't think he is, then bracing him is not the way to go about it."

"Since when did you become scared of a punk like Beaudine? You used to take on three Beaudines before breakfast without missing a beat."

Tollin tensed, then forced himself to relax and reluctantly nodded. "Okay. But for Christ's sake, if you're going to do it, do it right."

Lou grinned. He'd won. "How?"

"I don't know yet," Tollin admitted. "I need time to work it through. To figure out a way."

"I haven't got time."

"Make the time."

Lou shook his head. "I can't. There's only one way to deal with scum like Beaudine and you know it."

Lou crossed to the door and walked out, slamming the door behind him. Tollin turned to Chris. "If you like him at all, rein him in."

"You really think he'll listen to me?"

"He'd better or there's nothing either of us can do for him."

Chris stopped at a red light and turned to Lou. "He has a point, you know," she said.

"Bullshit."

"Must you talk like that?"

Lou ignored her jibe. He had been thinking back over the years in the Department even since they had left Tennant.

"It's funny what you become in this job," he finally said. "How it changes you. It's as if it's all you are. It devours you. You were right the other day. What you said. I thought I wanted to retire. To get away from police work. But without it my life's been nothing. Working on Shawn's murder…hell, I don't know."

"And I thought that glow was because of me," Chris blurted out before she could stop herself.

"Pull over," Lou ordered.

Chris pulled to the curb. Lou got out and walked away. She waited to see if he was coming back, saw that he wasn't, got out of the car and followed him. Before she caught up with him, he turned and waited for her to reach him.

"Look, it can't happen between us," he said when she had stopped in front of him.

"Okay," Chris said amiably.

"I'm old enough to be your father."

"True."

"I'm just not cut out to be a husband."

"Uh huh."

"What the hell is it with you? I'm telling you there can be nothing between us and you keep agreeing."

"What the hell do you want me to say?"

"Get pissed off! Get angry! Tell me how wrong I am."

"You're wrong," Chris said softly, then turned and walked back towards the car. Lou watched her go and realized that he still didn't understand women and this woman in particular. The one thing he did know was that he wasn't sure whether or not he wanted to understand this one. Then he realized he was sure and that thought scared him.

They both studiously avoided looking at one another as she drove back into the city. Chris finally decided to break the ice. "We going anywhere in particular?"

"I don't know about you, but I'm looking for a bar."

"What about Beaudine?"

"I don't know. Maybe we should wait. See what Tollin comes up with."

"Forget Tollin. Do what you think is right. You can work the streets without Tollin telling you how to do it."

"What do you know about it?"

"I know you're a lot better than you think you are."

Lou turned to face her. "Who appointed you my cheerleader?"

"Me. All by myself. And I don't care if you like it or not."

Lou turned away. "Do what you want."

"And one more thing," she said. "Get rid of all that baggage you're carrying. Get it out of your system once and for all before it destroys you. Have it out with Darleen or forget about it."

Chris pulled up in front of Lou's motel room and stopped. When he didn't move, she reached across him and opened his door. "You can't just sit there all night."

"Pick me up early tomorrow. I want to catch Morrison before he goes in to work."

"You got it."

Lou started to get out but Chris grabbed his arm forcing him to turn back and look at her.

"I'm sorry about what I said back there. About the baggage. It's none of my business."

"But you were right," he said and removed her hand from his arm and got out of the car.

Lou stepped out of the shower and heard the phone ring. He draped a towel around his waist as he crossed the room and picked up the phone. "Lou Parker."

"Lay off the case, Parker," a voice warned. "Or what happened to that bitch'll happen to you."

Before Lou could respond he was listening to the dial tone. He quickly dialed Chris's number and listened to the phone ring four times before her answering machine picked up.

"Chris? It's Lou. Are you there? Pick up the damn phone." There was no response. He slammed the receiver onto the cradle and grabbed his clothes.

Chris opened the front door of her apartment house and trudged up the steps to her third floor apartment. It was at times like this she'd wished she'd opted for a newer building with an elevator. But she had always liked the ambiance of the older buildings in the city and when she'd found an apartment available in this one she had jumped at the chance to rent it.

She pulled the key to her door out of her purse as she reached her landing. She noticed that the hall light was out again and made a mental note to tell the super to replace it.

She slipped her key into the lock, turned it, opened her door and walked in. The next second she was knocked sideways off her feet.

Instinctively, she forced her body to relax and rolled as she hit the floor while at the same time reaching for her gun.

She pulled it out of her holster and then cried out in pain as a shoe came out of nowhere and kicked her hand, sending the gun flying.

It was only then that she realized there were at least two of them.

She rolled to her left and started to get up but was knocked back down as one of the men landed full length on her body.

She went for his eyes but her wrists were grabbed from behind and stretched above her head.

She was powerless.

There was enough light coming through the window for her to make out the outline of the man who was on top of her. He sat up, straddling her body.

"Give it up, lady," he said.

"Fuck you," Chris hissed.

"Your choice," he said, and slapped her hard across the face.

Chris's head whipped to the side from the force of the blow and it took a moment for her head to clear. When it did, she looked back at the man on top of her. He was grinning at her. "Just relax and enjoy it."

He reached out and tore Chris's blouse open revealing her bra. He liked what he saw. Nice body. They hadn't told him that. He was going to enjoy this.

Chris saw him reach behind his back and come out with a wicked looking knife. The blade sprung out and he placed the sharp tip against her cheek right below her right eye.

"Now you're not going to give us any trouble, are you?"

Chris knew if she moved her head a fraction of an inch she'd be cut. There was only one thing she could do. Go along with them. Buy some time. Look for an opening.

"No," she whispered.

The man drew the blade slowly down her face, along her neck and onto her chest.

"I figured you were smart enough to go along. Don't worry. As soon as we're through with you, we'll take what we came for and you can go on with your life as if nothing had happened."

Chris looked into his eyes and knew he was lying. They were going to rape her and then kill her. It would look as if she had come home and surprised a burglar who then raped and killed her.

She also knew the police would never find her killers as another part of her brain registered that the man on top of her was wearing surgical gloves. There would be no fingerprints left behind.

Chris felt the knife slip between her breasts and under the clasp of her bra. She heard the knife cut through her bra. The man moved her bra apart with his knife, uncovering her breasts. He stared at them, licking his lips in anticipation.

"Come on," the man holding her arms over her head said. "Lets get it done and out of here."

"Ease off. I want to enjoy this."

Chris closed her eyes and felt the cold tempered steel of the knife as the man ran his knife over first one, then her other nipple. Chris tried to sink deeper into the carpet, to get as far away from the knife as she could, but there was nowhere to go.

She felt the man move back along her legs and then attempted to open her slacks. He had trouble doing it using only one hand.

Chris opened her eyes and saw him lay the knife down and then reach for her belt with both hands. As he did, his weight shifted and Chris seized the opportunity.

Chris drove her knee up into his crotch with all the force she could muster. The man screamed and fell forward across her body.

At the same time, Chris pulled one hand downward hoping that his partner's scream would give the man holding her arms a second's pause. It did and Chris had one arm free.

She felt for the knife on the floor, found it, picked it up and drove the blade into the side of the neck of the man laying on her. She felt warm blood spurt onto her body as it pierced the artery.

Chris pulled the knife out and swung it over her head towards the man behind her but he pulled back, away from the arc of the knife and rolled to one side out of her reach.

Chris pushed herself out from under the bleeding man and scrambled to her feet in time and saw the second man go for his gun.

She looked around frantically for her own gun. It was on the floor next the couch. Too far away to get to. She had no options left to her. Except one.She rushed the man with the gun.

He fired just as Chris plowed into him, his bullet missing her head by a fraction of an inch. Before he could fire again Chris embedded her teeth into the wrist holding the gun. The man cried out but kept his grip on the gun.

Chris was then pulled back by her hair until she was looking into the wild eyes of the man she'd stabbed. Blood was still spurting from his neck but somehow he was ignoring it. She screamed as he picked her up and tossed her across the room as if she were nothing more than a rag doll.

Chris hit the wall and slid to the floor, dazed. She looked up and saw the bleeding man hold out his hand to his partner.

"Gimme the gun," he said.

His partner tossed him the gun and he turned to Chris leveling the gun at her head. "You fuckin' bitch!"

Chris saw his finger tighten on the trigger. She rolled to the side and the bullet plowed into the couch inches from her head.

She saw him taking aim a second time and knew that this time he wouldn't miss.

Then the door burst open and the killer whirled towards it. But he was a fraction of a second too late.

Lou fired and the force of the bullet from his 9mm threw Chris's would-be killer backwards.

"Look out!" Chris yelled seeing movement out of the corner of her eye.

Lou turned just as the second man drove his shoulder into Lou's rib cage, knocking him hard against the wall.

The man then turned and raced out the door.

Chris ran to the couch, grabbed her gun. "Go!" she shouted.

Lou ran out into the hallway and stopped. Chris came up behind him. "Up or down?"

"Listen," Lou said.

They heard footsteps racing down the stairway. They ran for the stairs and sprinted down them. Reaching the front door first, Lou pulled it open and ran outside. He looked around. There was no sight of the man. In the distance he heard a police siren coming their way.

"There's a back way," Chris said, and ran back inside.

Lou followed Chris down the hallway and out the back door into an alley. There was no sign of the man here either.

Chris fell back against the side of the building. She could feel her heart pounding and knew that shock was starting to set in. She forced herself to breath slow and easy and tried to fight it off.

She heard Lou talking to her from what sounded like far away but something in her mind told her he was standing right next to her.

"You okay?" Lou asked again.

Chris nodded. She felt him staring at her and frowned. She was sure he wouldn't be this concerned if she weren't a woman.

"I told you I'm fine."

Lou gestured towards her with a grin. "I'm sure. I was just wondering if you wanted to face the whole Department with your blouse like that."

Chris looked down. Her blouse was torn apart. What was left of her bra was hanging down and her breasts totally exposed for the world to see. Lou was trying hard to keep his eyes on her face and losing the battle as his eyes kept drifting down to her naked breasts.

Embarrassed, she pulled her blouse shut and marched back into the apartment house.

Chapter Fourteen

Lou leaned against the wall next to the window and looked down at the army of police vehicles blocking the street. Off to one side, the Coroner's men were loading the body of the man he'd shot into the rear of their van. They were being watched by what looked like the entire neighborhood. Even though it was the middle of the night, a murder and the ensuing police presence always made for a good show.

As the Coroner's van pulled out, Lou saw they were followed by a couple of the radio patrol cars who were going back to their normal sector duties while the unmarked cars of the detectives remained. The detectives themselves were standing behind him, patiently waiting for Chris.

She had gone right into her bedroom when they'd gotten back to her apartment and had closed the door behind her. Lou had heard the shower turn on and used her phone to put in a call to the Department.

"Well, I hope you're happy now," Lou heard from behind him. He turned and saw Morrison standing a few feet away.

"Not really. One's dead and the other got away."

"You'd think that a cop and an ex-cop would be able to do better than that."

"I knew you'd think that." Lou could feel the exhaustion through his entire body. He needed a good night's sleep and Morrison's second guessing his actions was keeping him from it.

Morrison looked around the room and then back at Lou. "The way I get it from the uniforms you talked to was that Chris surprised two men burgling the place and shot one while letting the other get away."

Lou shook his head. "No. I shot the one they carried out of here. She just stabbed him."

"What's the difference?"

"Plenty, if you took the time to think about it."

"This had nothing to do with your investigation of your son's death. It's a straight forward case of attempted…"

"There's a connection even if you're too stupid to see it," Lou said wearily.

"I don't see it. There's no evidence that points to anything else either."

"Then let me give you some," Chris said from the doorway to her bedroom. She walked over to them. "They were here when I got home. They jumped me. They were going to kill me. They wanted it to look like I surprised two men robbing my place and killed me to cover their tracks. The rape was an afterthought."

Morrison frowned. This wasn't what he'd expected. "You sure about that?"

Chris nodded.

"You feeling okay?" Lou asked.

"Better," Chris said, and looked around her apartment. "How long before I can clean that blood off my carpet?"

Morrison turned to one of the homicide detectives who was standing nearby listening to their conversation.

"We're through here," he told Morrison and satisfied, Chris headed for the kitchen.

Morrison turned to Lou. "If this went down the way she thinks then you've gotten closer to finding out who killed Shawn than I thought."

"How long before there's a make on the dead one?"

"I don't know. Forensic'll send me a report when they're done."

"How about ten in the morning? Your office."

"I might not have it by then."

"Sure you will. All you have to do is make sure that the prints are expedited. Pull some of that rank you're so proud of having."

Morrison shook his head. "Even if I did, I couldn't give you the information."

"One way or another I'll get that information. And by tomorrow. Now we had a deal. You want to stick by it or do I go it alone and shut you and the department out?"

Morrison slowly nodded. "You'll have it."

"I thought so."

Lou stepped away from Morrison and looked into the kitchen. Chris was rummaging in the closet under the sink obviously looking for something to clean the blood off the rug with. He turned back to Morrison. "Do me a favor, will ya'?"

"I thought I was already doing that."

"Order her off the case. Put her back to work on something else."

"I can't do that."

Lou exploded. "Why the hell not? She was almost raped and killed tonight. It's not worth it."

"It is to me. If you find the killer I want one of my people there to make sure things go the way they should. Which was your idea in the first place if memory serves. She stays!"

Morrison didn't give Lou a chance to argue and walked away. Lou started after him but found his path blocked by an angry Chris. "I'm on it whether or not I have his permission. You should have gotten that through that thick skull of yours by now."

"But look what happened tonight."

"Goes with the job."

"I'm not going to risk it happening again."

"No? Think about this. You have no say in the matter. None at all. It's my choice and I'm in!"

"Just like that."

"Just like that," Chris agreed. "And tell me something. Would you be saying the same thing if it were Tollin?"

"Of course not."

"Why? And you'd better think hard before you answer."

Lou started to respond and then thought better of it. She had boxed him in and was standing there just waiting for him to say that Tollin was a man and she was a woman and that was the difference.

"Look," Chris said, letting him off the hook. "I'm a cop. I chose to be one. I knew the risks when I took the job and I know them now. I live with them. Why can't you?" She turned away, went over to the middle of the room and started to clean the blood from her carpet.

A strange feeling came over Lou and it took him a moment to identify it as admiration for Chris. She had acquitted herself pretty damn well tonight. But he couldn't shake the fact she was still a woman and that he didn't like a woman putting herself in harm's way. Then the picture of her standing in the alley with her breasts exposed popped into his mind and he wondered how much an affect that had on his feelings...or what she'd said in the park.

Lou looked around the room and saw everyone had left. He started for the door. "I guess I should be going. You should get some rest."

"Funny thing is I'm not tired anymore. I was before, but I'm not now."

Lou knew the feeling. He'd had it himself after a chase or a shoot-out or a fight. The adrenaline was still pumping and he knew it'd be some time before Chris came down.

"Hungry?"

Chris grinned. "Famished."

Lou sat across from Chris and marveled at what she was putting away. She had devoured two burgers and two orders of fries and was now impatiently waiting for desert. The waitress brought over a piece of apple pie topped with a scoop of vanilla ice cream and set it on the table.

"She's starting her diet tomorrow and wants to get her last licks in," Lou told the waitress who nodded knowingly before walking away.

"Maybe you should take a couple days off. Rest up a bit," he said.

"We already settled that," Chris told him as she eyed the desert in front of her in anticipatory delight.

"Think about it. Maybe you'll change your mind."

"There's nothing to think about."

Chris cut a piece of pie with her fork and scooped some ice cream on top. She put it into her mouth and savored the sugar high she was getting as it hit her system.

"You about through?" Lou asked.

"What's the hurry?"

"My bed is calling me," he explained. "I'm not as young as I used to be. Or you are. My body needs rest. It's tired."

Chris glanced up at him and grinned mischievously. "How tired?"

Lou caught the look and had to force himself to ignore it. Chris was still young enough to be his daughter and that was something he just couldn't get past.

"Pretty tired," he said. "I'll walk you home. You sure you want to sleep there tonight?"

"I have no problem with it. Unless you've a better thought of where I should sleep."

Lou pretended he didn't catch her flirtatious double meaning. "If you're comfortable at home then it's probably the best place for you to be. I'll meet you at Morrison's office at ten."

"No. I'll pick you up. Two cars are too much of a temptation for you to go your own way."

Morrison was waiting for them when they got to his office. He tossed a file folder across the desk. Lou picked it up, read it and then handed it to Chris.

"You still think the attack on Chris last night was just a coincidence, right?" Lou asked.

"Nothing in that report says different," Morrison said.

"Read it again."

Morrison looked over at Chris and wondered if she knew what Lou was talking about because he certainly didn't.

"He was released from jail yesterday afternoon," Chris said.

"So what?"

"So," Lou answered, "the guy who blew himself up the other day had also just been released from jail."

"How'd you know that?" Morrison asked.

"I know. Doesn't it strike you as strange that two men are released from jail and go right out and try and take us out?"

"You saying that someone in the Department got them released just to go after you? That's crap and you know it."

"I don't know a thing. But it does make one think."

"It's bullshit," Morrison said.

"It's called a clue," Lou said sarcastically. "Look up the definition in the police detective's manual. You might learn something." He winked at Chris, then walked out of the office. Chris followed in his wake.

"You notice anything else of interest in that file?" Lou asked Chris as they walked down the hallway.

"Only that the asshole was in for attempted rape, assault with a deadly weapon and that he'd been up on the same charges a couple years back."

"Notice who made bail?"

"Yeah…uh…Paulie something or other."

"Paulie Lambert."

"So what?"

"So guess who bailed out our erstwhile bomb expert?"

"Paulie Lambert?"

"Now that's what I'd call quite a coincidence."

Lambert Bail Bonds was a small store front office, a block and a half from the downtown jail. Its windows looked as if they hadn't been cleaned in years and kept most of the daylight from seeping in.

Paulie Lambert looked up from behind his desk as Lou and Chris walked in. He made them both for cops immediately. "What's the bad news? Which one of 'em took a powder?" he asked, fearing the worst.

Lou knew what Lambert was feeling. To him, it could only mean that they were there to find out if the bondsman had heard from one of his clients. Which meant the client had run. Which meant that he was probably out the bond he'd put up minus the five percent fee that he had already been paid.

Lou gave him the name of his dead client and watched as Paulie breathed a sigh of relief. If the guy was dead the court had to cancel the bond. The bond wouldn't be forfeit. He was safe.

Paulie leaned back in his chair and lit up a cigar. "So what's the occasion? You didn't come in here just to tell me that?"

"True," Lou agreed. "We want to know how he came to call you."

Paulie shook his head. "Beats me. My name and number is on the wall next to the phone in the holding tank. Maybe he got it from there."

"Bullshit," Chris said.

Paulie shrugged. "Believe what you want."

"This is the second guy you had a bond on that's turned up dead in the last week," Chris told him.

"You thinking I killed them both to save my bond? You're nuts."

"Uh uh," Lou said. "One blew himself up. I killed the other one last night."

"Oh," Paulie said. "I guess I should thank you then. I kinda figured neither one of them was the greatest risk in the world. This way it takes a load off my mind."

"If you thought that," Chris asked, "why'd you sign off on a bond in the first place."

"He wouldn't've unless someone else was guaranteeing any loss," Lou said, and sat down on the man's desk. "Who was it, Paulie?"

"I don't know what you're talking about."

"Sure you do," Lou said. "For one thing I'm talking about coincidences. I don't believe in them. Two guys come to you for bail money. You give it to them. They both wind up dead. Nope. That's too much of a coincidence."

"Hey, listen," Paulie said. "I'm just doing my job here. Somebody wants bail I give it to them."

"We know that," Chris said. "What we want to know is who referred them to you."

"Now that shouldn't be too hard even for someone with your limited intelligence to do," Lou said with a grin.

Paulie looked from one to the other and didn't like what he saw. They both had an attitude and if it was one thing he hated, it was cops with an attitude. "What's in it for me?" he finally asked.

"The chance to do your civic duty," Lou said. "And being able to go home in one piece," he added.

Paulie suspected as much and had already made up his mind to tell them what they wanted to know. He'd been stomped on by the best and had hated every moment of it. After the last time he had vowed not to allow it to happen again.

"I got a call from a lawyer on both of them."

"This lawyer have a name?" Chris asked.

"I'll do you one better." Paulie reached over and thumbed through a stack of business cards on his desk. He pulled one out and handed it to Lou. "That's him. He guaranteed both their bonds."

Lou and Chris waited in the outer reception area of the Law Offices of Koven, Myerling and Bass until a very attractive secretary came from somewhere inside and told them that Mr. Koven could spare them a few minutes. They followed her down a long paneled hallway to Koven's office, where she announced them and then shut the door as she left.

Koven's six foot frame was well suited to carry the three thousand dollar suit he was wearing. He didn't bother to offer them his hand. Instead, he just gestured for them to take a seat in front of his desk. Once they were seated, he leaned back in his oversized leather chair and clasped his hands behind his head. "Now what's so damn important that you were willing to spend the day in my waiting room until I saw you?"

Lou looked admiringly around the room as if he'd never even heard the question. "This is a very nice office. Very nice. You must have a good practice."

"Good enough," Koven said, wondering where this was going. "All criminal?"

"Very little criminal as a matter of fact."

"Oh," Lou said, surprised. "I thought you were a criminal lawyer."

"If you're looking for someone to represent you on that level I would've thought that the Policemen's Association would supply you with one."

"Well, to tell you the truth, we're not here for that. You see, we're not the one in trouble."

Warning bells went off in Koven's head. "Perhaps you'd better tell me what you want."

"Just some information," Chris told him.

"What kind of information?" Koven asked warily.

Lou sat forward and his voice changed. Now it was hard and cold. "You arranged bail for two men. One blew himself up the day he made bail while placing a bomb in a car. The other was shot and killed last night, the day he made bail, while attempting to kill a police officer. You're the common thread between them."

Lou watched the blood drain from Kovin's face. It took the lawyer a moment before he regained his composure. "Are you accusing me of doing something illegal?"

"The two men never even knew each other. Yet the day they got out they were both attempting murder. As I said, you're the only link between them."

"That proves nothing," Koven said, wondering if they had any solid evidence that might link him to what had happened.

"We didn't say it did," Chris said.

"But it is a coincidence, wouldn't you say?" Lou asked dryly.

"Coincidences happen in this world."

"In murder cases coincidences usually have other meanings," Chris told him.

"Okay, what is it you two want?"

"Look at it from our point of view. You don't practice criminal law, yet you arrange for bail for two criminals who then go out and attempt murder. Seems a bit strange."

"You think that I got them released so they could go out and kill someone?"

"I'd say that was a fair assumption," Lou said.

"And you want to know who hired me to represent them."

"They certainly couldn't afford you themselves."

"I can't tell you."

"Can't or won't?" Chris asked.

Koven turned to her. "It's the same thing. The fact is I just don't know. Ten thousand dollars was delivered to my office with instructions that to earn it I was to arrange bail for someone who couldn't raise it himself. The same thing was repeated yesterday. I did as I was asked. As simple as that."

"And kept the money," Lou said.

"It's was a fee for my services."

"And you didn't think anything was strange?" Chris asked.

Koven shrugged. "Maybe I did. So what? I didn't break any laws."

"I'm not so sure of that," Chris said.

"I am. Now since I can't tell you anything more about who hired me I think it's time you left."

Driving away from the lawyer's office Chris ran the meeting over in her mind. "He could be telling the truth, you know."

"I've been thinking the same thing," he admitted.

"Where're we going now?"

Lou looked around, spotted a gas station with a public phone and gestured towards it. "Pull in there. Over by the phone."

"Tennant?" Chris guessed.

Lou nodded. "Hopefully, he's gotten the rest of the information for us."

Chris stopped the car next to the phone and waited while Lou made the phone call. She saw him hang up and dial again before slamming the phone down and hurrying back to the car. He opened the driver's side door. "Slide over."

"What for? What the hell happened?"

"I'll tell you on the way. Move."

Chris stayed put. He thought about pulling her out from behind the wheel before deciding he hadn't the time and ran around to the passenger side. "Get over to Tennant's home," he said as he scrambled into the car. "As fast as you can."

Chris slammed the car into gear and pulled out of the station. "What happened?"

"His office told me he was working at home today and when I called there a cop answered and demanded to know who I was and wouldn't tell me why he was there except that there'd been an accident."

"Jesus. Not another J.J.," Chris thought out loud as she whipped in and out of traffic towards the parkway entrance.

They arrived at Tennant's house to find the gate open and a uniformed police officer guarding it. Chris flashed her badge and they were waved through. Three other patrol cars were parked in the driveway near the main entrance. A rescue ambulance was directly in front of the door. When they walked into the house, they were met by a plainclothes detective whose I.D. was pinned to his coat pocket and said his name was Connors.

Lou walked up to him. "What happened?"

Connors glanced from Lou to Chris and relaxed when Chris held up her badge. "The owner of the place got himself shot."

"How bad?" Chris asked.

"As bad as it gets," Connors told them. He turned around and gestured towards a room off the main entrance. It was where Lou and Chris had met with him. Two paramedics were wheeling a gurney out from the office. There was a black body bag on it. All three waited for the paramedics to wheel the gurney outside before the detective turned back to Lou and Chris. "What's your interest in this?" he asked.

"He was helping us out on a case," Chris answered. Lou walked away from them and into Tennant's office. He crossed to Tennant's desk and stood there, staring at it.

"He was killed right there," Connors explained, coming up behind him and pointed to the chair behind the desk. "We figure somebody came in to rob the place figuring he'd be at work. When they found him home, they killed him, robbed the place and then split. We're canvassing the neighborhood now to see if anyone saw anything suspicious."

"Anything taken?" Chris asked.

"Not that we can tell. It looks like the killer panicked after the killing and ran."

Lou walked behind the desk. "I wonder." The desk was filled with stacks of papers just as it'd been when he'd been there the other night. Except for the area right in the center where someone would place things that they were working on.

Lou looked over at the computer. It was still on. He glanced up at Chris. "He might've been working on the computer."

Chris moved around the desk and looked at the computer screen. It was blank. She hit a key and the screen refreshed. "See this?" she said pointing to the screen. "He was knocked off the service he'd been calling. If you don't access anything in a certain amount of time they terminate your call."

"Can you tell who he was calling?" Lou asked.

"Sure. It's right there in the "thank you for calling" message. It looks like a financial service of some kind."

Lou nodded as if this confirmed his own thoughts. Chris hit another key trying to get the program to scroll back and show what he'd been doing on the service but got nothing except the log-on screen.

"Let's go," Lou said, and walked out of the room.

"Hey," Connors said when Chris started to follow him out. "If you've got some information that I should know about this guy, I'd really like to hear it."

Chris turned back. "I'm not sure there's a connection."

"But there might be, right?"

"Anything's possible. Tell you what. I'll go back to the office, pull the file, and give you a call. How's that?"

"I have a feeling I have no choice."

Chris grinned.

"And that you know more than you're ever going to tell me," he added.

"Ever's a long time. But believe me, I find out who did it, you'll know."

Lou was waiting for her in the car. Chris got in and drove off the property. "I figure that he was working on the printout when he was killed," she said when they'd gotten onto the Expressway again.

"Yeah."

"I think we've got them scared."

"They're covering their tracks all right," Lou agreed. "Somehow Shawn was onto something much bigger than he probably thought it was. And that's what got him killed."

Chris nodded. "Where to now?"

"Back to my motel."

"What's there?"

"My car."

"Come on, Lou," she warned.

"I'll call you later and we'll pick up where we left off."

"You going to try and cut me out again. Are you really that slow a learner?"

"I've got an appointment. It's personal and you can't be there," he said flatly.

Chris glanced suspiciously over at him.

Lou caught her look. "Okay?" he asked.

Chris nodded. She wasn't sure why she had agreed but her instincts told her not to push him on this one.

Lou saw Darleen waiting for him at the entrance to the coffee shop. He walked up to her and nodded his head by way of a greeting.

"Well, at least you're better at being on time these days," Darleen said.

This was not going to be easy, Lou thought. He'd been surprised that she'd even agreed to meet him. The waitress led them over to a table and they sat down opposite one another and ordered coffee.

Lou looked at Darleen and despite himself had to admit that she was still a very pretty woman. They were almost the same age, but she looked a lot younger. It was something she had told him ran in her family. They sat in silence until the waitress brought their coffee and had left.

"Well," Darleen asked in a tone that still jarred his nerves. He'd forgotten how condescending she could be using just her voice and body language. He took a deep breath and plunged ahead.

"Look, I don't want to fight."

"Good. Neither do I," she agreed. "So what is it you want from me?"

"I just wanted to talk to you. About us. About what happened."

"We got a divorce, Lou. We decided we weren't right for one another and went our separate ways."

"You decided, you mean."

"I thought the divorce was a mutual decision."

"Only after you cheated on me."

"I didn't cheat on you, Lou."

"Really? Then what would you call what was going on with that guy and you?"

"The guy's name is Warren and you well know it."

"Fine. Then what would you call what went on between you and that guy Warren."

"I never cheated on you. What I did with Warren was only after our marriage was over."

Lou frowned. He had never understood her way of looking at things and still didn't. "And who decided the marriage was over? You? How come you never let me in on that little fact?"

"I thought it was obvious. We weren't getting along. Hadn't for years."

"So you go and have an affair and it's morally okay because you decide the marriage is over even though you never bother to tell me about it. Is that it?"

Darleen thought for a moment and then nodded. "Something like that."

"Doesn't your word mean anything to you?"

"Is that what this is about, Lou? You're hurt because you think I cheated on you and now you want to tell me how much of a shit I really was."

"When you put it that way it does sound a little ridiculous, doesn't it?" Lou admitted.

"I came here because I thought enough time had gone by that perhaps we could at least be friends. I guess I was wrong."

"Why the hell would you want to be friends with me? You divorced me to get me out of your life."

"I'm not sure, Lou. Maybe because we have a history together. Memories. We go back a long ways."

They did. Lou knew that. And maybe that was the reason that he was still carrying the baggage Chris said he was. When he'd first gotten the divorce he'd shut Darleen completely out of his mind. As if she'd never existed. As if the marriage had never even happened. But it had. And there'd been some good times and some bad times. But they were a part of his life and to deny their very existence was denying those years of his life. He suddenly realized that shutting those memories out wasn't the smartest thing to do. He should've allowed himself to remember them. The good times and the bad. If only because they did happen.

Looking at Darleen now, Lou found that for the first time since the divorce he could do so without anger, without those ugly feelings that had always turned his stomach into knots.

"You're right, Darleen. We do have a history together. And I do remember it. But I'm also sure that as time goes by I'll forget most of it if only because time does that."

"I know," she agreed. "But you don't have to let it."

"But I will let it. It's the past and I don't like living in the past. Not anymore."

Lou took a deep breath and continued, sure of himself with her for the first time in years. "And as far as being friends is concerned, I really don't want to be your friend. I don't think we were ever friends and so there's certainly no reason to start now."

"Maybe not, Lou. But I'd like to be."

Lou shook his head. "I don't. I'm not your enemy but I don't want to be your friend either."

"I'm sorry," she said softly.

"To tell you the truth I'm not."

Lou got up from the table and tossed a couple of bills down for the coffee. "Take care of yourself, Darleen."

Lou walked out of the coffee shop feeling extremely good. Better than he had since the divorce. It was as if a huge weight had been lifted from his shoulders.

Chris had been right. Again.

Chapter Fifteen

Chris walked into Lou's motel room determined not to ask him where he'd been. So the first thing she did once she had closed the door was to ask him. He had flat-out refused to discuss it and she let it drop.

Lou took a sip from the container of coffee that Chris had brought him and then looked over the top of it at her. "You think we have enough to move on? I know there're some pieces missing, but there may be enough to get a warrant and apply some pressure."

Chris thought about it and then shook her head. "Tell you the truth, I'm not sure. How about we get another opinion?"

"Tollin?"

"I was thinking of Morrison. He'd love to get all the credit for wrapping this thing up so he'd be the toughest to convince. I say we lay it all out for him and see what he thinks."

"He can be pushed."

"Not far enough that he's going to risk his job."

Lou nodded. "Let's do it."

"Just try and stay cool."

"I'm always in control with Morrison."

"I know. Right up until the time he presses your buttons and you lose your temper."

Morrison sat at his kitchen table, the morning paper to one side unread and a pot of coffee in his hand. He refilled his cup and gestured to Lou and Chris, silently asking if they wanted more. Both shook their heads. They'd had enough coffee over the past two hours to last them a lifetime.

The computer printouts were scattered in the middle of the table. In between reading them Morrison had questioned Lou and Chris intensively about what they'd learned.

Morrison took a sip from his cup, leaned back in his chair and fingered the printouts. "And this is all you have?"

Lou glanced over at Chris. "This has been a waste of time."

"Damn right," Morrison agreed. "Of my time and yours. You expect me to move on this crap?" he said, gesturing at the printouts. "The DA would laugh me out of his office."

"Forget the DA" Lou said.

"Then what is it you want," Morrison asked.

"I want to know what it is that you're holding back."

"I've told you everything I know, Lou," Morrison protested. "Believe me, if I knew more I'd tell you."

"I haven't believed a word you've said from the moment I first met you."

"Then get the hell out of my house!" Morrison shouted. "I offered you my help…"

Lou cut him off. "So you could get your name in the paper when I broke the case."

"Big deal," Morrison shot back. "You'd get what you wanted and I'd get what I want. Quid pro quo, Lou. What difference does it make what my reasons for helping you are?"

Reluctantly Lou nodded. "You're right."

"Thanks," Morrison said dryly.

Lou got to his feet. "But if I ever find out that you've been holding back on me you'll be my next target."

"I'm not, Lou. I'm really not," Morrison assured him.

Lou walked into his motel room and threw the copies of the printout across the room where they bounced off the wall and scattered as they fell to the floor. He started pacing back and forth and Chris seized the opportunity to slide into the chair.

He stopped his pacing and looked at Chris. "We're missing something."

"Like what?"

"If I knew that it wouldn't be missing."

Chris ignored the sarcasm and tried again. "How about you try it out on me?"

"Okay," Lou said. "Shawn's dead and J.J.'s dead and Tennant's dead. They're connected. How?"

"The Swiss bank account," Chris answered.

"Right. It was in Shawn's name and J.J. and Tennant were trying to get the specifics of it. That ties in fine. But we still don't know where the money in the account came from."

"Or where the cocaine came from," Chris offered.

"And both the money and the coke are tied in to Shawn."

"And maybe to each other."

"The money came from dope?"

"That's the way I'd look at it," Chris said.

"Me, too. We find out who planted the dope and maybe we'll find out who funded the Swiss account."

Chris ventured a guess. "Beaudine?"

Lou shook his head. "He doesn't have the smarts. Not to set Shawn up. The dope's another matter. And if we go with that it stands to reason that someone's running Beaudine. That's who we've got to find."

"Okay. I'll buy that. Now how're we going to do it?"

"All I can think of at the moment is to keep rattling the cage and hope that the door will eventually open."

"That's not very promising."

"You got a better idea?"

"Nope. It's what I'd do, but that doesn't make it any more promising."

Frowning, Lou looked away from Chris. "There's one other thing that I keep avoiding and perhaps it's about time I faced it."

Chris nodded. She knew where he was heading and she'd been avoiding the same thing. "The Department."

"Yeah, the Department. They've accepted that Shawn was involved in drugs. That the money from the Swiss account was payoff money for inside information."

"Pure bullshit."

"Exactly."

"Then why?"

"The only thing that I can come up with is that Shawn was fingered to take the fall for someone else. Someone high up in the Department who's dirty."

Now that he had said it out loud, Lou felt a sadness come over him. It was bad enough having his son accused of being dirty, but if the Department was involved it just made everything worse. He loved the Department and no matter what it did or how much he disagreed with its policies, he still loved it. It was his family, for better or worse.

"So you think it's all a cover up?" Chris asked.

"And you don't?"

"It certainly looks that way."

"How about we find out?"

"Okay. But how do we get to him," Chris said.

"Get to who?"

"Foster."

"How'd you know that's who I was thinking of?"

Chris grinned. "You may have carried a badge longer than me but that doesn't give you the corner on who's who in the Department. And I'm betting you know a way to get to him."

Lou walked into the bar and spotted Terry Lapp, a man in his late thirties, and strode over to him. Chris stayed two steps behind so she could cover his action.

Lou came up to Lapp and grabbed him by the back of his jacket and lifted him off the bar stool. The two men he'd been talking to jumped to their feet.

"Stay put!" Chris ordered.

They turned to look at her, saw that she had a badge in one hand and her other hand on her gun and decided to slide back onto their bar stools.

Chris watched Lou half-walk and half-carry Lapp towards the men's room and leaned against the bar to wait.

Lou opened the men's room door and threw Lapp inside. He followed him in, picked him up from the floor where he had landed and slammed him against the wall.

"Remember me, asshole?"

"Uh huh," Lapp said. "Lou Parker." Lapp was scared out of his wits. Not only of Lou, but also of the two men outside. He'd just accepted four ounces of prime cocaine from them and hadn't paid for it yet. If Lou took the dope from him he'd either have to pay the two men and have nothing to show for it or refuse to pay and he'd end up in a gutter somewhere. Neither appealed to him.

"I need a favor, punk."

"Hell of a way to ask, man," Lapp said, trying to breathe through Lou's chokehold on his throat.

Lou released his hold and stepped back. Lapp took a moment to catch his breath, then looked at Lou. "It's your move, man."

"All I want is for you to make a call for me. To your friend downtown. I want you to convince him that you have to meet with him. Today. Right now."

"I don't know…"

Lou stepped forward and slammed him against the wall again. "You've been Foster's snitch for years. It must be nice having the head of narcotics as your protector. Only he's not here right now to protect you."

"Let me go. I can't breathe," Lapp pleaded.

"Only if you do me this one little favor."

Lapp nodded. Setting up a meeting was a thousand times better than having to deal with the two waiting outside or having Lou bang him around again. Lou turned him loose. "And make sure he knows to come alone," Lou warned him.

Lapp nodded again and Lou pushed him over to the pay phone on the wall. He dug into his pocket and pulled out a quarter. "Here. My treat."

Chris pulled in behind the Hall of Science building in Flushing Meadows and turned off the ignition. She checked her watch. "You think he'll show?"

"He'll show," Lou said confidently.

"I still can't believe that the Chief of Narcotics is at the beck and call of that character you braced in the bar."

"Lapp's been Foster's main informant for years. His tips are what got the man his last two promotions."

Chris leaned against her door and grinned. "You're loving this, aren't you? In fact, I'll bet you haven't had this much fun or felt this alive in years. Not since you retired."

"Don't do your shrink stuff on me."

"It's not shrink stuff. Remember, I saw you when you first got here. You looked down, depressed, lost. Now you're rearing to go. There's a spring in your step. You're looking forward to each day, each hour of that day, each minute of that day, with an enthusiasm you didn't have before."

"You never give up, do you?"

"I'm right, aren't I? You can feel it inside. Why you won't admit it is beyond me."

Lou turned to face her. "Admit what? That I'm enjoying myself? You're damn right I am. I'm on the streets again. Doing what I do best in this life. It makes me feel good and I guess it shows. Big deal."

"Calm down," she told him, surprised by the vehemence of his outburst.

"Don't tell me what to do."

"I don't understand you."

"Join the end of the line, kid."

"No. I think I want to be in front."

Lou frowned. "Look. I don't know what you want from me. You wanted in. You're in. Now you want to understand me. That's not possible. I don't even understand me."

"Bullshit. That's just what you want people to think."

"Is it now?"

"You bet. You know yourself better than you let on and why you insist on hiding behind that facade you've so carefully erected is beyond me. Especially since you're so big on truth and honesty."

Lou was losing this one and he knew it. She was too perceptive for his money. She saw him for what he really was and he didn't like it. It was too unnerving.

"Why'd you become a cop?" he asked.

Chris smiled at him. "Nice change of subject."

"Thanks," he said, and went back to his question. "How come?"

Chris wondered if he was really interested or if he was just using it to get her off the subject of him. It was the first time he had asked her anything about herself. He looked interested enough, but with Lou you couldn't always tell.

"A patrolman came to visit my school when I was a kid. I liked the uniform. I liked the gun he carried. I liked the power and the confidence that seemed to come from him. I equated that with the badge he was wearing. Right then and there I decided to join the force when I was old enough."

"But you went to college first."

Chris nodded. "My parents had saved their entire lives for me to go. I couldn't disappoint them."

"Then what? Out of college and into the Academy."

"I joined the next day."

"Any regrets?"

"You kidding? The first day I went onto the streets I knew I'd made the right decision."

Lou smiled. He knew the feeling. He had felt the same way.

"It was something that I've thought about a lot," Chris said. "How I felt that first day. There was an anticipation, sure. Even a fear. But above that was the excitement. An adrenaline rush way beyond anything I'd ever experienced before. I'll never forget it and I feel it every day that I come to work. I live on the edge and I love it. I took a vacation a couple of years ago and was bored silly. Without that edge, life just doesn't seem exciting enough. I have to live on that edge, Lou. Without it, I know my life would be miserable. I think it's why you were so miserable on your boat. You need it, too. And now you feel it again. It's why you feel so alive."

Lou knew she was right. It was why, way down deep, he didn't want the case to end and have to return to his boat. Out of the corner of his eye, he saw an unmarked police car pull into the museum lot and forced his thoughts back to the problem at hand.

"Foster," he said, gesturing with his head.

They watched Foster drive to the far corner of the lot. Chris started the car and followed in his wake, coming up behind Foster's car and stopped, blocking him from backing out and getting away.

"Let me handle this," Lou said.

"No way."

"He's your superior. He'll want to save face in front of you. He doesn't have to with me. Think about it."

Lou didn't wait for her to decide. He got out of the car and walked over to Foster's car. Chris remained where she was. She knew Lou was right. Foster would probably tell him much more than he would if she were there.

"What the hell?" Foster shouted when his passenger door opened and Lou got in.

"Lapp couldn't make it, Chief."

Foster knew he'd been had. "I'll have his ass for breakfast."

"Don't blame him. I didn't give him much of a choice."

Foster nodded. He knew Lou and knew that Lou'd do whatever it took to get what he wanted. In a strange way he almost felt sorry for Lapp. "Okay. I'm here. Now what?"

"Now you tell me what the hell is going on?"

"With what?"

Lou twisted around to face him. "Don't fuck with me, Chief, or I'll bury your sorry ass along with everybody else who thinks they can screw with me and get away with it!"

"Take it easy. I'm not fucking with you."

"Then talk to me," Lou said harshly.

"What is it you want to know?"

"Who killed Shawn for starters?"

"We don't know."

Lou shook his head. "You sound like Morrison."

"He knows just as much as I do. Or as little."

"The two of you together haven't enough brains to know which way is up. Morrison knows as much as you tell him and not a thing more."

"I can see why he doesn't like you, Parker."

"Who gives a shit? Now what the hell is going on? And this time think before you answer or I swear I'll tear you a new asshole!"

"Honest, Lou," Foster pleaded. "We just don't know."

Lou believed him. He didn't know why but something in his gut told him that the man opposite him was telling the truth. "How about the Swiss account? And the cocaine?"

Foster took a deep breath and exhaled. "We're working on it."

Lou sat back and tried to make sense of it all. Foster hadn't told him anything. But there was something else. In Foster's attitude. He was too guarded. What the hell did he have to be wary about? Something about Shawn, sure, but what? And Foster seemed to know Shawn. Did he maybe know him better than the difference in their rank usually allowed. Suddenly, it all made sense to him. He turned to face Foster again.

"Shawn was working undercover, wasn't he? Trying to nail the coke dealers for you."

Foster sighed.

"And you were letting me run to see if I could do what they'd stopped him from doing."

"Something like that," Foster agreed.

Lou didn't like his agreeing so quickly. He was still holding something back. But what? What was so important to the Department that they'd let an outsider do their work for them? And that's what he was now. An outsider. A civilian. Yet Foster was telling him that they were allowing him to investigate something they should be doing themselves. Why were they afraid of using Department personnel to do the job? And then the rest of it fell into place.

"Shawn wasn't working undercover to nail the coke dealers. That was just a cover story."

"Was it?"

"You bet it was. Morrison told me that the Department had a leak. And he believes Shawn was that leak and that's why you've covered everything up."

"He's right."

"No, he's not. Shawn wasn't the leak and you know it. He was working for you. Undercover to find the leak in the Department. To find a rogue cop."

Foster refused to meet Lou's eyes and Lou knew he'd hit the nail right on the head.

"And I'll bet that nobody else knows about it, either. Nobody knows you gave Shawn the assignment to ferret out that rogue cop. And you're covering the whole thing up to save your own ass because you never got permission to give him the damn assignment in the first place."

Foster looked admiringly over at Lou. The man was still the best detective he'd ever seen. "You're close. It's true we've got a leak. A big one. And it's someone under my command. Every time we raid a dealer we come up blank. They're being tipped off."

"And you pulled Shawn into it because you couldn't trust your own men and didn't want I.A. crawling all over you."

"Too many good reputations have been ruined just by being questioned by them.

"Too fuckin' bad. If they're clean, they're clean. No, you wanted to keep your record clean so you went outside your command for help. To my son."

Foster shook his head. "He came to me. He'd been working undercover on the street and heard something. He put two and two together and asked me about it. I decided to tell him what I thought and he volunteered to find out who it was." Foster shrugged. "What else could I've done? I needed help and Shawn was there to give it and I took him up on it. You would've, too, if you were in my position. You know something else, Lou? If you were in Shawn's position you would have done the same thing he did. He had the same moral code that you do. Right is right and wrong is wrong and you do what you can to correct the wrongs."

"And it cost Shawn his life," Lou said.

Foster nodded. "I figure that whoever is leaking the information caught on to him and either killed him or had him killed."

"And planted the money and the drugs so if he had found out something and had told anyone he wouldn't be believed because he was a dirty cop."

"Yeah. Something like that," Foster agreed.

Lou sighed. At least his son's name was cleared. That counted for something.

"It almost worked, too," Foster said. "I almost believed that Shawn was the leak and got himself the job as a cover. Then I thought maybe it hadn't gone down that way. Maybe he just did have a falling out with the bad guys he was working and they had killed him."

"What changed your mind?"

"His partner. She wouldn't let it go."

"And you believed her?" Lou asked unable to keep the surprise out of his voice.

Foster shrugged. "She didn't give me much of a choice. She was poking around and I couldn't stop her."

"But you still don't know who killed Shawn?"

"We're working through Interpol on the Swiss account, but it takes time. You know how the Swiss are. The coke? Could've come from anywhere."

"And you've still got a leak somewhere in your command," Lou pointed out.

Foster nodded.

"You're an asshole, Chief. You made rank, but you never did find out how to be a police officer. How you live with yourself is totally beyond me."

Lou opened the door and got out of the car, turned and leaned back in. "That rogue cop in your division?"

Foster looked over at Lou.

"Don't worry. I'll find him for you."

As they drove back, Lou replayed his entire conversation with the Chief to Chris. She took it all in without any questions and then thought about it for a couple of minutes. "It makes sense," she finally said.

"I know."

"Then what's troubling you?"

"I don't know who I want more. The guy who actually pulled the trigger and murdered my son or the cop that set him up."

Chris nodded. She didn't know which one she wanted more either.

Chapter Sixteen

Chris was stretched out on the bed in Lou's motel room waiting for him to return with some coffee and hoping he remembered to bring some sweet rolls to go with it. She needed a sugar fix.

The phone rang just as Lou came back. He handed Chris the bag and picked up the phone. Chris opened the bag and pulled out a sugared doughnut. She took a large bite out of it and felt her body react to the sugar. Lou hung up the phone, dialed nine for an outside line and dialed again.

"What's up?" Chris asked.

"I'll tell you when I know," he answered, listening to the phone ring. After three rings, he heard a familiar voice.

"Hello," Dee Dee said.

"Dee, it's me."

"Thank God. It's about time. Get over here as fast as you can, Lou. Please."

"Where's here?"

"Fawn's."

"I'm on my way."

Lou hung up and looked for Chris but she had heard him and was already out the door and heading for the car.

Chris drove while Lou stared out the window trying hard not think the worst. The anxiety in Dee Dee's voice had stopped him from asking any questions, but now he wished that he had. There were too many possibilities that came to mind and none of them were good.

Chris pulled up in front of Fawn's apartment house and Lou was out of the car before she could shove the gear into park.

Lou barged past the doorman and was impatiently pushing the elevator button when Chris caught up to him. The door opened and they got onto the elevator. Neither of them said a word on the ride up to Fawn's floor. After what seemed like an eternity the elevator door opened again and they hurried over to her apartment. Just as they reached it, the door opened and Dee Dee stood there.

"I heard the elevator," she said by way of explanation before stepping back and gesturing them inside. They walked into an apartment that looked as though it had been through a cyclone. Everything that could've been smashed, was. Broken pieces of pictures, vases, sculpture, china and crystal were all scattered about. The sofa and chairs had been ripped apart with what looked to have been a very sharp knife.

Lou raised his eyebrows at Dee Dee.

"She's in the bedroom."

Lou took one step into the bedroom and stopped. Fawn was stretched out naked on the bed, her body a mass of welts and bruises. Her face was twice its normal size and her eyes were swollen shut, her lips brutally cut. She'd taken a vicious beating.

"I fixed her up the best I could," Dee Dee said, coming up behind him. "She refused to go to the hospital."

Chris sat down on the bed next to Fawn. She picked up her hand and softly stroked it. Fawn tried to open her eyes but all she could manage was a small slit out of the right one. It was just enough to recognize Chris, however, and she tried to smile but flinched from the pain the movement caused.

"It's okay. You'll be all right," Chris said gently.

"Someday maybe, but not right this second," Fawn whispered.

Lou walked over and stood by the side of the bed. He looked down at Fawn. "You know who did this?"

"They were here when I got home. I walked in, saw the damage, then they jumped me."

"They? You sure there were two?" Lou asked.

"There could've been a dozen. I wasn't really paying attention."

"You should be at the hospital," Chris said.

Fawn took a slow deep breath, fighting the pain it caused. "No way. I'm getting out of here. Right now. Help me up. Please?"

Dee Dee came over and placed a hand on Fawn's shoulder, keeping her down. "In a couple of days, maybe, but you're going to stay here until you're better."

"Help me up," Fawn insisted.

Lou bent down and gently helped Fawn into a sitting position. He swung her legs over the side and then, grasping her under her arms, pulled her to her feet. Fawn looked at Chris and Dee Dee. "You guys help me dress, okay?"

"Where're you going?" Lou asked.

"I'm not sure. Anywhere else but here. Home, maybe. Montana."

"I don't think you can make it," Dee Dee told her.

"I'll make it," Fawn said, with a determination that left no doubt in any of their minds that not only was she going to go, she was going to make it, too.

"I'll wait in the living room," Lou said, settling the issue for all of them.

Handing Lou a piece of paper with the information he had asked for, Chris went back into the bedroom. Lou reached for the phone and dialed, reading a number from the paper. First he called Fawn's parents and told them that their daughter had been mugged in the big city and was coming home to recuperate. They had sounded pleased that she was coming home. Next he called the airlines and booked a first class seat for Fawn to Montana and then called her parents back and gave them the flight number and arrival time. By the time he finished, Chris and Dee Dee had Fawn dressed and the three of them helped her down to the car. They eased her gently into the car. Dee Dee hugged her friend and elicited a promise from her to keep in touch. Stepping back from the car with tears in her eyes, Dee Dee stood there and watched the car drive off. She remained standing motionless, looking down the street, long after she had lost sight of the car.

Fawn sat in front with Chris while Lou sat in the back, hating every moment of it. Not only wasn't he driving, but he'd been relegated to the rear seat. He leaned forward next to Fawn ear. "I figure if you're up to this trip you're up to answering a couple of questions."

"They wanted to know what I'd told you about your son's death."

"Damn!"

"What'd you tell them?" Chris asked.

"The same thing I told you. Nothing else. Hell, I don't know anything else."

"Then why'd they trash your apartment?" Chris wondered.

"As an object lesson. They said that's what happens when people get involved with an asshole like Lou Parker. At first I thought they were going to kill me but they seemed to change their mind when they realized I didn't know anything more that could help you."

"So all they did was beat you up," Lou said disgustedly.

"It was enough."

Lou nodded. First J.J., then Tennant, now Fawn. Somebody was right behind him and cutting off all his contacts. If he didn't get to the bottom of it soon they'd be right up next to him.

Chris got to the airport with six minutes to spare. She badged the first airport cop they saw and he made sure they made it to the gate in time. Fawn forced a tiny smile at both of them before allowing the stewardess to help her onto the plane.

Lou and Chris walked away from the gate and started down the airport causeway side by side. Suddenly, Lou stopped in mid-stride. Chris turned to him. "What?"

"Dee Dee."

"Oh my god," Chris said as she grasped the implications of the name. She spotted a wall phone and pointed. "There."

Lou ran over to the phone, dialed Dee Dee's bar and got the bartender who told him Dee Dee had called in and said she was going home to change and was going to be late. Lou hung up on him and called Dee Dee's apartment. He let the phone ring a dozen times before he disconnected.

"No answer?" Chris asked.

Lou shook his head. "So she's not at the bar and not at home."

"She could be in between."

"Let's hope so. If they went after Fawn like they did who knows what they'd do to Dee Dee. Damn! I should've thought of this earlier."

"You didn't. And neither did I. So let's do something about it now."

Lou lost count of all the traffic violations Chris was piling up on the trip from the airport to Dee Dee's. He doubted a patrol car with its red lights going and siren wailing would have made it any faster. Chris pulled up and they both ran inside, up the stairs and over to Dee Dee's door. Lou rang the bell. There was no answer. He then balled his fist and banged on the door.

"Maybe we just missed her," Chris said.

"Maybe." Lou moved back from the door and sniffed the air. "You smell something?"

Chris inhaled and her eyes widened as she recognized the scent. "Smoke."

Lou looked down. A small wisp of smoke was coming from under the door to the apartment. He stepped back and was about to slam his foot into it when Chris pushed him aside. She grabbed the door knob, turned it and pushed the door open. Smoke rushed out of the apartment into their faces.

"I don't have a choice," Lou said, and ran into the apartment.

"Neither do I," Chris said, and followed him in.

Inside, flames were already licking their way up the wall, crawling towards the ceiling. Lou ran through the living room into the kitchen. Chris went for the bedroom.

"Lou!" Chris called out.

Lou ran through the smoke into the bedroom. Dee Dee was on the bed, the front of her dress soaked in blood. There were powder burns around the gunshot wounds.

Lou picked Dee Dee up in his arms and carried her out of the bedroom, through the smoke-filled living room, into the hall and on down the stairs. Chris stopped to pull the fire alarm mounted on the wall next to Dee Dee's apartment and then raced after Lou.

They emerged from the building and Lou gently laid Dee Dee down on the sidewalk. Kneeling down next to her, he felt for her pulse. "I'm not getting anything," he said to Chris.

"Let me try," Chris said, placing her finger on the carotid artery.

"Feel it?" Lou asked hopefully.

Chris frowned, moved her finger and tried again. "There's something. Faint, but there."

A radio patrol car pulled up and stopped while down the block a fire truck turned the corner and barreled towards them. Lou ran to the patrol car and shouted at the driver. "Get ESU rolling. We've got a gunshot victim over there.".

"Gunshot? I thought this was a fire call?"

"Make the call, asshole," Lou growled, "or I'll make it for you!"

"Back off, mister," the cop said, and started to open the car door. Lou slammed it shut with his knee and leaned into the car, his angry face inches from the driver's. "Make the fucking call! Now!"

Lou stopped pacing when he saw the doctor coming down the hallway towards him. The doctor had come down straight from surgery and his gown was splattered with blood from the work he'd just done there. Chris moved to Lou's side as the doctor reached him.

"She'll make it," he said.

"How close was it?" Chris asked.

The doctor shrugged. He'd been working the hospital's trauma unit for years and had seen it all. "Compared to what? She had three bullets in her. One hit a rib, cracked it, and caromed off and out. Easy fix. Another went through her shoulder. Clean through. Another easy fix."

"And the third?" Lou asked.

"That one was a dilly. It bounced around inside the rib cage for a while before settling down in the lung. It missed the heart by a fraction but tore everything else up pretty bad."

"And?" Chris prompted.

The doctor smiled. He was a good surgeon and he'd just saved a woman's life and was proud of his work. "I put all the pieces back where they belonged and sewed them together again. A couple of months and she'll be as good as new."

"Thanks, doc," Lou said, and held out his hand. The doctor shook it and then looked closely at Lou. "You could use some rest," he said, before turning and walking away.

Chris opened the door to the car, started to get in and noticed that Lou was just standing there, not making any move to get in his side.

"You coming or what?" she asked.

Lou shook his head. "Go home. Get some sleep."

"And what're you going to be doing?"

"I don't know."

"I'm not just driving away and leaving you here."

"Look. I just want to be alone for a while. I want to walk. To think. It's nothing personal, I just want to be alone."

"Then what?"

Lou looked over at her and sighed. "I'll meet you in the morning. We can decide what to do then."

"What time?"

"How the hell do I know?" he shouted, then forced himself to lower his voice. "Early. I'll call you about seven and we'll go from there."

Lou turned and walked away, his hands buried in his pockets, his head bowed. Chris watched him go and wondered if she should go after him. Finally, she decided that maybe the best thing she could do for him was to allow him to go off by himself and wrestle with whatever demons were working on him at the moment. She got into the car and drove off, passing him as she did. Lou never looked up.

Chapter Seventeen

Tucking her blouse into her slacks with one hand, Chris picked up her holster and clipped it to belt with the other. She slid her gun into the holster and turned to look at herself in the mirror. The weight of the gun and holster made one side of her slacks droop, something she had always ignored before, but today it seemed important not to. She pulled the blouse over her head and tossed it onto the bed. Her slacks quickly followed.

She opened her closet and ran her eyes over the clothes hanging there. She pulled out a dress, held it up against her body and looked at herself in the mirror. This was more like it, she thought. She removed the hanger from the dress, slipped into it and turned to look at herself in the mirror again. This time she liked what she saw.

She picked up her gun and holster from the bed and grimaced. There was no place for her to put it when she wore a dress and the thought of carrying it in a purse, where she'd never get to it unless she was given a week's notice, didn't appeal to her. She smiled as the solution came to her. She went back to the closet, grabbed the sports bag laying on the floor there, unzipped it and rummaged through it until she found what she was looking for; a .32 automatic with a covered hammer. She didn't like the firepower of the .32, but knew it would do the job if she used it properly.

Lou was already finishing his third cup of coffee when Chris walked into the doughnut shop. He noticed there was something different about her and then realized that for the first time since he'd met her, she was wearing a dress. And he had to admit she looked good in it and wondered if he should tell her that, then decided it wouldn't be a good idea.

Chris sat down opposite him and Lou pushed a container of coffee towards her. She nodded in appreciation and then looked closely at him. His eyes were red and he looked as if he had slept in his clothes. She decided not to quiz him about it. He had been hurt by what had happened to Dee Dee and she thought he probably blamed himself for it. She hoped he would eventually see that it had not been his fault. Perhaps he had even figured that out himself during the night. She took a sip of coffee and then set the cup down. "You figure out our next move yet?"

"We're close. I can feel it."

"I agree. So what're our choices now?"

Lou took a deep breath and exhaled. He had been sitting there trying to decide if he should tell her of the decision he'd come to during the night. He had gone back and forth on it, but now, with her sitting across from him, he knew he had to tell her.

"I want you to understand something," he said. "I find the people who killed my son and shot Dee Dee and the others and they're dead. No questions. No Miranda rights. They're dead."

Chris nodded. She had expected it. "I asked what our choices are?"

"Just so there's no misunderstandings later on."

"You going to answer the question or not?"

Lou had been worried she wouldn't accept what he intended to do. Now that she had, he felt relieved. "Either we go and find out if Tollin's gotten anything of use for us yet or we go for the gusto and brace Beaudine."

"Tollin would've called if he had something for us."

Lou nodded. Tollin was never one to sit on things. "The thing is Beaudine knows I'll be coming back at him if for nothing else than the beating."

"But he doesn't know when."

"True."

"You really think you can make him talk?"

"For all his drug money and his so-called power, Beaudine is still the scared little punk I used to wipe the streets with years ago. He'll talk."

"Because of his fear of what you'll do if he doesn't?"

"Something like that." Lou smiled at her. "Sometimes having a reputation, true or not, can work for you."

"Especially if you make sure to foster it enough," Chris laughed.

"Hey, whatever works."

Lou reached over and tossed the remains of his food into the trash bin behind the table and looked back at Chris. "You done?"

Chris shook her head. "Not so fast. There's something we need to discuss first."

Lou rolled his eyes skyward. What now?

"I think we should go see Morrison," Chris said. "Tell him what we're planning to do."

"What the hell for?"

"Because I work for him. I'm a police officer under his command. And long after your gone and sitting around on your boat in Florida, I'm still going to be here working for the Department. It's not going to stop us, but I want him to know."

"To cover your ass."

"No. To keep my job. There's a difference."

"I suppose," Lou agreed reluctantly.

"And we might get him to come through with some back-up," she added.

"What we want, what we're asking for, is back-up," Chris said to Morrison. She was sitting across from him in his living room. Lou was standing, looking out the front window while listening to Chris explain things to her boss.

Morrison looked away from Chris and over to Lou. They'd put him in a bind and he wasn't sure he could get out of it. If he didn't go along with them and they made good on their promise to go ahead without his help, he'd be shut out of any good that came of their actions. On the other hand, if he did help them and they fucked up, he would be left holding the bag. "And you're sure a member or members of the Department are involved."

"Which is all the more reason that the Department should find out from you instead of it coming from a civilian like Lou," Chris told him.

Lou frowned. He hated being called a civilian. Inside he was still a cop even though he didn't carry a badge anymore and not to be thought of as one rankled.

Morrison wrestled with a decision he really didn't want to make. "I suppose if you do get the evidence, it would be good for the Department in the long run. Especially if we were there to make the actual arrests."

"Yeah. You'll look great on the six o'clock news," Lou said.

Morrison ignored the sarcasm and instead, visualized himself in front of the television cameras. Suddenly, what they were asking him for seemed much more palatable. If they pulled this off, he'd get the credit. He nodded his agreement. "When do you intend to brace him?"

"Like I told you before. I never liked waiting," Lou said.

Chris got to her feet. "Thanks, Captain."

"Keep me apprised," Morrison said with a warning tone.

"I will," Chris said.

"Now do your part and get that back-up rolling," Lou said, and he and Chris walked out.

Morrison watched them go, then reached for the phone and pulled it over to him just as his wife, Susan, came in. He forgot the phone for the moment and pulled her to him. Susan stood there while Morrison ran his hands up the back of her robe, pulling it up, exposing her buttocks and the sharp tan lines there. He leaned forward to kiss her stomach but she pulled away and reached for her cup. Disappointed, Morrison picked up the pot of coffee and filled her cup before turning to the phone.

Chris watched as Lou pulled the snub-nosed .38 from his waist holster and slipped it into his jacket pocket. They had been sitting across from the country club for the better part of an hour watching employees arrive for work. Lou checked his watch and realized he was as antsy as a rookie on his first bust. It wasn't the coming action that was making him nervous, it was something else entirely and he decided he'd better get it off his chest.

"You know," he said slowly. "What I said the other day...I changed my mind...I think you're extremely feminine."

Chris's eyes widened. This was something she had never expected to hear him say and she didn't know how to respond. He had caught her completely off guard.

Lou saw Riley and two of his men pull up to the country club entrance and park. "Here we go," he said, thankful that Riley's arrival prevented a discussion of what he'd said. He watched as the three men pulled some cartons out of the trunk of their car and carried them inside. "Somebody's planning a move."

"Which means Beaudine's probably already there, waiting for them."

"Yeah," Lou agreed. "No way would he allow those three to pack his personal stuff."

"How long you want to give them?"

"I say we move now."

Chris had expected him to push things, but not this soon. "I don't suppose you'd consider waiting for the back-up?"

"And I like that dress, too," Lou said as he got out of the car.

It took Chris a moment to realize that Lou had complimented her again and by that time he was halfway up the driveway. Chris hurriedly got out of the car and sprinted to catch up with him. She caught him right at the entrance. "The back-up?"

"Probably on the way."

"We should wait."

"And if Beaudine decides not to? We go. Now!"

Chris nodded. The time for talking was over. She stepped to Lou's side and they walked in together. It was way too early for club members to be there and most of the staff was just arriving.

Lou and Chris walked across the lobby and into the hallway leading to Beaudine's office. They could see Riley and his two men lounging in the reception area. Riley saw them coming and quickly got to his feet, grinning in anticipation of taking Lou apart again.

Lou never broke stride. He entered the reception area and fired right through his jacket pocket.

Riley rocked back. Shock registered on his face. He stared down at the blood starting to pour out of his stomach and spread onto his shirt and pants.

Lou continued on, past Riley's two men, who had backed off at the sound of Lou's gun firing and were now staring at him as if he were crazy.

Lou reached Beaudine's door and kicked out. The jamb shattered and the door swung open. Lou walked in.

Chris came as far as the doorway and turned around. She raised the gun she'd been carrying in the folds of her dress since they'd left the car and motioned Riley's two men down to the floor.

Lou looked around the lush office. Beaudine was nowhere in sight. He walked to the private bathroom, opened the door and glanced in. Beaudine wasn't there either.

Lou walked out of the office and back into the reception area. He moved over to Riley and hauled him to a sitting position. Sweat poured from Riley's face as the pain from Lou's gut shot coursed through his body. He looked up at Lou. "What'd you do that for?" he groaned.

"I got tired of you pounding on me," Lou told him, and pulled him to his feet. He dragged him over to the couch and pushed him onto it. Riley looked up and saw Lou draw the .38 out of his jacket pocket. He watched in disbelief as Lou then took careful aim at Riley's kneecap.

"Where's Beaudine?" Lou asked, his voice a deadly calm.

Riley tried to inch away, scared out of his mind. The quiet tone of Lou's voice when he asked the question made a believer of him. He knew Lou would shoot. He was certain of it. He was also certain that Lou had gone over the edge. That he was totally and completely mad. So he did what he thought anybody would do in his position. He told Lou exactly what he wanted to know.

Lou shoved Riley into the freezer vault and stepped back. Chris motioned with her gun for his two men to follow their boss in. Once inside, Lou locked the vault shut behind them. He turned to the cooks who had been watching the proceedings.

"Who's got the key?"

One of the cooks pulled out a key ring. He tossed it to Lou who pocketed it. He and Chris then turned and walked out.

Lou hung up the pay phone next to the market, strode back to the car and got in. He sat there for a moment digesting what he'd just learned.

"Well?" Chris asked. "What'd Morrison say?"

"That he'd already dispatched the back-up to the country club, but he'll re-route 'em our way."

Chris noticed something in Lou's voice that didn't quite ring true. "So what's troubling you?"

"How long you suppose we were in there? Ten minutes? Fifteen?"

Chris shook her head. "Less than that. Maybe five at the most."

Lou agreed, which cleared up what Morrison had told him over the phone. He had said that he'd had some trouble getting permission to release the cars from patrol duty but had finally gotten it and they were on their way. That and the fact he and Chris had only been inside for five minutes explained why they never saw their back-up. Lou turned to Chris.

"You waiting for anything in particular?" he asked with a grin.

Chris grinned back at him. "Just for you to come back to Earth."

They pulled into the curb across the street from the meat packing plant where Riley had told them Beaudine had another office. Chris shut off the ignition and sat there wondering if Lou was going to shoot the first person he came upon as he did at the country club.

"What'd'ya think?" Lou asked her.

"It's perfect."

"Yeah," Lou agreed. "Stuff the drugs inside sides of beef and then ship the sides all over the country."

"You got to give him high marks for ingenuity."

"I give him nothing. Beaudine didn't figure out this method of distribution all by himself. Somebody's running him. Doing his thinking for him. Has to be."

"But who?"

"That I don't know. Yet."

Chris turned and looked at the meat packing plant. "Now how the hell are we going to get inside?"

"Good question. You got any ideas?"

"Nope. Do you?"

"Not a one."

"Okay. Then what do we do?"

"Let's wing it," Lou said and winked at her before getting out of the car. "Maybe something will come to us along the way."

They crossed the street and walked up to the loading dock where they stopped to watch men in blood stained white coats pick up sides of beef, hoist them onto their shoulders and carry them into the plant.

"It certainly looks legit from out here," Chris said.

"It would have to. Operating in the open like this. I'll bet none of those guys even have an inkling of what Beaudine's doing with that beef before it gets shipped out."

"You're probably right."

"And that, my dear, is what's going to get us inside."

"Really?"

"Let's go," Lou said and walked across the yard. He jumped up onto the dock and reached back to give Chris a hand up. He then went over to one of the men who had a side of beef on his shoulder. ""Where's Beaudine's office."

The man looked at Lou, then at Chris. "You state or federal?"

"Does it make a difference?"

"Nope. I just like to know which inspectors are which. You guys change so often it's hard to keep track."

"That's why we do it. Keeps you guys on your toes."

The man nodded his head in Chris's direction. "She your supervisor?"

"You kidding? New man…ah…woman. Breaking her in," Lou answered.

The man looked Chris over from head to toe thinking that he'd love to break her in himself. Chris returned his look with an open innocence.

"Beaudine's office?" Lou asked again.

The man tore his eyes from Chris's body and gestured into the plant. "Take a right after you get inside. It's down in the corner. You can't miss it."

Chris and Lou walked into the plant. Once inside, Lou looked over at Chris and spread his arms. "Easy, huh?"

"You're breaking me in?"

"What'd you expect me to say? That you were breaking me in?"

"Why not?"

"He never would've believed it for one thing."

They walked on, deeper into the huge plant. From the loading dock they had gone through a heavy plastic curtain that was slit every eight inches to make access easier while at the same time, the curtain prevented the cold air from escaping and the heat from outside getting in.

Once through the curtains, Lou and Chris had felt the immediate drop in temperature and the further in they walked, the colder it seemed to get.

Beaudine's office was in the far end of the building. From the amount of room that had been carved out from the floor of the plant Lou and Chris could see that either the office was bigger than the one Beaudine had at the country club, or it was a series of offices. They reached the outer door and Lou opened it. It was an empty reception area. They went in and when they closed the door behind them, the noise from the plant outside completely vanished.

"Soundproofed," Lou said.

They looked around the room. The offices off the reception area all had glass windows set in their doors and they saw they were as empty as the reception area. A large oak door was set into the center wall opposite them. It was slightly ajar and they could see Beaudine behind a desk just slightly less ornate than the one he had at the country club.

Lou and Chris watched Beaudine unplug the external hard disk from the computer on his desk and place it inside an open briefcase. He left their view for a moment, then came back with stacks of hundred dollar bills wrapped and marked. He took the top four stacks and tossed them across the desk.

Four men, who had been hidden by the door, stepped up to the desk and each picked up a stack.

"A bonus," Beaudine told them, and dropped the rest of the cash into his briefcase. "When I get set up again I'll call. Count on it."

"Nothing for me?" Lou asked as he stepped into the office.

All five men turned. Four of them went for their guns in the same motion. Beaudine hit the floor.

Lou and Chris had entered with their guns already in their hands. As soon as they had cleared the doorway, Lou dove to the left, Chris to the right.

The room exploded in gunfire.

Then just as quickly as it started, the firing stopped. Smoke from expended gunpowder hung in the air.

Lou and Chris got slowly to their feet, weapons still at the ready, covering the room. Beaudine's four men were on the floor. All four were dead.

Lou stepped over one of them and walked to the desk. He looked behind it and motioned with his gun. "You can come out now." he told Beaudine.

Chris walked out of the room, across the reception area and opened the door to the plant. Apparently the rooms were not as soundproofed as they had thought. Some of the meat packers had heard the gunfire and were starting to drift towards the offices to see what was going on.

"Get the hell out of here," Chris shouted to them, and gestured them away with the barrel of her gun. "Police business," she added, and held up her badge. Seeing the gun and the badge and wanting no part of either, they backed off. Satisfied, Chris went back into the office.

Lou looked at Beaudine and pointed to the plant outside with his gun. "Good distribution idea. I'm impressed."

"What is it with your family?" Beaudine asked, with a mixture of frustration and anger. "This place's been running free and clear for years and all of a sudden, first your son, then you, make it."

Lou whipped his gun up into Beaudine's face. "And that's why you killed him," he said, the soft tone in his voice even more menacing than if he had shouted.

Beaudine thought he was about to be killed. Beads of sweat broke out on his face. "It wasn't me. Honest. He was dead when we got there."

"Bullshit!"

"It's the truth. Please. Don't shoot me. I didn't do anything."

"Then who did?"

"I don't know."

"Don't play me for an idiot. You know who did it and whether you want to or not you're going to tell me."

Beaudine looked around the room for some help.

"And don't think about Riley coming to bail you out of this. He's locked safely away in a freezer back at the country club."

"You took Riley?"

"I just told you."

Beaudine shook his head. "I don't believe it. He hates your guts. He'd sooner put a bullet in you than see you."

"He never had the chance," Chris said. "Lou put a bullet in him before he could even say 'hi'."

"You're crazy. The two of you," Beaudine said. He looked over at Chris. "But you're a cop. You can't let him do this."

Chris shrugged. "I wouldn't want to get in his way. Not in the state he's in. Would you?"

Beaudine looked back at Lou. He saw nothing but hatred coming from Lou's eyes.

"Talk to me," Lou said, and pulled the hammer back on his gun, the sound unnaturally loud in the room.

Beaudine stared at the barrel of the gun and made his decision. "Your son had found this place. How we were using it to distribute our goods. We had to stop him. There was no other choice. But the thing is we never had a chance to. Somebody got to him before we did."

"That's bullshit," Chris said.

"It's the truth! That's what happened!" Beaudine shouted back.

Lou took a step towards Beaudine who moved back against the wall, raising his arms in a futile attempt to protect himself.

Lou and Chris heard the sound at the same time. It was coming from behind them and they whirled in unison.

Tollin stood in the doorway, a wicked-looking 9mm machine pistol in his hand, pointed at the floor.

Lou grinned, relieved. His old partner hadn't let him down. He had come to back him up as he had done all the years they had been together. "It's about time. You missed all the fun."

Tollin looked at the bodies on the floor. "It took me a while to realize what you were going to do." Tollin shook his head. "You always were a hothead, Lou. I could never hold you back."

"You did a pretty good job when we worked that homicide in College Point."

Tollin laughed. "Yeah. But I had to get you drunk to do it."

"What is this? Old home week?" Beaudine complained.

Lou turned to him. "You in a hurry?"

"You know it," Beaudine answered.

Lou looked at Chris and nodded towards the phone. "Make the call."

"I don't think so," Tollin said.

Chris had started for the phone on Beaudine's desk, but stopped when she heard Tollin's words. She turned and looked at him. The .9mm was no longer at Tollin's side. Now it was pointed straight at her.

"Don't even think about it, Lou. I even feel you start to move I fire."

Beaudine walked from behind his desk and pulled the gun out of Lou's hand before doing the same with Chris's.

"He's got another in an ankle rig," Tollin warned, and watched as Beaudine got that one, too.

Lou felt as if he'd been struck in the stomach with a two-by-four. All the fight had gone out of him when Tollin had showed his hand and his mind was still trying to comprehend the incomprehensible.

Chris stared at Tollin and realized that Lou had been right. Beaudine wasn't smart enough to go it alone. He had a partner and that partner was Tollin, one of the smartest men to ever carry a badge.

Lou was unable to mask the sorrow and disgust he felt towards his former partner and couldn't help thinking that it was the same feelings he'd had when he found out Darleen was cheating on him. Then he realized why. It was the same thing. Tollin had cheated on him. Only this time there'd be no resolution as there had finally been with Darleen. This would be settled here and now. And only one of them would survive and walk out alive. But there were things still unanswered and he needed to know.

"Why?" he asked Tollin.

Tollin shrugged. "Why not? We always said that the line between us and them was awfully thin."

"That's crap and you know it."

"Why? We knew as much about the world of the crooks as they did. More. The only difference between them and us was that we were on the other side."

"By choice."

"What difference? We always knew we could do it better than they could. Besides, nobody ever said we couldn't change sides."

"You sold out," Lou said sadly.

"Have it your own way, Lou. You always did think you knew more than anyone else."

"You still haven't told me the reason."

"You're so smart. You tell me," Tollin challenged.

"I think you just couldn't stand being off the streets. They retired you and you hated them for it. The streets were your world, your life. Without it you were nothing."

"It's who I am. Just like you. You couldn't stay away either."

"You're right. I couldn't. But I didn't step over the line then and I wouldn't now. That's the difference between us." A sadness entered Lou's voice. "Frank, you threw away thirty years of your life. What gave it meaning."

Tollin smiled. Lou was right. What he'd done had a down side, something he had always refused to think about. Lou stating it angered him.

"It was my life," Tollin said defensively.

"And you destroyed it. What the hell were you thinking of?"

"Of doing something with the rest of my life. You think I could sit on a boat like you? Doing nothing but living in the past. I made myself a future."

"Right," Lou said derisively.

"And it was so easy, Lou. All it took was a beer or two. I was amazed how much cops talk. About dope shipments coming in. Raids about to go down. Did we talk that much, Lou? Did we?"

"Probably."

"I can't remember. No matter. I was so far out in front of them, it was pathetic. I have this town by the balls. Just like it used to be."

"Until Lou showed up," Chris said.

Tollin nodded and took a step closer to Lou. "I tried to warn you off, partner. But you wouldn't listen."

"You killed J.J., didn't you?" Chris asked.

Tollin nodded. "I had no choice. Lou was using him to trace the money. I couldn't allow that."

"I wondered why people got killed around me, but all I got was a bruise or two," Lou said.

"A weakness on my part," Tollin said. "We'd gone through too many doors together. But now you've given me no choice." He turned to Beaudine. "You got the money?"

Beaudine gestured towards the desk. "In the briefcase."

"And the hard disk?"

"Same place," Beaudine assured him.

Tollin shifted the machine pistol until it was aimed at Beaudine and pulled the trigger. Beaudine was lifted off his feet and blown back against the wall. Tollin quickly shifted his aim back to Lou and Chris. "Sorry, Lou. I really am."

"Lou...," Chris cried, and ignoring Tollin's gun, ran to Lou, pressing her body tightly against his and burying her head in his chest, her arms around him.

Tollin waited. He figured he owned Lou one last moment with the girl.

Lou wrapped his arms around Chris and suddenly realized how much she had come to mean to him. And now, having admitted to himself just what she did mean to him, there was no time left to do anything about it. Tollin was going to blow them both away and that would be that. Lou decided he was not going to just stand there and allow himself and Chris to be killed without putting up a fight. When Chris moved out of his arms he would go after Tollin. He didn't think he'd get to him, but maybe it would buy Chris enough time to get away. He pulled her tighter against him and marveled at how good her body felt pressed up against his. She must be feeling the same thing, Lou thought, because she was moving one leg around his, pressing it into his groin. Then he felt something else. He slowly lowered his hand along Chris's back and down along her buttocks.

Tollin watched Lou run his hand over the girl's ass and knew that he had been right all along. Lou did like her. He probably loved her. But it was too late for them now. He decided to give him another minute with her, just for old time's sake.

Lou moved his hand across Chris's ass, then across her thigh and around to the front of her body. Once there, he worked her skirt up and felt her naked thigh. He ran his hand along the smooth skin to the inside of her thigh. He continued upward until he came to the edge of the holster strapped upside down to her thigh. He slid his fingers around the butt of the .32. It was what he'd felt when she first pressed up against him. What she had wanted him to feel.

Tollin decided that he had given them enough time. Besides, if he didn't get out of there soon the police might arrive. "Time's up. I'll make this as quick and painless as possible."

With Chris still pressed tightly against him, Lou whipped the .32 out and fired.

The bullet slammed into Tollin's stomach.

Tollin's eyes widened in surprise. He looked down at his stomach. Blood was starting to flow.

Tollin looked up at Lou with admiration. At the same time, using all the strength he had left, he tightened his finger on the trigger of the .9mm.

Lou fired again.

This time the round went high into Tollin's chest. He fell back against the wall and the machine pistol dropped from his grasp. He fought to stay on his feet, lost the battle and slumped to the floor.

Chris, sensing that it was over, pushed out of Lou's arms and turned around and saw Tollin was laying there, motionless, yet still alive and in obvious pain.

Lou walked slowly across the room and stood over Tollin. He looked down at his former partner. Blood had started to trickle from Tollin's mouth. Lou knew Tollin's lungs were filling with blood from his last shot. It was over. There was nothing that could be done. He was dying.

Kneeling down, Lou gathered Tollin in his arms. Tollin opened his eyes and he looked up at Lou.

"I thought I could scare you off… should've known you don't scare…," Tollin whispered, forcing the words out. "We did make a great team back then… didn't we?"

Tollin grinned, remembering, then his memories clouded over and he died.

Lou reached out and ran his fingers over Tollin's eyes, closing them. "The best," he said softly, and gently laid his former partner down.

Chapter Eighteen

Chris walked out of the packing plant and looked around for Lou. She finally saw him standing by her car, head bowed, staring down at the ground, totally withdrawn from his surroundings. She realized she was looking at a totally defeated man. She understood how the loss of his son and Tollin's betrayal could extract a toll, but it was not the end of the world and she was not about to allow Lou to think it was.

Chris walked across to her car and stopped in front of it. She took a deep breath, steeling herself for what she was going to do. "Self-pity sucks," she said harshly.

For a moment Lou didn't move, then he slowly straightened up and looked at her. Chris smiled warmly and he looked away and over to the meat packing plant. Police cars were scattered all around the building. Lou could see the coroner's wagon near the loading dock and he wondered if old Amos would be back in time to perform the autopsy on Tollin. Maybe it was better that he was out of town on his forced vacation. Amos had once told him the one thing he hated was having to autopsy someone he knew. Especially someone he liked and Lou knew that Amos and Tollin had been friends for years.

"Hey!" Chris called.

Lou tore his eyes away from the packing plant and over to Chris. He shook his head. He didn't want to talk about it. He just wanted to be left alone. No time worn platitudes. No nothing, but being alone with himself and his memories. "Let it go, Chris. Not now."

"Okay. But you did find you're son's murderer and no matter who it was, you got him. You did it."

Lou nodded. He did do that. It was something. Something to perhaps hang on to now that it was all over. But there was also something nagging at the back of his mind. Something he couldn't quite get a handle on. Something not right about the whole thing. He looked over at Chris.

"I don't think so," he said slowly.

Chris grimaced. What now?

"Follow me on this," Lou said. "Tollin was the brains behind the drug operation. He'd had Shawn and J.J. and Tennant killed to protect the operation. And he knew exactly what was happening because I'd tell him our every move. Right?"

"Agreed. So?"

"So look over there. At the plant. What's not right?"

Chris looked at the packing plant. At the coroner's wagon, the patrol cars, the detectives swarming all around. It was all normal police routine. And then she saw what Lou had seen and she hadn't until now.

The police had all arrived after she'd called them. After Tollin had been killed. All from the local precinct. There were none of the back-up units from downtown that Morrison had promised them. She turned to Lou, who was watching her intently and tossed him the keys to her car. "You drive."

Lou caught them in mid-air and tossed them right back to her. "You forget how to drive?"

Without waiting for an answer he turned and got into the passenger seat of the car.

Chris pulled up in front of Morrison's house. Lou got out, waited for Chris to come around the car, then started up the walk to the front door. When he got there he reached for the doorbell.

"It's open," Chris said, gesturing towards the door. It was slightly ajar, no more than an inch.

Lou started to push the door open, but Chris grabbed his arm. After all, this was Morrison's house. "Ring it anyway."

Lou rang the doorbell and the sound of the door chimes inside carried out to them. They heard nothing else. Lou looked at Chris and she shrugged. He pushed the door open. There was nobody in the hallway.

"Anybody home?" Lou called out.

Silence.

They walked into the house and down the hallway. A quick glance into the living room showed them that it was empty. They looked in the kitchen but nobody was there either. Lou opened the door to the bathroom and looked inside.

"In here," Chris called out.

Lou walked over to Chris who was staring into the bedroom. He followed her gaze and then quickly brushed past her into the room.

Morrison's wife, Susan, was laying across the king-sized bed. Bullet holes riddled her body. Blood stained her white outfit. Lou didn't even bother to check for a pulse. She was dead.

Morrison sat in a chair opposite the bed. A .38 in his hand. His service revolver. Held loosely in his lap.

Lou moved slowly, cautiously. The man was holding a gun and although it looked as if he had used all the bullets in it on his wife, Lou didn't want to chance spooking him and taking a slug for his efforts.

Morrison felt Lou's presence and looked up. He tried to focus on Lou, but the tears in his eyes made everything blurry. He squinted and finally recognized the figure next to him as Lou, then looked back to the body of his wife laying on the bed.

"She was leaving me," Morrison said, his voice choked with emotion.

Chris noticed there was an open suitcase on the floor.

"She said she didn't love me anymore. And nothing I could say or do would stop her from going. But I had to do something."

Morrison looked up. "I stopped her, Lou. She can't leave now. Morrison turned and looked at his wife. "I love her. She's my whole life. I couldn't let her leave. I put up with so much. Her running around. Seeing other men. But I forgave her because I loved her. You can understand that, Lou, can't you? I love her so much." Morrison's body shook as his emotions overcame him and he burst out crying.

Lou moved closer. When he spoke, his voice was calm. Soothing. Comforting. "I know. I know."

"I'm sorry about Shawn…but she gave me no choice."

Lou looked over at Chris. He saw that the irony of the situation was not lost on her either. The entire drug operation had nothing to do with Shawn's death. Sure, Shawn had probably gotten too close to Beaudine and therefore to Tollin and they had wanted him dead. But Tollin hadn't killed Shawn and somehow that made Lou feel better. Shawn had been killed by Morrison. Not because of drugs. Not to cover a rogue cop in the Department. Morrison had killed Shawn because he had been having an affair with his wife. Because she was cheating on him and he blamed Shawn instead of his wife.

"She wouldn't stop seeing him," Morrison said through his tears. "I had to end it. You don't know how painful it is knowing your wife is with someone else. And now she can't hurt me anymore. But how come I still hurt, Lou? Inside."

Lou slowly reached out for the gun in Morrison's lap. "Because you loved her," he said gently.

Morrison looked up into Lou's eyes. It was as if he were seeing him there for the first time. His eyes shifted over to the bed. To the dead body of his wife. "My God…," he said as the realization of what he'd done hit home.

Before Lou could touch the gun, Morrison brought it up, and into his mouth. He pulled the trigger.

The back of Morrison's head was blown away. Bits and pieces splattered against the wall behind him. Lou winced. Chris turned away.

Chapter Nineteen

Lou and Chris walked out of Morrison's house together. They looked around at the quiet unsuspecting neighborhood.

"Sometimes I wonder if we ever really know what good healthy love is," Chris said.

"Beats me. All I know is what makes me feel good."

Chris took a deep breath, gathered her emotions and took the bait. "And what's that?"

Lou turned and looked deep into her eyes. "You like fishing?"

Chris grinned. "I could learn."

"I'm warning you. There's not a lot of room on my boat. Just one bunk."

"How many do we need?"

Lou nodded. He turned and walked towards their car, Chris at his side. After a couple of steps, Lou slid his arm around her shoulder. As Chris felt his arm she moved closer, slipped her arm around his waist and hugged him tightly to her.

About the Author

James Schmerer was born in Queens, New York and graduated from New York University. He has been the producer of three television series and executive story consultant on half a dozen others. As a freelance writer, he has written primetime television, soaps, animation and features. He lives in Southern California.